REVIEWS

THE LIGHT AFTER THE DARK I and II:

The Jewish Post & News: Winnipeg, Manitoba
"These stories enlarge our understanding of both history and humanity. Irving Abella writes that books like this one are profoundly important. I agree. This testimony is powerful and moving – a most worthwhile read."

Bob Hawkins

Jerusalem Post: Jerusalem, Israel
"We knew her as The General and made fun of her. But we didn't know, we didn't know. The incredible tale of Batia Malamud is told in a recent book by Alvin Abram…This old woman, the butt of indignity on Prince Charles Street was the greatest hero we ever met. And we never knew."

Sam Orbaum

The Leader Post: Regina, Saskatchewan
"Abram relates true-life accounts of men and women who lived through the Holocaust…Abram collected and published these poignant and inspiring stories in hopes that they would change the perspective of people who hear them."

Nick Miliokas

The Canadian Jewish News: Toronto, Ontario
"Alvin Abram has fashioned a book to be cherished. It both nourishes and enlarges the spirit."

Rabbi Bernard Baskin

London Jewish Community News
"In The Light After The Dark, Alvin Abram has collected six true stories of men and women who, through determination, courage and luck survived the dark years of Nazi barbarism to build new lives for themselves in Canada…Abram must have needed infinite patience to draw the details of each of these stories from their narrators. He has certainly exerted all his talents in retelling them, using a flashback technique to set the scene for each one, but otherwise letting the stories of the individuals' Holocaust experiences and subsequent lives speak for themselves."

Susan Merskey

"These are powerful stories and for the most part you have told them well. In a market place that is crowded with Holocaust manuscripts, I think yours stands out…I was initially dubious about the Holocaust conveyed by means of something fictionalized short narratives, but the result is a powerful manuscript, so how can I argue against the basic premise. This is one of the best Holocaust manuscripts I've read."

Greg Ioannou
Manuscript Evaluator, Toronto, Canada

REVIEWS

WHY, ZAIDA?

Jewish Free Press: Calgary, Alberta
"Author uses metaphors from nature to explain the Holocaust. Why, Zaida? explains the brutality of the unnamed Nazi regime and its collaborators by drawing another analogy as they see a dog attempting to prey on a squirrel. Likewise, he likens evil to weeds, which threatens the good grass if left unchecked. Alvin Abram's sensitive exploration is beautifully illustrated by Judy Willemsma. Interspersed with illustrations and text are the Yiddish words for Why, Zaida?...Abram generalizes the story – perhaps to provide a gentle more universal approach to young readers first being introduced to the potentially traumatic subject matter."

Maxine Fischbein

The Canadian Jewish News: Toronto, Ontario
"The book "Why, Zaida?" by Alvin Abram, illustrated by Judy Willemsma, talks about that kind of person – a grandfather who talks about the Holocaust only after his grandson asks and asks. Nevertheless, the grandfather has to answer his grandson. He does this with the time-honoured technique of parables, stories that help teach a lesson – a robin eating a worm, a dog chasing a squirrel, a leaf caught in a stream, a grassy bank. Every page has beautiful illustrations in lush greens, blues and browns."

Leila Speisman

SHORT STORIES

KUGLER
"Wonderful usage of actual events. Definitely a good understanding of history. Brought a few tears and a sniffle upon first reading."

A. Lange

COLOUR THEM DEAD
The characters and plot of this story show that it has the potential for a powerful and dramatic piece. The theme, though common in our society accustomed to grisly crimes, is still relevant and needs to be retold – even if it's only to keep the general public alert. And the author has the imagination and talent to tell it in a suspenseful way."

L. Pompa

GUILT!
I believe that this particular writer is destined for greatness and must pursue his ability to achieve these ends."

M. Goatham

TA-TA-T-A-TA
"I have to say I really liked your prose. It has a maturity that's refreshing to see. Your opening is nice, setting the mood, the loneliness, fear, reluctance of the situation at hand."

Clair Anderson

The Unlikely Victims

by Alvin Abram

AMA_Graphics_ Incorporated
Toronto   Ontario   Canada

National Library of Canada Cataloguing in Publication Data

Alvin Abram, 1936-
The Unlikely Victims

ISBN 0-9692398-6-6

I. Title

PS8551.B49U55 2002   C813'.6   C22001-903516-0
PR9199.3.A1715U55 2002

Published by AMA Graphics Incorporated
Toronto, Ontario, Canada

Cover design by Charlotte Launø
Page design and typesetting by Tara Fortnum

Printed in Canada

BY THE SAME AUTHOR

Non-Fiction Books:

THE LIGHT AFTER THE DARK I (Soft Cover) (244 pages)
6 True Stories of Courage During the Holocaust *published by Key Porter Books*

THE LIGHT AFTER THE DARK II (Soft Cover) (272 pages)
6 True Stories of Courage During the Holocaust *published by The Incredible Printing Co. Inc.*

Fiction Book:

WHY, ZAIDA? (Hard Cover) (32 pages)
Children's illustrated book, using metaphors to explain the Holocaust *published by AMA Graphics Incorporated*

Fiction Short Stories – Tabloids and Magazines:

KUGLER
FORGIVE ME
A TOUCH OF LOVE
GROWING OLD
REMEMBER: COME HOME
WHAT IF...
THE CLOTH COAT
WHO'S THERE? A YID.
THE PHOTOGRAPH ALBUM

Fiction Short Stories – Anthologies:

JEALOUS BULLET
THE PHOTOGRAPH ALBUM
THE CREDIT CARD CAPER
LATE AGAIN HARRY
JONAS: THE BAKER
TA-TA-T-A-TA
GROWING OLD
A STORY IN TWO WORDS

IN APPRECIATION

An undertaking such as this required the assistance of several key people and I wish to thank them for their time and patience.

ALLAN BERNSTEIN, retired sheriff, New York State, for telling me about some of his cases that I altered to fit my manuscript.

MAHLON WATSON, retired Toronto Homicide cop, trained and experienced in all aspects of major criminal investigations, who authenticated police procedures to make the cases more realistic.

CARLOS KIRK, retired Narcotics cop from Trinidad who gave me invaluable assistance for a story and read the story for accuracy.

IRIS FORESTER, aka a female police officer whose name I cannot reveal for her insight and assistance as it applied to the women on the force.

HOWARD CLEMENTS, 32 Division, a member of the Toronto Police Force who gave me some insight into patrol procedures.

And to the many police officers I would stop at random and ask if they would tell me a story.

and to

MARYAN GIBSON, Editor, who made my jumbled thoughts flow like water and it didn't hurt that she has a couple of cops in the family.

And this one for
those that mean the most to me

Marilyn
Lisa
Lori, Phil and Ally
Jason
and
Mystic, the Wonder Dog

The
Annie
Weisz
Case

A *jagged bolt of lightning split the black sky, followed by a sharp crack of thunder. Short gusts of wind blew loose leaves over mani-cured lawns and well-kept walkways; rain fell, first in large drops and then in a deluge. An old woman moved slowly along a deserted residential street. She brought a hand to her chest, hoping to calm her racing heart. Glancing at the creased scrap of paper clutched in her right hand, she read the address once more. The rain pelted the writing, causing the ink to run, distorting the words. But it made no difference to her, for she knew the address by heart. She smiled in spite of her exhaustion. He was waiting for her. Fifty-nine years,* *five months and six days had passed since she'd last seen him. Her beloved husband was alive. Her smile broadened.*

She glanced quickly at a small, darkened bungalow opposite her to see the number, then forced herself to approach until she stood before the front door. She swept her matted hair away from her eyes. Was he really there? Everyone had said he was dead, but he wasn't to her. She had always felt his presence, no matter where she went, no matter what she did. She refused to accept any answer but the one in her heart. She looked at the windows for signs of movement – there were none. Why did the house appear deserted? The man on the telephone had said he lived here. For almost sixty years neither she nor her husband realized the other had survived the war. Not only survived, but lived in the same city! She knew miracles happened. This was to be hers. She gazed down at her wet clothes. She must look terrible. He'd be so disappointed seeing her this way. She took a couple of deep breaths and faced the door.

She knocked.

The steady drum of rain on the roof of the small porch was her only answer. "Please, open the door. It's me, Annie." She knocked again, then hesitantly tried the handle. The door swung open. Peering into the darkness, she called weakly, "Hello, Hershl, are you here?"

Once again the sky lit up and in that instant, she saw that the interior was empty. She stepped over the threshold, leaving the door open, placed a trembling hand on the wall and followed it to an adjoining door, only to find another empty room. "Hello," she called again. "Hershl?"

She was crying, although she was scarcely aware of her tears. She turned towards the door and watched the fury of the rain. Her tears became sobs that wracked her fragile body, and from the centre of her being came a wail of pain. "No-o-o!"

She lowered herself to the floor and buried her face in her hands. He wasn't here. He'd never been here. The man on the telephone had played a cruel joke on her. How had he known so much about her Hershl?

Her tired body sagged against the wall, and she ignored the sharp pain in her chest. She drew in short shallow breaths, letting her mind take her on the familiar journey back to when she and Hershl had first met at the University of Warsaw in Poland. She worked as a file clerk, but spent many nights in the library reading. She was sitting at a long table, an assortment of books scattered before her, when Hershl sat down across from her. He smiled, and she smiled back. She felt embarrassed when he continued to stare at her, making no attempt to look in the book he had opened in front of him. He suddenly got up to get another book and she watched him. Lord, he was handsome! Tall, hair black as coal, blue eyes and a dimple in his chin that deepened when he smiled. She dropped her eyes to her book when he returned and pretended to read. She could sense his gaze on her.

"Hello," he said.

She looked at him.

"My name is Hershl Weisz. I've seen you here several times and I finally had the courage to sit at your table." He laughed nervously. "I apologize for being so forward. I've never done this before, but I can't get you out of my mind. Would you tell me your name?"

"Uh-h-h," she stammered, "Annie Kapinsky."

"Hello, Annie Kapinsky."

"Hello," she said. Her eyes sparkled, and then she laughed.

Hershl laughed, too.

Over the next five months, their romance blossomed. They were married in June of 1939 – she was twenty-one, he twenty-four – and the next two months were sheer bliss. She would rush home from work, desperate to be in his arms. Each night a memory to cherish.

In September the Germans invaded Poland.

They took him away. She screamed to go with him, but the officer kicked and punched her into unconsciousness. She was told he had been taken to a concentration camp in Germany called Dachau. The Germans sent her first to a labour camp, and then to Stutthof, a camp for women in Poland. The war ended, but Hershl never returned. She searched the names of the dead from the Dachau records posted every day by the Jewish Congress in Krakow. His name never appeared. She asked those who returned from the camp, but no one knew Hershl Weisz. Thousands had died and were buried in unmarked graves, she was told. Was he one of them?

No!

She knew he lived.

She came to Canada – to the city of Toronto. She worked as a seamstress and saved her money, always believing that some day they would be together again. A few days ago a man had phoned. A stranger. "Is Weisz your married name?" he'd asked. "Is your maiden name Kapinsky? Did you come from Warsaw?"

"Who is this?" she had responded.

He would say only that he was a private investigator. He worked for a search bureau and was instructed by a client about six months ago to find a woman from Warsaw, Poland, by the name of Annie Kapinsky Weisz.

Annie couldn't contain her excitement. The investigator asked more questions. He fumbled with his words, but Annie heard only what she wanted. "Who is this client?" she asked. Her fingers gripped the telephone receiver so hard they turned white. "Where is he?"

"I'm sorry," the man said, "I'm not at liberty to say at this moment."

"Can I not speak to him?"

"No. We're still not sure you're the right person. I'll call again tomorrow night," and he abruptly hung up.

Annie was devastated by the delay. When every second is count-ed, a day can feel as long as a year. When the man did call, he told her that he was instructed to reveal his client's name. It was Hershl Weisz. Annie gasped. Her body shook with apprehension. Tears rushed down her cheeks. "Is he coming here?" she whispered.

"No. Mr. Weisz has been confined to a wheelchair for more

than fifty years. Recently he won a lot of money and he hired our bureau to find any information we could on what had happened to his wife. We sent one of our field agents to Warsaw, then to the German archives and located your name. The Jewish Congress in Europe assisted us, and to our surprise we discovered you lived in the same city as our client."

All of Annie's strength seemed to leave her. She gripped the table hard on which the telephone rested to prevent herself from slipping to the floor. Her heart raced and her body shook uncontrollably. "Please…I want to talk to him," she whispered.

"Mr. Weisz said to tell you he sees you as when he first saw you in the library in Warsaw and that is the way he will always see you." The man had laughed nervously. "I hope I said that right. I've never played Cupid before."

Annie had beamed with joy. "Yes, yes. Thank you."

"Mr. Weisz would like to see you right away. I believe he is arranging for a limousine to pick you up tomorrow morning and bring you to his house."

"Oh! Why can't I talk to him? Can't I phone him now?"

"I'm sorry, I'm just the investigator. I don't have all the answers. Maybe he wants to talk to you in person the first time. But wouldn't it be marvellous if you showed up tonight and surprised him? What a great idea! Do you have a car?"

"No," she said.

"I suggest you take a taxi, then."

"Where does he live?"

The man had given her an address and she'd written it on a pad before she realized the location. "That's all the way downtown," she had said. "I don't think I have enough money with me to take a taxi that far. I'll have to take a bus."

"His house is not too far from the bus route," and again he'd encouraged her to surprise his client.

Annie shifted her body against the wall. She'd begun to shiver. Her thoughts focused on her present predicament. Why had this "investigator" been so cruel? The neighbours who knew her story told her to forget the past, but how do you forget such happiness? How do you ignore your feelings? She couldn't. All she had from her all-too-brief marriage was a photograph of Hershl. They had lived in Praga, the gentile section of Warsaw, and fortunately the building in which they'd rented an apartment had survived the war. She had returned to Warsaw after her release, to their old apartment, hoping to find something, anything that belonged to him. The tenant had allowed her to look about. Her stubbornness had been rewarded when she discovered a faded photograph between a shelf and the wall in the closet. It was discoloured and stained; one corner was missing and the image blurry, but she'd recognized Hershl.

Annie noticed the rain had stopped. She felt her exhaustion. Her damp clothes were uncomfortable, and the pain in her chest was more pronounced. She was frightened by the pain. She struggled to her feet, and with small steps, made her way out of the house and back to the bus stop. It took forever to reach her apartment. She had considered going to a hospital, but she wanted to change her clothes. Besides, she felt foolish. She was eighty, for heaven's sake; she should have known better. It was too late for her miracle to come true. She had let her emotions crowd out her common sense. She should have realized that Hershl was alive only to her.

Annie fumbled in her purse for her key. As she was about to place it in the lock, she noticed the doorknob was broken and hesitantly pushed at the door. It swung open. Her heart pounded anew when she saw the living-room floor strewn with her possessions. The drawers to her china cabinet were open, and her new radio, which should have been on the small table by the couch, was gone. Annie screamed, her thoughts on Hershl's photograph.

She raced to the bedroom. The drawer of her bedside table was open and the silver-framed photograph, which always sat on top, was gone. A cry of agony escaped her lips as she dropped to her knees and peered under the bed. She saw the frame and reached underneath, drawing it towards her. An overpowering pain stabbed her chest. Her strength evaporated and she sagged to the floor, clutching the photograph. Her eyes closed as her last breath left her.

The tenant in the next apartment heard the scream. He looked out into the hall, noticed that her door was wide open and cautiously entered. When he saw her crumpled on the floor, he ran back to his apartment and called the police.

THE WAIL OF a siren woke me and I listened with my eyes closed, as it grew louder and louder – stopping right outside my apartment building. I knew it was a fire truck. I've heard enough of them over the years. More than likely an elderly tenant had had a heart attack or fallen. I live in a building with a lot of elderly people and it's happened before.

I kept my eyes shut, not wanting to come fully awake, but then about ten minutes later I recognized the whine of a police siren and opened my eyes. I lay in bed waiting to see what other sounds I might hear, still not wanting to bestir myself.

Another ten minutes passed, and I heard the approach of yet another siren. I sat up and swung my feet off the bed. This latest siren I recognized as coming from the coroner's car. I went to my window and sure enough a fire engine, a squad car, a coroner's car and, to my surprise, an ambulance, with lights flashing, had pulled up to the front door. I must have missed one siren. I put my robe on over my pyjamas and tied the belt, barely. I'd been gaining weight again and it was either get another robe or lose weight. The former seemed more appealing. I went down to the lobby to see what the fuss was about. I'm a homicide detective, a thirty-year veteran of the Metropolitan Toronto police force. Gabriel Garshowitz is my name. I'm a widower, my wife of twenty-five years died five years ago, and I have one daughter who lives somewhere. That's not to say I don't care where she lives, I just don't know.

It stands to reason that being a cop, tired or not, I would go see what was going on. I had just finished a long shift and went to bed early. When I say early, I mean before midnight. I've just turned sixty. I don't think my age is a factor, but it's having its drawbacks. Being tired after a long day is one of them. It's happening more often. Superintendent Holloway keeps telling me to lose weight, but what does he know? In the lobby, an officer told me everyone had gone to the third floor. I got off the elevator at the third floor and followed the sounds of voices to the apartment, passed the curious who'd come out into the hall, and then stood by the door until a cop emerged from the bedroom. I recognized him. "What have we got here, Howard?"

"Hi, Gabe," he said as he approached. A grin appeared as he scrutinized my baby blue pyjamas and a matching robe. "Did they actually drag you out of bed for this call?"

"No. This is my night uniform. It's more comfortable." I tried to tighten the belt, but there was hardly anything left of it by the time it circled my girth. "Heard the commotion outside," I said. "Went down to the front door, and a cop told me what apartment, so I came up to see what was going on."

"I never realized you lived here."

"I moved in last month," I said. "So what have you got?"

"Break and enter, and a dead old woman."

"Homicide?"

"The apartment's messed up, but not the victim. My guess is she died of a heart attack."

"Before, during or after?" I asked.

"Can't say. One thing I do know for sure is she was a Holocaust survivor."

"How do you know?"

"The tenant next door told me."

"The buildings full of them. What's her name?"

Howard opened his notebook. "Annie Weisz, eighty years old, lived alone."

"What else?"

"Call came at 11:46 p.m. A tenant heard a scream. Called 911. I was down the street. When I arrived, saw the old woman on the floor. Paramedics did CPR, but couldn't get a heartbeat. The fire department was right on their heels. Confirmation of death was made by telephone hook-up to Branson Hospital by a Dr. Lew Snyder. I notified Homicide, and Forensics arrived at 12:16." He closed his notebook. "The old woman's clothes were soaking wet. Must have been out in the rain. A silver picture frame with an old photo in it was in her hand. I didn't see any bruises on her."

"That's why you figure it was a heart attack?"

"Yes. She could have died witnessing a break-in, but I think she saw the place as it was and died of shock. Also, she was married, but lived alone. No children."

"How do you know?"

"The neighbour. I asked."

Detective Stella Morgan emerged from the bedroom and stopped dead in her tracks, staring at me. Stella was with Forensics and we go back a few years. She approached, a huge smile on her face. "Nice, Gabe. Stylish."

"Hello, Stella. You heading the forensic unit?"

"This your case?"

"No, curious."

Stella fingered my robe sleeve between two fingers. "Good stuff. It fits you well. It has a balloon effect." She burst out laughing. Howard grinned. "You don't look bad for a guy who's seventy."

"Sixty." I pointed to the bedroom door. "You belong in there, I believe."

Stella returned to the bedroom but stopped at the door. "How about I take your picture?"

"How about you go inside?"

Laughing again, she did. "There's always a joker around. You can expect this when you make detective," I said to Howard.

"When I do, will I get a uniform like yours?"

"The divisional detectives should be here soon. I'm changing into my civvies, then I'm coming back."

"How come?"

"I told you, curious."

I made my way back upstairs. It's not often a crime is committed in an apartment building that has a cop as a tenant. Being so close to home, I was curious to see what had taken place. Besides, I was having a bad time sleeping, anyway. Being sixty was only a number, I told myself. It is. I also knew the pain in my knees was not from fatigue, but maybe arthritis. When I had a headache, I took an aspirin. Aspirin doesn't work for this type of pain. And the mornings are the worst part of my day. Maybe that's why I couldn't sleep, knowing what I'd be waking up to.

I didn't know Annie Weisz, but I knew many Holocaust survivors, my late wife being one. To go through the hell Annie did and then die because her apartment was robbed pissed me off. Maybe being curious was not my real reason.

I put on a shirt and trousers. I kept my slippers on. I wasn't intending to leave the building. I made my way back to the scene of the crime. "Divisional detectives not here yet?" I asked Howard.

"Yep. You're it for tonight. I told Superintendent Holloway you were here and he said for you to take over. He wants you to make out the initial report and bring it in tomorrow. He'll allocate it then. It's a busy night. In case you complain, to remind you, you're on call this week."

"No complaint. Forensics got something?"

"Nope."

I looked at my watch. It was going on one. "Was the neighbour who put in the call told to wait for the detectives?"

"Yep."

"I can tell you've had a university education. You're so eloquent."

"And with honours."

"I'm surprised you didn't become a lawyer." I grinned my farewell and went next door. I listened to the neighbour tell his story before returning to the Weisz apartment. He had very little to offer. He heard, he saw, he ran, he phoned. It took a half hour for him to tell me that. He was positive Annie Weisz was still home at seven-thirty. He'd smelled her dinner. I returned to Annie Weisz's apartment. How did the thief know Annie was going out? I don't believe in luck. This robbery was planned – but maybe without considering her bad health.

There was no doubt in my mind that whoever broke in, his actions contributed to her death. What did he steal that was worth a life? I found her furniture puzzling – old fashioned, heavy dark wood. The living room, kitchen and bedroom had a European flavour. Most people are prone to so-called modern furniture, but this apartment was right out of the thirties. She had modern appliances, though, and a 32-inch television. Too big for one person to carry out alone, which made me suspect the crime was committed by a single individual. An old-fashioned record player was still in place. There were no CDs or videos. Chances were Annie Weisz had never owned any. There were books on the floor, thrown from a wall unit. Must have thought something was hidden behind the books, but what? Jewellery? Seemed unlikely she owned anything really valuable. At her age and living alone, she probably rarely went out socially. Why buy jewellery? Whoever broke in knew she had something he wanted. To get what he wanted he had to make sure Annie Weisz was out of the apartment. Why and how did he lure her out in the middle of the night?

I had to wait for confirmation that a warrant had been granted before I could search the apartment. I dared not touch anything, because if I did, the search might be deemed unlawful and any evidence I found inadmissible in court. There've been times when I've taken risks, but only if I'm positive the victim lived alone and would have wanted the person responsible caught. Still, I've seen bad guys get off on technicalities before, so this time I waited. At last I got the call that the warrant had been issued and we all went to work.

After the silver frame had been bagged, I asked Stella for a look. I stared at the photograph, wondering why such an expensive frame enclosed such a poor-quality picture. The image was barely discernable. It looked like a man or a woman wearing slacks. The background was a wall, and the paper the picture was on had definitely seen better days. I rummaged in the bedside-table drawer after Stella had finished with Annie's bedroom and the body had been removed. In it I found an old vinyl passport wallet. I flipped through it, admiring the young woman's photo, then opened Annie Weisz's immigration papers and read the letter congratulating her on becoming a Canadian citizen. Howard said the old woman was married, and yet there was no pictures or anything showing a husband. Even if deceased, there would be photographs. I checked her immigration papers again and noted that she could have been married before the war. That could be the answer why no photographs of her husband, unless the picture in the silver frame was all she had. I looked at the image in the frame again, but it was too hard to tell what or who it was – another victim of the war, I figured. A young victim.

There wasn't much more I could do until Forensics was finished with their investigation, and Stella thought it would take the rest of the night. I'd looked in drawers, closets and the bathroom. The medicine cabinet had been trashed, the floor littered with its contents. What was it that attracted a thief to her apartment? Was he after her drugs? The vials were for high blood pressure, water pill, stuff for woman problems and some vitamins. Everyone was popping vitamins. I always wondered if they really worked. There was nothing there worth stealing, unless of course he got what he wanted. I wasn't accomplishing much. Until I had the freedom to do what I wanted in the apartment, it was useless sticking around, and besides I was tired, so I told Stella I was going and returned to my own apartment. Howard stayed at the door to protect the crime scene.

It was after 3 a.m. when I undressed and lay in my bed, but sleep was elusive. What had the old woman been doing out in the rain? I sat up quickly. My brain must have been asleep because I suddenly had a thought that should have come to me earlier. How did she get where she was going? Bus stop was right outside the front door if she wanted to go south, and a taxi stand was only a block away. Subway was about fifteen minutes from the corner by bus. I slipped on my dressing gown and slippers and returned to the crime scene. I approached Stella Morgan.

"Stella, were there any bus tickets or subway tokens in her purse?"

Stella grinned at me. "Did I tell you, Gabe, how much I like your new uniform? You'd look quite distinguished if you weren't so overweight and your moustache looked less like a push broom under that big schnozz of yours."

"Smart. So were there?"

Stella checked her clipboard and read silently until she

came to a sheet with the information. "Three bus tickets, no subway tokens."

"Okay, good chance she was on a bus. But she was wet. When did it start to rain?"

Stella grinned. "Sorry, Gabe. Not my area of expertise. Want me to call a forensic Climatologist? He'd know."

"What? Oh, no. I was just thinking out loud."

"I do have something that might prove interesting." She crossed to a table where she had an assortment of evidence bags and picked one up. "This pad has been written on recently. Good indentation on the top sheet. I can barely make out a number and word. Could be an address. I'll get a good reading once I get back to the lab."

"Good." I stared around the room again, just trying to get a feel for the place and the occupant.

"Going outside in that costume, Gabe?" she asked, still grinning.

"No. As a matter of fact, I'm going to bed. And because you're a naughty girl, I'm going alone."

3

POLICE HEADQUARTERS WAS in a relatively modern building in downtown Toronto. Homicide was on the third floor. A wide room with clusters of workstations with desks, computers on most, and uniformed personnel operating the dancing screens. There was a steady drone of voices, a mix of police business and profanity, indistinct from afar and not worth hearing close up. There was a good deal of movement, too, as the officers went about their work, some leaving, others arriving.

I was finishing a prior case report. I had already sent Superintendent Holloway my notes on last night, along with a recommendation. I made my final peck on the keys and hit "print." A crazy world, I thought as I looked at my words spewing from the machine. I arrest the guilty and I could count on a lawyer plea-bargaining the penalty. Lawyers were not my favourite people. I had a reputation as a plodder when it came to investigating. "Methodical" was what I called it. I crossed my t's and dotted my i's, took each step cautiously, not wanting to make mistakes that allowed a guilty person to walk free. Which was why I hated typing reports – my fingers were clumsy and often tapped the wrong key.

My telephone rang. I pressed a button and spoke into the receiver. "Yes?"

"My office, Gabe." It was Superintendent Holloway.

"On my way." I stood and groaned. Goddamn knees were acting up again.

For sixteen years, Greg Holloway had been my partner. Three years ago, he was made superintendent. Since then I hadn't had a permanent partner. Didn't want one. Holloway looked up from his work as I entered. I sat on the only other chair in the room.

"I read your preliminary report on the Weisz case. What's with the memo at the end?"

"I'd like the case," I said.

"If I read your report right, death was a result of a heart attack. The most you could charge the guy with might be manslaughter."

"Yeah, but he will be caught. You know what the stats are on catching someone who did this? Give me the case and I'll catch him."

"You know the victim?"

"No."

Holloway stared at my solemn face.

"The old woman was a Holocaust survivor," I said. "After what she'd been through, this was not the way for her life to end."

"You still hung up on that?"

"Your words, not mine."

"It's time to let go, Gabe. You can't hold yourself responsible forever."

"It's my cross to bear," I said. "Do I get the case?"

"Sure."

"Good. It was strange that the old woman was out last night. Weather is always unpredictable this time of year, but rain was forecast. She more than likely left her apartment before it started. I figure wherever she went she took a bus. There were bus tickets in her purse. She had less than twenty dollars on her, otherwise she could have taken a taxi. Wherever she went was farther than the money she had."

"Do you know where she went?"

"Not yet."

"How about a bank card?" the superintendent asked.

"Nah. At her age I would be surprised if she used an ATM. No such card in her purse anyway, but I'm checking that out. I find it strange that she'd leave her apartment without rain gear or an umbrella. Tells me she must have left in a hurry. Who knew she wouldn't be home, and why break into her apartment?"

"Prescription drugs?"

"Maybe. I'll get a list from the drugstore she used. But I don't think it's a junkie. Junkies react, they don't plan beyond the first step. This was well planned. No, I don't think the main reason was drugs. It was robbery. But what?"

"I see you've given this a lot of thought."

I nodded. "I put myself in the prick's shoes. The old lady has something I want. How do I get it? Daytime's no good. Building's too busy. Too much coming and going. Good chance she'll be home. If not, someone on her floor might spot him and know he doesn't belong. I figure the person we're looking for is young or middle-aged. Most of the tenants are seniors. And they go to bed early. Get her out at night when the building is quiet, that's what I'd do. But how? How do you get an eighty-year-old woman to leave her building and head out into a rainy night?"

"Just keep your time on this case in perspective. We have more cases than cops."

I nodded again and stood to leave. I was glad I had the case. One rule a cop learns is don't make a case personal. For reasons I didn't fully understand I was breaking the rule.

"Uh, Gabe. I have another matter that has to be handled."

I waited. I could tell that whatever Holloway wanted to say wasn't going to be something I wanted to hear. Good news has a way of being accompanied by bad.

"I'm partnering you with a recruit."

"No!"

"Yes."

"You know I don't want another permanent partner," I protested. "I'm too set in my ways. Has anyone been complaining?"

"No. Listen, Gabe. You could have had my job. It was yours for the taking, but you turned it down. You were senior man. You could be telling me what to do."

"You were better qualified, Greg. When Edith died, I didn't want four walls. I'm not cut out to sit in an office while others are doing what I want to do. No, the position was yours. I had enough sense to back away from something I didn't want."

"You taught me everything I know."

I grinned because it was the truth. When Greg and I teamed up he was greener than a banana in a refrigerator car. "I'm glad you appreciate that. So do me a favour and let things be as they are until I retire."

"Can't. I have another detective with good potential, and you're best suited to help her."

"Her?"

"Yes, her. Her name is Iris Forester. Six years on patrol and three at Thirty-one Division investigating break-ins and robberies. Black belt in karate, reasonably good shot and easy on the eyes."

"How old?"

"Thirty-two."

"Why me?"

"Right now, she needs a mature person to guide her. Not just a partner, but a friend and mentor…her stand-in *zaida?*"

"I'm not anyone's *zaida.*"

Greg laughed. "You're retiring in five years and passing her your experience would be a good way to end a good career. She'll make an excellent pupil."

"What's she to you?"

The grin on Greg's face broadened. "She's my brother's kid."

"That Iris? Married?"

"Didn't last. You know what a cop's life is like. He didn't like her hours. They broke up relatively amicably. No kids. So this is a favour to me. Besides, when I told her I would partner her with you, she seemed pleased."

I grinned. "I'll tell her stories about you."

"Good. My brother and I have a…problem that's put a wedge between us, and I was hoping you'd help remove it."

"When did this happen?"

"The year I got promoted. Timmy and I had words. I'm going to be counting on you. She'll be here in a couple of days. Is it a go?"

"You don't think I have enough on my plate?"

"From where I sit, it's a small plate. Do you want my job?"

"Never. Okay, but you owe me."

"Anytime."

THE NEXT DAY I dropped into Stella's office and read her report. She had been able to decipher the address from the pad. It was a downtown street. I drove to the house. The rain was intermittent. It hadn't gone away. Before I got out of the car I knew the house was empty. I knocked, then tried the door. It opened. I returned to my car and retrieved my flashlight, then went back and shone it on the walls and floor. I could tell this house had been unoccupied for some time by the smell of decay. My flashlight picked up a crumpled piece of paper, and when I unravelled it, I saw it was the original sheet from the pad. The wall was stained near the paper and I patted it. It was damp. Annie Weisz had been here. Why?

On the way back to the apartment, I mulled over what I had discovered. Annie Weisz had been lured away from her apartment. Someone knew her or knew enough about her to get her to that empty house because she had something in her apartment that was valuable, and whoever it was wanted to take it without fearing she'd catch him. What? Why go to such lengths? Maybe I'd learn something at the apartment building.

I talked to the janitor and to all the tenants on Annie Weisz's floor. I didn't learn anything. This was a friendly building; most belonged to a recreational club on the main floor. They did things together, like talk about their various ailments and compare notes on their meds. I hadn't joined. They looked so much older than me. And besides, sixty is not old. The word got out that I lived in the building, and I could tell some of the women were sizing me up. Since this morning, I already had three invitations for dinner. Been living in the building a month and never talked to anyone. Now, I'm the single cop on the second floor, with the emphasis on single. They believed the old adage: the fastest way to a Jewish man's heart was through his stomach. I begged off, claiming I was too involved in this case. Everyone gave me a rain check.

I was now going to see Annie Weisz's hairdresser. If there was anyplace women talked freely, it was at the hairdresser. I know from my late wife, Edith. She would come home and tell me stories that were worthy of a daytime soap opera. And jokes. For example, there was a seventy-one-year-old named Yankel who considered himself the building's stud. Whenever a new single female tenant moved in, he would tell her of his qualifications, hoping she would be interested. Well, one day a new tenant was. They met in her apartment at ten. It was a bachelorette, bed, kitchen and chesterfield in one room. He removed his shirt, she her blouse. He took off his under shirt, she her bra. He stared at her chest as he undid his pants and let them fall to the floor. She dropped her skirt. "Before we get too involved, Yankel," she said as she placed her fingers inside her panties. "I have to tell you something." "What?" he asked, his eyes focused on her bared chest. "I have acute angina." Yankel raised his eyes and smiled. "Thank God! Because your breasts aren't much to look at."

The hairdresser was only a few blocks from the apartment. In fact, it was the same one my wife had gone to on Saturdays. Although we had lived farther south then, Edith drove up here because a lot of her friends lived in the neighbourhood. Being a cop, I preferred to live closer to the heart of the city. That took Edith away from friendly territory and placed her in surroundings that were cold. I had discovered that the closer to the heart of the city you lived, the more alone you were. I don't know if this was true for everyone, but it was true for Edith.

Realizing my thoughts were drifting to memories of my wife, I pushed them away, reluctant to relive what had happened. I didn't want to think about the way she had died.

I entered the salon, not sure what kind of a reception I was going to get, and looked for Judy Weiner, the owner. She appeared from a back room when she heard the buzzer.

"Gabe! It's been a while. How are you?"

"Fine. Yeah, it's been a few years."

"Five, to be exact," she said. "What brings you here?" She smiled warmly.

The look she gave me was tender. I knew she had a "thing" for me. One of the reasons I was reluctant to see her. "I'm here about Annie Weisz."

"Dear God!" Judy exclaimed. "Wasn't that awful?"

"I'm the investigating officer. I understand Mrs. Weisz was your client. Is there anything you can tell me about her?" I watched Judy absorb my request. She still looked good, I thought. Trim. Doesn't show her age, which I knew was early fifties. I could see she was disappointed that I hadn't come to see her.

"I don't know what I can tell you," she said. "She was nice. Not a complainer like some I know. Been coming here for over ten years. Lived alone, but you must know that."

"Yes. She was widowed, I figured. Do you know anything about her husband?"

Judy nodded. "Everyone did. He died in the camps during the war. I got the impression it was a Harlequin romance with a sad ending. I think she lived her love story in her mind. Had many friends, no one close. I'd say she was pretty predictable. She was a sweet old woman."

"Any changes in her living pattern or her behaviour recently?"

Judy frowned. "You know, maybe there was. Last Monday she seemed very preoccupied. I asked her if I could help. She said she was waiting for an important telephone call that night."

"Anything else?"

"You might check with Sam."

"Who's Sam?"

"Sam Belmont, the mailman. If anyone knew anything about her, he did."

"How's that?"

"Thought maybe he was interested in her, but they never went out together. He helped her with her correspondence a few years ago. Helped write to places for documentation on her husband's death. Being a mailman, he had access to information about who and what. Annie sent out a lot a letters with his help. Poor soul, never gave up hope her husband was alive."

"Her apartment was broken into. Do you know of anything that she had that might interest a thief?"

"What could she have? Old age pension? She wasn't rich."

"Anything else?"

Judy thought a moment. "No, I don't think so."

"Well, thanks, Judy. You've been very helpful." I smiled.

"I'm glad I could help." There was an uncomfortable pause in the conversation before Judy asked, "Care to come for dinner later this week?"

This was what I was afraid would happen. She was ready to pick up where she left off five years ago. "I'm pretty busy with this case. In fact, I have several cases I'm working on. Been making a mess of my personal life. Can I have a rain check?"

"Sure, anytime." She extended her hand.

I took it and gave it a squeeze. Judy didn't release my hand right away. I was becoming uncomfortable. She was sending me too many messages and they all said the same thing.

"Don't be a stranger," she said.

"I won't. Thanks again." I turned and left. Maybe I should say escaped.

Oₙₑ ᴏꜰ ᴛʜᴇ things about being a homicide detective I liked was I didn't have to punch a clock. I could call it a day when my shift was over if I wanted, but I rarely did. I often worked longer than I had to because I enjoyed the action. Sounds corny, but in truth, pitting myself against someone who took the law into his own hands and catching him was a rush. Working around obstacles, finding the missing pieces, even making wrong deductions were all part of the game. And luck plays a small part in investigations. There were always moments of disappointment. Times when I had to back off because I was going in circles, but they were few and far between. I had a good track record of winning. That meant spending a lot of time playing the game. That meant being absent from those who needed me more. Hindsight, as everyone knows, is twenty-twenty. My long hours were a major factor in my wife's untimely death. After twenty-five years of marriage, I had developed a work routine and had believed my wife understood, had accepted my unpredictable hours, my moodiness, the lack of affection. It was self-discipline. I witnessed the ugliness of life every day and was unable to turn off the feelings of anger and disgust. My only daughter became a stranger to me. Without realizing it, I had pushed my wife and daughter out of my life, and now I was paying for my neglect. Now I worked longer to avoid going home to the loneliness, to the memories, to the self-pity. My wife was dead, and my daughter was gone.

Edith had been an orphan. Her parents had died in the war. She was eleven when she was found wandering the streets in Krakow after the war ended and handed over to a Jewish agency. It was assumed that a gentile had hidden her for four years, then abandoned her when her parents didn't return to pay him and take her off his hands. It wasn't unusual. It had happened often. She came to Canada in 1953. We met at the Spadina Y and were married a year later. She wasn't big on sex and I could accept that. We had our daughter, Miriam, about two years later. When Miriam was ten, Edith started having nightmares. At least, I called them nightmares. Who would have thought that nightmares were an illness?

I used to wake her when she thrashed about next to me. I always asked what her dreams were about. Her answer was always the same – she couldn't remember. I didn't really believe her, but I never pushed it. I had my life of fighting crime, while my wife fought her nightmares – alone. One night I came home late, expecting to find her asleep as usual – and found her dead. She was in bed fully clothed. She had swallowed an overdose of tranquillizers and antidepressants. Her doctor told me a few days after the funeral that my wife had confided in him that she had been sexually molested as a child – often. She wouldn't elaborate further, but said she'd never forgotten those painful memories. The doctor recommended she see a psychiatrist, but she wouldn't, nor did she want me to know.

There had been signs. I had seen them and ignored them. She'd become melancholy and withdrawn. I should have known something was seriously wrong, but I was too preoccupied with work. Still, I was a trained detective. It was my job to recognize when something was out of the ordinary. Edith had been too young to die. Only fifty-five.

I knew a lot of Holocaust survivors, and they had seemed no different from anyone else, but since Edith's death, I had learned otherwise. Many never forgot the pain. They tried. I hadn't realized what they lived with. Not long after Edith's death, my daughter left home when I was at work and never returned. No note, nothing. She didn't understand what it was that her mother lived with, but I knew she blamed me for her death. I shook my head to rid it of such thoughts, and tried to focus on the present.

As the lead investigator, I attended the post mortem. The pathologist's report on Annie Weisz was as I expected, death from a heart attack. Apparently she had clogged arteries, and her breathing must have been a problem for a while. We Jews have our own ethnic cleansing. It's called shmaltz. My mother would make chicken soup every Friday and if it didn't have at least three rings of fat floating in the liquid, it wasn't thick enough. I had spent the morning at her apartment looking through the drawers to see if there were any clues that would steer me in a direction I could follow. I found nothing. She liked things being neat. I could tell by how her clothes were hung and the way the contents of drawers, the ones not turned inside out by the intruder, were kept. There was the normal accumulation of odds and ends, some photographs, always with people her age, a comfortable place that must have resembled the occupant. Her neighbours said she was a quiet person. Played bingo in the social room, a member of the Bernard Betel Centre at Steeles and Bathurst, went on bus trips and liked to read. I found enough evidence of that in her apartment – a bookcase full of romance novels.

The stolen items were not expensive, hardly worth taking. A neighbour had looked around the rooms to see if she could tell what was missing: a sterling silverware set in a walnut box, she said, silver-plated Sabbath candlesticks, several ornate dishes with an unusual pattern and a new radio. Value in the low four-figure range. She had a record player and quite a few old thirty-threes – Frank Sinatra, Perry Como, Andy Williams. Ballads and love songs. No one stole vinyl records anymore. Most drawers were pulled out. The thief had been looking for something he knew was in the apartment. Could she have hidden a lot of cash in the apartment? Old people do that. Doubtful. If she had any in the apartment, why did she have only twenty dollars in her purse? She had a savings account at the bank at the corner plaza, some Canada and Israel Bonds, GICs, but no big money. No more than what I expected from someone who had worked all her life for minimum wage and scrimped to save. So, now the sixty-four-thousand-dollar question – why her?

What Judy Weiner had said about the mailman, Sam Belmont was interesting. When I returned to headquarters, I ran his name through the computer. No criminal record, not even a parking ticket. A phone call later to a friend in Personnel at the main post office, and I knew a little more. Belmont had been employed by the post office for thirty-odd years, was a hard worker and divorced. Had one kid. A boy. I went to Family Court to learn the details of the divorce. It seemed that Sam's wife had committed adultery. He had held down two jobs, and while working his ass off, his wife was exposing hers to others. When Sam learned this, he threw her out; his son went with her. Sam Belmont appeared to be just one of the drones who made the system work. Still he might know something useful about Annie Weisz.

Back at the office, I typed everything I knew into the computer, then leaned back on my chair and closed my eyes. Too many things needed attending to, but I had run out of gas. I was finding it harder to finish my day. I couldn't tell whether it my age or depression. More than likely it was both. Holloway figures I suffer from Jewish guilt. He hasn't a clue what Jewish guilt is. Tomorrow I begin babysitting Iris Forester, a divorced woman, no less. I don't need this.

"Sleeping, Pop?"

I looked up at Homicide Detective Simon Munz, the department's biggest *putz*. He stood out; a goliath of a man with the arms, neck and shoulders of a wrestler, small beady eyes and, I figured, the brains of a gnat. "Welcome back," I said. "Have a good trip?" I straightened myself in my chair and pulled the sheets from the printer.

"Yeah. I see you've been busy. Do you know I asked to be your partner after I returned from Vancouver?" I could feel Simon's hostility.

"I have a partner."

"So I heard. I think your buddy arranged that, knowing about my request."

I looked up again. "I hadn't realized working with me was so enviable."

Simon grinned. "I like you, Pops. You're good at what you do – whatever it is."

"I like you too, Simon – but from a distance."

"Pops, you've got a few years left," Simon snarled. "Make your life easier and get rid of the guy who's coming to work with you. You got me. I'll hurry your retirement for you, then the department will have one less old fart stumbling around here, taking up space and doing fuck all."

"The guy's a gal."

"Really? Then it won't last. I'll make sure of that."

I looked into Munz's grinning face and said nothing. He walked to his desk and began flipping through the papers that had accumulated since he'd left for Vancouver to pick up a prisoner. I got up and left the office. Munz was trouble even when he was pleasant. "As if I don't have enough on my plate," I grumbled to myself.

I WAS AT my desk all morning, mostly on the telephone getting information from Forensics. At noon Iris Forester appeared and headed straight for me. I could see every pair of male eyes following her as she manoeuvred around the desks. She was attractive – too attractive for a cop – maybe five-eight, and carried herself well; she seemed to glide over the floor. Her hair, long, brunette, eyes bright and smile engaging. Her short skirt revealed more than two attractive knees. She reached my desk and extended her hand. "Hello, Gabe. Good to see you again."

I took her hand. She had a firm handshake. I retrieved a chair from another desk and indicated that she sit. She crossed her legs and I felt my testosterone stir. I needed this like a hole in the head, I thought. "So, you're in Homicide? Your uncle has said some nice things about you. He's very proud of you."

"That's nice," she said.

The way she said it, it sounded like it wasn't. Family troubles, I remembered. Shit! I'm running in circles trying to figure solutions to my cases and now I've got to deal with someone else's family problems. "Well, I understand you wanted to partner with me. How come?"

"At the Police College, you have a reputation. You've handled just about every type of case. I want to learn, Gabe. It's important to me. Holloway said you were going to be my *zaida*. What's that mean?"

"He's just being cute. I'm no *zaida*."

"Is that a Jewish man?"

"No, a grandfather. Someone who's old. I'm no grandfather. At least I don't think I'm one. My kid's not married – wasn't when I last saw her. Okay. Let's get down to business. I've several cases, but one in particular I want to concentrate on – a B and E that resulted in the owner, an old woman, having a fatal heart attack. At the moment, I have no suspects, but I need to talk to her mailman. Seems they were friendly. He might be able to –."

A shadow fell across them. "This your new partner?" Munz interrupted.

Iris turned her head and smiled.

"You two will make a good combination. Beauty and the Beast." He laughed at his joke.

Iris's smile disappeared.

"Maybe you'd like to apply for a transfer and be my partner. We'd make a better team. More…intimate."

Iris's gaze was cold.

"So, are you single?"

"Why?"

"Babes like you shouldn't have to stay home alone." His grin had ugly overtones.

"Thanks for your concern."

"So, you single?"

"It's none of your business."

Munz's features turned ugly. "I'm Simon Munz. You must have heard of me."

"I don't believe so. Are you the janitor?"

Munz's lip curled. "You got a smart mouth."

Iris stood and faced Munz. "Whatever I got, none of it is yours."

"I don't like smart mouths. I was just trying to be friendly, but I see you and the old man are two of a kind. You being a broad means nothing to me. Smart-mouth me again and you'll find out who Simon Munz is."

"I already know what you are and I'm not impressed."

Munz sneered. "You and I ain't finished. I'm putting you in my book with the old man. Count your days here. They won't be many." Munz turned and left the room.

Iris sat down, scowling furiously. "God, what an asshole. Who was he?"

"Trouble."

"I didn't instigate this. He did. I gather he doesn't like you."

"He doesn't like anybody." I stood. "Let's go. We have work to do." Without waiting for an answer, I walked around Iris and headed for the door.

Iris followed.

I DROVE. THE silence was heavy in the car as we headed north to Sam Belmont's address. A few times I glanced at Iris but said nothing. I could tell she was percolating.

"You don't want me as a partner, do you," Iris said.

"It's not personal."

"Of course it is. Do you have a problem with women?"

I snorted. It wasn't what I thought she was going to say. "No more than you have a problem with men. I noticed you went for the jugular when Munz came on to you."

"I've met his kind before. Neanderthals. All balls and no brains. The standards for being a detective had to be low when he signed on. The man's a *putz.*"

I laughed. "You'll get no argument from me."

"Why take me on if you don't want me?" Iris asked.

"Not everything is black and white, sweetie."

Iris glared at me. "I'm not anyone's sweetie, Gabe. I'm Detective Iris Forester and I earned that title. I didn't sleep my way to here, I worked harder than any man to get where I am, and I don't like being patronized. By you or some pre-historic dick."

I drove a block before pulling over to the curb. "It's not personal, Iris. I prefer working alone, but I'm not allowed.

Greg asked me to work with you, so I am. I understand there's a problem between you, your father and him. I'm sorry about that, but it's not my problem. It's obvious Greg cares about you. You could have asked for another assignment if you and your uncle were not getting along, but you didn't. I figure whatever it is between you can't be serious, because you're here. That's what a detective does, kid – figure. I need to get used to you. I'm sure I will, I just need time. I have a daughter your age. We didn't get along. In fact, I've not seen her in about five years. So I, too, have problems. I try to leave mine at home. Understood?"

Iris nodded.

I put the car back in gear and continued on to the Belmont house. The tension was still there. It was hard enough living with myself, and now I had to contend with someone else's problem.

Sam Belmont's neighbourhood had a reputation for being a trouble spot. Too many people in too little space can become a breeding ground for the ills in society: prostitution, drugs, excessive alcohol consumption, a lot of drunken fights and nasty domestic scenes, to name just a few. It was a high-density apartment area with semidetached houses separating the tall, unattractive structures. A large unemployment ratio, an ethnic mosaic that resulted in racially divided gangs. The crime was controlled by a few misfits who used the poverty and despair as a weapon, selling false dreams in a nickel bag as a means of escaping the invisible walls that locked the parents and kids in their self-imposed prison, and their victims to a way of life that usually ended tragically. The Belmont house was a semi-detached two-storey, looked like every other semi on the block. It seemed the craze years ago. Built them fast, build them cheap and sell fast.

We parked on the opposite side of the street. When we rang the doorbell, no one answered. Sam Belmont finished work about one in the afternoon. It was half past the hour now. As we waited in the car for him to arrive, Iris sat, silent and stiff as a board. The fire was still burning. I ignored her, preferring the silence.

At about two, Sam pulled into his narrow driveway, got out of his car and entered the house. I turned to Iris and said, "When we get inside, just sit and observe, I'll do the talking. After we leave, give me your impressions. Okay?"

Iris nodded, her lips pressed into a thin line.

"Right, let's go." We walked across the street. I rang the bell again. The curtain covering the window in the door was pulled back and a man peered out. The door opened slightly. "I'm Detective Gabe Garshowitz, this is Detective Iris Forester." I showed him my identification and Iris did also. "Are you Sam Belmont?"

"Yes. What's this about?"

"Can we do this inside?"

"What's this about?" Belmont asked again, making no move to let us enter.

"I'm investigating a break-and-enter."

"My son's not home. Why you hounding him again?"

I didn't know the kid was with his father. I tried not to show my surprise. "I'm not. I'm here because you knew the victim, Annie Kapinsky Weisz."

Belmont's eyes were hard and unyielding. He looked at us as if deciding whether or not to close the door in our faces. At last he stepped back and opened the door wider, then indicated that we enter. The living room was small and well kept. I scanned the room looking for signs that might give me some indication of the sort of man who lived here. The furniture was old, but polished, and the couch and tub chair had slip-covers. There was a modest-sized television against the wall, flanked by bookcases. There were few books but many bowling trophies. The scattered pictures appeared to be of Sam Belmont and various friends, but none of a man young enough to be his son. I sat down in the tub chair. Iris remained standing. Belmont went to the couch and sat, moving an open book of crossword puzzles to one side. That answered the first thought that came to my mind. He had answered 'Yes,' not 'Yeah,' which told me he might have a good command of English. The crossword book confirmed that thought.

Another soon-to-be pensioner, I figured. His skin was lined from age and weather. Most of his hair was white and, lucky for him, he still had a lot of it. He had a slight stoop to his left shoulder, which I presumed was from carrying a mailbag for so many years, and he looked to be in good physical condition. Considering what he'd been doing for so many years, I didn't expect otherwise.

"Been a postman long?" I asked, wanting to ease the tension.

"Over thirty years."

"Must have had opportunities to get off the streets. Were you ever interested? Had to have been in some miserable weather over the years."

He nodded. "Some."

I could tell that I would have to squeeze him to get any information. He wasn't the talkative type. His eyes seem to bore into me and it was apparent he didn't trust me.

"What is it you want to know?" Belmont asked.

"I understand you helped Mrs. Weisz with some correspondence about her late husband."

"Yes. For about a year. The governments we wrote to don't always answer back. We kept trying. It took time to get any kind of answer. Annie always thought her husband went to Dachau, but we couldn't get any confirmation from the Dachau records that he was ever there."

"Do you think he's dead?"

"Sure, but I can't prove it. That's not unusual, considering what went on back then."

"Did she believe he was dead?"

Belmont shook his head. "No."

"Why your interest in Mrs. Weisz?" I saw the solemn look

on his face turn to anger.

"What do you mean by that?" he asked.

"Just a question."

"Your question is out of line. She was a nice person. No other reason."

"Did she pay you for your services?" I figured I already had him mad at me, so what was there to lose.

"Of course not."

I decided to jump into the puddle with both feet. "Did you talk to your son about her?"

Sam leaped to his feet. "What's my son got to do with any of this? Is he a suspect? Can't you cops leave him alone? He's not a bad kid. It's you cops that gave him a bad reputation. I want you to leave."

I rose slowly to my feet. "Everyone's a suspect, Mr. Belmont. That includes you and your son. Mrs. Weisz is dead and someone was responsible. It's my job to try to find who that was and arrest him or her. This is done by elimination. Cops don't give people bad reputations – people give those to themselves. You and your son are names on my list. What I do know is that you knew the woman's history better than most. I'm not hounding your son, Mr. Belmont. I'm investigating a crime."

Belmont went to the front door and opened it. As I passed him, he said, "Detective Garshowitz, my son had nothing to do with Annie's death."

Back in the car I turned to Iris and asked, "Well, what do you think?"

"Seemed all right to me. What was I supposed to be looking for?"

"Listen, sweetie. You were supposed to hear his voice, watch his mannerisms, notice his eyes and look the room over. That's for starters. So, what do *you* think?"

Iris's lips tightened. If looks could kill, my car would need a new owner. "I believe him. What do you think?"

"I'm the one with the experience. I wanted to know what you thought." I started the car and pulled into the street.

T HE NEXT THING I did was run a check on Alex Belmont. The way the father had defended him meant that the kid had been in trouble before. What I needed to find out was how much. What I discovered didn't surprise me. Alex had a rap sheet as long as my arm. Busted for dealing drugs when he was sixteen. Juvenile Detention. Probation. Juvenile Detention. When he was eighteen, charged with assault. Believed to be an enforcer for some hood until arrested. Had a reputation that stunk. His mother had her boyfriends sleep over a lot. Apparently the kid went back to live with his father last year, after his mother left the city with some guy without telling him. He was now twenty-one. My sources told me that Alex used the water fountain at the corner mall as his meeting place. I showed Iris the rap sheet. "It's time to see Alex Belmont."

"Goin' to bring him in?"

"No, I just want to watch him. See what he's like in his own environment. You can learn more about a fish watching him swim than by catching him and looking at his features. I'm interested in watching this fish swim. Maybe into my net."

I parked my car near the main entrance to the mall. Someone had sprayed a swastika on the telephone booth. I shook my head in disbelief. "That's stupid," I said to Iris, "if they think the swastika is a symbol of power. It was a symbol of decay. The only power it had was to destroy the believers."

"Did you lose any family in the war?" Iris asked.

"Almost every Jew lost someone. We lost them in the Holocaust, too. Remember that. Millions of Jews died in the Holocaust."

"Touchy."

"No, sensitive."

We entered the mall and I stopped inside the door and took a newspaper out of a waste receptacle. "See that bench in front of the fountain? I'm going to sit there. You stay here and watch. Move around but don't go too far."

"Why are you going to sit?"

"I'm going to be conspicuously inconspicuous. I want him to notice me while I'm observing him. This is a get-acquainted trip. This is his element. I'm not interested in messing with him, just observing him."

"Why can't I sit with you?"

"Look. You watch me. If I get into trouble, then come. Don't make a big deal out of this. If he doesn't show in an hour, I'll get up and leave."

Iris stalked off, then turned to glare at me. I smiled, but she didn't.

I made my way to the fountain. The mall was quiet. Being a weekday, there wasn't much pedestrian traffic. Some of the shops had sales, but for me, the richness of the stores' decor belied the fact that a sale was really a sale. I sat on a bench, opened my newspaper and pretended to read. Alex was not here yet. Others were – two white guys, two blacks. One smoked. There were signs all over the mall clearly stating No Smoking, but that didn't make any difference to the one puffing. Another tough kid who would spend more of his life behind bars than outside them, I thought.

I'd been sitting for more than an hour and noticed that the four had glanced my way a few times. I figured I'd been made. Alex must be late, otherwise his friends wouldn't have stuck around as long as they had. There was a little excitement among them when a young man sauntered in their direction. From the look of him, it wasn't his brawn that made him a leader, it was the confidence on his face. I'd seen his type before. They thought they could walk on water. His friends crowded around him. I could hear raucous laughter when one black guy pointed in my direction. Two of them strutted around Alex in an exaggerated imitation of a chicken. I was about to become their sport.

Alex ambled over to me, a grin on his thin pockmarked face. Dark glasses hid his eyes and his short stubbled haircut had two arrows cut into it, meeting at the base of his head. His fingers continually opened and closed, as if he was testing the joints.

"Hi, Pop," Alex said. "I hear you been around here for a while today."

"Killing time," I said, keeping my voice expressionless.

This brought a laugh from his friends, who had moved up behind Alex.

"You a cop, Pop?" More laughter. Alex's grin widened.

"Do I look like one?" I answered.

"Kind of old for a cop, but maybe they upped the age limit. You an old cop?"

Alex's friends were enjoying the entertainment he was providing.

"I'm just minding my own business," I said calmly.

Alex had removed his glasses. His beady eyes assaulted me. "Are you? So…who are you?" The grin had changed to a smirk.

"What you see is what you get."

"And what have I got? Are you a pensioner doing your thing? Are you a slow reader?"

I shrugged.

"You're not afraid of me, are you?"

"Should I be?"

Alex nodded. "Yes. This is my turf and this bench is mine."

"Oh, I didn't know." I stood and folded my newspaper. During the entire confrontation, Alex's hands had not once stopped their opening and closing. Odds were he was on drugs, I thought. "I'm not looking to cause any trouble," I said.

"I'm glad. Maybe you'd like to get lost."

"I'm finished, anyway." I took a step, but Alex blocked my way. We stared into each other's eyes. Alex had to have the last word, even if it was silent. His face slowly broke into another smile and he stepped aside. I proceeded to walk away.

I had gone about ten feet when Alex called. "Hey, old man. Don't come back."

I stopped and turned to face him. "I can't promise you that, Alex." I saw the surprise on his face before turning and leaving the building, passing Iris on my way out. I waited for Iris to catch up and we walked toward the car. "What did you see, Iris?"

"He shot you."

"Must have missed."

"Two shots. In the back. He extended both his arms forward, cocked his thumbs as if they were triggers and bent them down, one at a time. Never blinked an eye, but he had a grin on him that said he was enjoying himself. What now?"

"Learn some more about the Belmonts."

The next day Iris and I made the rounds of the pawnshops.

A few had reputations for buying merchandise without trying too hard to confirm ownership, mostly items too inexpensive for anyone to go looking for, except a cop on a mission. I had also heard they were going to bury Annie Weisz tomorrow. The neighbours were arranging her funeral. I wanted to be there. There was something I had to do.

At the third pawnbroker, we hit pay dirt. There were a lot of musical instruments hanging on the walls, in display cases and out in the show window. "A reminder, Iris," I said. "If you go into the music business, make sure you have a sugar daddy."

"Not to worry. I don't even sing in the shower."

I grinned.

"You can take that grin off your face. I shower alone."

"Too bad."

"Excuse me for being so blunt, Casanova. I figure at your age, the only thing hard about you is your arteries."

I patted my chest. "Ouch. I hope I'm not bleeding."

I approached the wicket where the attendant sat, a burly, ruddy-faced guy with the broken veins and bulbous nose normally associated with too much drinking or boxing. His ears were normal, so I figured too much drinking. I produced my badge and Iris showed hers. "We're looking for some items that were stolen in a break-and-enter." I produced the list and pushed it under the bars. "Anything here look familiar?"

The attendant dragged the sheet towards him and gave it a cursive glance, then pushed it back. "Nah," he said. "Nuttin' I've seen."

"Nuttin'?"

"Nah," he said as he watched Iris wander around the shop.

I brought out a photograph of Alex Belmont. "He look familiar?" I asked.

The attendant gave the photograph a quick glance and shook his head. His eyes continued to follow Iris as she prowled about. Iris stopped before a shelf with several radios and picked one up. "Careful," he said. "You break it, you pay for it."

Iris replaced it on the shelf and picked up another, turning it over in her hands. "Gabe," she said, "come look."

I crossed to Iris. She handed me the radio and I looked it over, turning it around and under. It was the same colour and model as Annie Weisz's. The look in Iris's eyes told me she wanted I should bluff the attendant. We returned to the wicket. "Who pawned this?" I asked.

"I don't remember."

"I think that's the radio, Gabe," Iris said. "I'll call for a Forensic team to search the store for more items." She pulled out her cell phone.

The attendant glanced at the slip number and reluctantly opened his ledger. "John Smith," he said.

"Really? Was Pocahontas with him?"

"Who?"

"Do you have an address and telephone number?"

"No phone. An address." He showed what was written in his ledger. Iris copied the address down and went into the corner to use her cell phone.

I slipped the photograph under the wicket again. "Want to take another look?"

The attendant picked it up and stared at it, his mouth twisted in annoyance. "Could be."

Iris returned. "A branch of the North York Public Library on Steeles near Jane," she said.

"Anything else we might find here?" I asked the attendant.

"I don't buy hot merchandise," the man said indignantly.

"Did the seller want to sell something else?"

"I don't remember."

"Too bad." I turned to Iris. "Finish that call to headquarters and get a team down here to check the inventory."

"Okay," the attendant said. "Some silverware. I wasn't interested. Got too many now that ain't moving."

"You've been a big help. So much so, we'll be back. And if

you're smart, you'll take inventory."

Outside, Iris asked, "You think it's the Belmont kid?"

"Does Carter make little liver pills?"

I SAT IN my car across from the Belmonts' house. My meeting yesterday with Alex was enough to tell me the kid wasn't worth salvaging. I'm not supposed to judge, just arrest, but some criminals I take a dislike to and there's nothing I can do to change my opinion. It goes against what they taught me years ago, but I'm human, too. Alex's father would be the only one to feel the pain of his kid's arrest. Some parents were blind to their kid's behaviour, always hoping, like a battered wife who keeps going back to her husband, blaming themselves, hoping that love will make things better, only it never does.

There were a lot of pieces still missing in the puzzle, but I had enough to make an arrest. It seemed something had gone wrong with Alex's plan and whatever he had gone looking for he never found. What he got was me closing in on him.

It was time to make an arrest.

The street was cordoned off. He was a loose canon, maybe even had a gun. Chances were he did. I got out of the car and looked to see if the others were in place. Iris waved from beside the house. A shot rang out. "Shit!" I exclaimed, and raced to the house. Iris and I arrived at the door at the same time. A couple of cops were behind us. I pushed open the door, my gun drawn, and stopped short. Sam Belmont stood over his son's body, his face and shirt splattered in blood, his hands at his sides, a gun hanging loosely from his fingers. I edged closer and gently removed the weapon from his hand.

"What happened?" I asked.

He stared down at the body. "It was him," Sam said in a voice so soft that I barely heard the words.

"What happened?" I asked again as I bent down and felt for a pulse. There was none.

Two police officers held Sam Belmont's arms. "We argued. He brought out a gun and threatened me. He became enraged when I ordered him out of my house. He was going to kill me. I'm his father, and he was going to kill me. I wanted to help him. We wrestled. He fell over the couch and dropped the gun. I picked it up and pointed it at him, ordering him to get out of my house. He charged me, and I…I shot him."

Sam faced me. "He thought she had money in the apartment. After your visit I went into his bedroom to convince myself that he had had nothing to do with the robbery. I recognized a set of silverware in his clothes closet. I had dinner there a few times and commented on the pattern. It's my fault. I told him too much about her. I told him she was a wealthy woman. I didn't mean money, but memories. She was wealthy in that she possessed beautiful memories. I envied that. My son heard only the word 'wealthy' and thought I meant money and jewels, I guess, and robbed her. He laughed at me when I said he was cruel. He didn't care. Why? How did he get that way?"

I handcuffed Sam and told him to sit and say nothing. His lawyer would do the rest.

I STOOD OUTSIDE the ring of friends and watched the ceremony. The rabbi said some nice things about Annie Kapinsky Weisz. Her pain was over, her suffering at an end; the last page in the book of her life was closed. True, I thought, but at least she and Hershl were together now. I made sure that Hershl's photograph was put inside the coffin with her. I watched until the last shovelful of earth had been tossed into the grave before I went to my car.

I stood beside the driver's door and stared at the expanse of lawn with its many gravestones. The sky was overcast and solemn. Snow was coming; I could smell it. It would cover the scars of the earth, but only the physical scars. My wife was buried here, too. Before going to Annie Weisz's funeral, I had visited her grave. It was quiet. My thoughts were filled with guilt. I made the pilgrimage here only once a year during High Holidays. It was my penance. Edith had been a good person who deserved better. Normally I would just stand before the stone and stare. Today, I told her I was sorry. How many Annie Weiszes would I need before I could forgive myself?

I got in the car and drove away.

The Solomon Silver Case

7

Her expression was filled with contempt as she stared down at the body of the young man, the dead eyes open, his head in a pool of blood. She placed the revolver into her purse and looked around to see if there was anything that would reveal her presence. On the small writing desk by the bed she saw a single sheet of hotel stationery with her name on it. Her eyes widened as she read the words. She turned to look at the body again as she crushed the sheet into a ball with one gloved hand and stuffed it into her purse.

"After all I've done for you, this is my reward?" she whispered hoarsely. "We'll see. You could have had everything if only you'd *listened to me." Her hands were clenched into fists. She stepped around the body and went to the door, peering out into the corridor; it was deserted. Closing the door behind her, she listened to the lock fall into place. Knowing she needed to leave the fifth floor of the hotel without drawing attention to herself, she took the stairs to the second floor, made her way to the opposite end of the corridor and down the stairs to the ground floor, well away from the main section of the lobby. It was a busy hotel, so her presence should go unnoticed. She left the building and crossed the street to where her car was parked. As she passed a sewer, she dropped the gun and surreptitiously kicked it into the opening before continuing to her car. "The ingrate," she muttered as she pulled out of the parking lot. "We'll see who has the last word."*

She glanced at her wristwatch and realized the time: she would need an alibi. She would have to convince the police that she couldn't possibly have done this. She smiled, knowing who she would blame as she manoeuvred through the downtown Toronto traffic.

I CAME OUT of the coffee shop with a large cup of steaming coffee and a bag with a bagel, slid into the passenger side of the car, uncapped the container and took a sip. "I needed this," I said to Iris, sighing with pleasure as I savoured the flavour.

"You needed that like you need a hole in your head," she said. "You drink too much coffee and you're putting on weight because of all the junk you eat," she said. "Porky Pig was not a cop."

"I need my coffee to get me through the day and I like something with my coffee."

"Drink juice," she shot back.

"Iris, you're a nag. Start the car and let's get back to headquarters so we can finish our report. Then we'll go out for lunch."

"Wrong."

"About finishing the report?"

Iris snorted. "About lunch. The last time, you conned me into paying. Someone like you should eat at Bloomsbury's or Sunshine's. One price for all you can eat."

I smiled broadly, but it had no effect on her. I had become sloppy about my appearance, more so lately than before I hooked up with Iris. I didn't want anyone to think that working with a young attractive woman would change me, and to prove it, took the opposite tack. Dumb logic. I took another sip of coffee and watched as she wound her way through the traffic.

"Did you hear the story about the cop chasing a new Mercedes down the Don Valley Parkway?" I asked.

"No, and I'm not interested."

"The guy in the Mercedes realizes the cop is gaining and puts the pedal to the metal. The Mercedes shoots ahead. Then reality hits him. 'What the heck am I doing?' He pulls over. The cop comes up to him, takes his licence and examines it and the car. 'It's been a long day, this is the end of my shift and it's Friday. I don't feel like more paperwork. I know you could have outrun me, but you stopped. If I believe your excuse, I'll let you go.' The guy thinks for a second and says, 'Last week a cop ran off with my wife. For a minute, I thought you might be him and were trying to give her back!' The cop drove away."

"Where do you find these nuggets?"

"On the Internet," I said, covering my mouth with the coffee cup. "Iris, you have no sense of humour."

"Tell me something funny and I'll laugh."

"What're you doing after work?"

"Soaking in a tub," she said.

"You want company?"

Iris sighed in mock despair and shook her head.

"I didn't think so," I said. "Just testing the water."

"Why don't you call up Judy Weiner?"

"She has marriage on her mind. That's not for me anymore. She's nice to be with in public, but I've learned not to be alone with her."

"How so?"

"A lot of hints. Provocative ones. Her intentions are too obvious."

"Aren't you lonely?"

"Nope. Just don't always like being alone. Don't worry. You enjoy yourself. I'll survive."

"I hate it when you act like a martyr."

I chuckled, finished the last of the coffee and threw the cup into a bag at my feet.

"Tell me, Gabe, after you finish the bagel, what do you do with the hole?"

"Ha-ha," I said. "I save it for later."

The radio crackled and the dispatcher's voice came on. "Detective Garshowitz call in."

I unhooked the mike. "Detective Garshowitz."

"See the divisional detectives at the Park Hyatt Hotel on Avenue Road."

"On my way." I turned to Iris and grinned. "I guess you ain't soaking and I won't be alone for most of the tonight."

Iris rolled her eyes.

OUTSIDE THE PARK Hyatt, the usual media circus whenever there's a homicide was forming. Crews from the various television stations were blocking traffic with their vans. Police cars, their lights swirling red and white, were everywhere; cops controlled the gawkers and checked those entering the hotel to make sure they were guests. Whatever was waiting for them had obviously leaked out. We entered the lobby, which was already filled with cops and reporters, and made our way to an elevator being guarded by a cop. We showed him our badges.

"Fifth floor," he said. "Room 505."

We entered the elevator. "Must be a slow day in the newsroom; every station's already here," I said. "I don't like that."

"Why?"

"Too much media, too much attention on us. I don't like

people looking over my shoulder. I get bad vibes."

"Don't worry. I'll hold your hand."

I smiled. "Nice idea, wrong part of the anatomy."

"You're such a teddy bear, Gabe. If I ever came on to you, I think you'd panic and run."

"Wrong. I'd run, but I wouldn't panic."

We laughed.

The elevator door opened and we hurried down the corridor to the crime scene. A cop was at the door, and again we showed our badges. Forensics was already at work. I looked around to see who was in charge and was relieved to see Detective Stella Morgan.

I waved her over. "Hi, sweetie," I said. "What do we have here?"

"Hello, Gabe, Iris. This one yours?"

"Yes," Iris said. "Will this take time? I was hoping to soak in a tub tonight."

"Forget about the tub, Iris. What we have is a dead male, probably killed by a small-calibre bullet to the head. My guess it's a .22. There's an entrance wound but no exit. Age between thirty and thirty-five, weight about 175 pounds. White. Name is Solomon Silver and he lived in Hamilton."

"When did it happen?"

"Looks like death occurred some time early last night. The temperature of the body indicates that rigor mortis is leaving rather than entering."

"Can you be more specific?" Iris asked.

"Depends on the body weight, but we figure twelve hours for rigor mortis to enter and twelve to leave. The lower extremities are still stiff, so we're assuming more than twelve hours, but less than twenty-four. An autopsy will confirm the time more accurately."

"Lesson over. What else?" I said.

"The cleaner discovered him about eleven this morning. The door was locked. She said she heard the television. She used her pass key after she knocked and got no answer. There wasn't any Do Not Disturb card on the knob to indicate whether he was in or not."

"Was there a struggle?" I asked.

"Looks like it. Some furniture's out of place, but nothing heavy. The bedspread's been pulled off the bed, the lamp and the telephone were on the floor. There's powder burns on his temple where the bullet entered, which means the revolver was pressed against his head when it was fired – which is often the case in a suicide. But there's no revolver at the scene, which indicates maybe someone else pulled the trigger and took the revolver with them. Anyway, when we get the body to the morgue, we'll check his hands."

"Do you think it was robbery?"

"No. He still had his wallet and credit cards. Had about two hundred dollars in cash in his pocket, and he's still wearing a watch, nothing expensive but not cheap either. I'll talk to you guys later, have to start collecting." She returned to where she'd been when we arrived.

"Well, what do you make of it?" I asked Iris.

"The door was locked. The victim must have invited the murderer into his room, so that means it was someone he knew. The victim is not a big person. The killer could have been a man or woman. No robbery could mean the murder was premeditated. It's a bit odd that the report from the revolver wasn't heard, but then, these rooms are well insulated against sound. What did I leave out?"

"Nothing. We need more information." I called Stella back.

"You're keeping me from my work, Gabe," Stella said. "When we finish here, I'll give you my report."

"Are his clothes packed or in the drawers?"

"Haven't looked yet."

"Could you?" I gave her my cajoling smile. She rolled her eyes as she turned and went to the suitcase lying on the luggage rack across from the bed.

"Empty," she said, then began opening dresser drawers. "His clothes are in here," she said, pointing at the last open drawer. "Not much either."

"Count his underwear."

"Two pairs, both worn."

"Thanks."

"What does that mean?" Iris asked.

"People who stay in hotels for only one or two nights tend to live out of their suitcase. If they stay longer, the clothes usually make it into the drawers. This guy's been here for at least three days, if I'm right. What he had wasn't enough for three days. I know by the amount of underwear he had. He stayed longer than he expected. I'm going to talk to the people at the front desk while you knock on doors on this floor. I'll meet you back here."

"Why can't I have the front desk?" she said, a look of annoyance on her face.

I pretended surprise. "You want the front desk?"

"Yes."

"Too late. I got it." I laughed, leaving her sputtering.

There is no glamour in investigating a crime, just methodical and often monotonous work, but there is that surge of adrenalin when the pieces start fitting together and a whole picture emerges. It's no different from putting together a jigsaw puzzle. The trick is putting the right pieces together and hoping you can connect them. Premeditated murder occurs when the killer intends to kill and believes he has a foolproof plan. There's no such thing, of course. Sure, some do get away with it, but only because the investigating officer couldn't uncover all the pieces. Sometimes others interfere with the investigation, causing additional roadblocks, and of course there are times when the investigating officer is not on top of his game. I hesitate to call some cops incompetent, but I've witnessed some piss-poor investigations. Most times the murderer is just not as smart as he or she thought. Also the so-called perfect crime could be ruined by circumstances beyond the murderer's control. The sound of the report from the revolver could have brought someone to the door to look. There might have been unintentional shouting or an accidental passing in the corridor, an overheard name or words. These were the pieces that make a puzzle. A .22 bullet comes from a small revolver with very little punch, the sort of revolver a woman often uses, and it's small enough to fit in a purse or trouser pocket. More pieces. But they could be false clues. The worst thing an investigating officer can do is to speculate too early; it might lead the investigation off course. The smart cop follows the evidence and doesn't force it to follow his theory. If he manipulates the evidence, he generally has a case that is weak enough for a good attorney to pick apart. Of course if the investigating officer has tunnel vision, then he can make pork look like steak. I've seen it happen.

I approached the front desk. Two women and a man were behind the counter. I chose one of the women. I smiled. It always pays to have white teeth and fresh breath at such a time. The white teeth I can guarantee – they aren't mine. The breath is a matter of taste; probably today mine smelled of coffee and an empty stomach. "Homicide Detective Gabe Garshowitz," I said to the petite good-looking woman with whiter teeth than me. I showed her my badge. "I'm investigating the body found in room 505."

Her eyes became saucers. The man and woman next to her stopped what they were doing and stared at me. "Yes, sir," she meekly replied.

"Could I see the registration form and the hotel bill for that room?"

She punched the computer keys, printed out a copy of the bill and tore the sheet off the printer, then handed it to me. Then she excused herself and went to a side room and asked a man inside for something. I watched. She returned with a hotel application and a credit card imprint.

"Did Mr. Silver get any messages?" I asked as I looked over the hotel bill. It showed only the cost of the room plus taxes. My gaze took in all three of them behind the desk. They shook their heads. The credit card used was a gold card. There was a time when that would have impressed me, but not any more. I've heard enough silly stories about who gets the card to realize it was fool's gold. I heard a dog received an application once. I figured he must have had to give the bank a paw print to get his credit. I figured it was a he dog. If it were a she dog, the bank would want her father to co-paw it.

Several people approached the counter dragging their bags. Check out was by eleven in the morning. These people would be paying for a day they didn't stay. A dead body had a tendency to cause people to forget about costs and want to be elsewhere.

I smiled at the woman again.

"I don't know, sir, but I'll see," she said as she went to the back of the registration section and checked the pigeonholes where keys and messages were left. "No," she said when she returned. "Nothing."

I looked at the sheet again and saw that Solomon Silver had driven a 1998 Toyota Camry, not the top model. The licence-plate number was given too. "Where would I find his car?" I asked.

She took the sheet from me and examined it. "He didn't use valet parking, so it would probably be on the second or third level under the hotel. First level is valet."

"Thank you," I said. "Any incoming calls?" She checked her computer after punching some keys, then shook her head. "One more thing – does each room have a safe, or does the office hold the valuables for the guests?"

"Each room, sir."

I nodded my appreciation and made my way to the elevator. The hotel business today was a different world than it used to be; it was more personal and left a paper trail. Now everything was computerized. Admission, wake-up calls, safety-deposit boxes in rooms, eating in the hotel and even checkout. Once you show up, it's possible that the front desk might never see you again. The lobby was noisy, guests coming and going, what with the television crews clamouring to put words and people onto film for the next newscast; the cops had their hands full trying to keep them in line, along with the gawkers, anxious to tell their friends what they saw. I took a moment to study the scene. The piranhas were hungry. I wondered how many of the stories that would appear on the six o'clock news or in the morning newspapers would be based on facts and how much on wishful speculation. Well, they had their job – and I had mine.

As I got off the elevator, Iris was returning to room 505.

"Nothing," she said. "Some guests are out for the day. One thought he heard something last night, but figured it was the television from another room. He was watching the movie *Twilight,* and there were gunshots in that movie. I called the front desk to ask which rooms were occupied last night on this floor, and if any had already checked out. Seven had checked out before the body was found. I asked the clerk to leave me a printout of who when we leave."

We entered room 505 and Stella made her way over to us. "The guy was recently married."

"How do you know that?" Iris asked curiously.

"His wedding ring. It fit well. No trouble getting it off," Stella said. "Men always gain weight after getting married."

"Says who?" I grunted.

Stella stuck a finger into my stomach. "What do you call that?"

"Aging."

"Bull!" Stella answered. "Most married men come home to a wife who cooks. Cops may be the exception, eating on the run because of the hours. You live alone, but you remember the cooking and eat to remember. The trouble with you, it's the wrong food you're buying."

"Women don't gain weight after marriage?"

"Didn't say that. Men always gain weight is what I said. That tells me he's recently married, year, two, maybe three. No more."

"That's one theory that don't fly with me."

Stella grinned. "What else you want to know?"

"Is the safe open or closed?"

"Open. Nothing inside and the bar's been depleted."

"Did you find any car keys?"

"Yes. In his jacket."

"Care to send someone down to open it for us? I'd like to see if there's anything inside that might shed some light on what Mr. Silver was doing in a hotel for three days in Toronto when he lives just about seventy kilometres away and can get home in an hour."

"I'll send Jonathan Wye down in a few minutes."

"We'll meet him at the front desk." I turned to Iris. "C'mon, sweetie, our work is ahead of us." I headed toward the elevator. Iris followed.

"How many times have I told you not to call me sweetie? I'm not your girlfriend or your wife."

I didn't respond, just continued heading for the elevator.

"Hey, wait a minute," she called.

"What?"

"Let's walk down."

"Why, you need some exercise?"

"We're only five floors up, actually four, because the mezzanine is not a regular floor. The killer could have walked down without any trouble. The elevators are right in the centre of the lobby. Why would the killer look for trouble? Let's walk."

"Makes sense," I said. "Sorry about the sweetie."

"Mule shit," she responded, and passed me on the way to the sign that indicated the stairs. "Any ideas yet?" she asked over her shoulder.

"More like questions. What puzzles me most is why he was here. If he's seeing someone, then why no telephone calls from or to his room? His bill showed no outside calls. Is he selling something, and if so, why no lunch or dinner tabs with his client? Again, his room bill had nothing on it but the charges for the room. Maybe there's an answer in his car."

We reached the mezzanine. "He could have eaten in the hotel, but paid cash."

"Okay, check that out." I looked both ways. "Left or right?" I asked.

"Left. It's shorter to the main floor."

We followed the corridor to the end and down the stairs to the main floor, not far from a door exiting to the street. "Let's go outside and walk around to the main entrance," I said. Outside, we scanned the block as we walked to see if there was anything that might help us in our investigation. "There's a couple of underground car parks on the side streets."

"What can you ask the parking attendant? 'Do you remember a woman or man taking their car out yesterday in the early evening?' Kind of vague, I think," Iris said.

As we entered the lobby, I had a thought. I went back to the desk and waited for the young woman to finish with what she was doing. I smiled at her again. "Did anyone make any inquiries about Mr. Silver in the three days he was here?"

"I worked yesterday and today. I wasn't here the day he arrived. He registered at 1:10 p.m. The attendant who was working then is off today."

Jonathan Wye made his way over to them. I looked at Iris. "You check out the car. I'm going upstairs again."

"What now?"

"I have an idea. Maybe the victim has relatives in Toronto. Also, I want to find out if someone notified his wife, and if so, when she's coming to Toronto. When you're finished with the car, come upstairs. I'll wait for you. This case just gets curiouser and curiouser."

A MURDER INVESTIGATION is conducted using what is called the MOM principle – Motive, Opportunity and Method. I didn't know who the murderer was or why there was a murder, but I knew when and how. Whoever Solomon Silver was meeting was someone who had to be confronted in Toronto. Toronto and Hamilton were too close to each other to be a real inconvenience for anyone to go from one city to another. So was the killer from Toronto, or was it someone who had followed him from Hamilton?

Mr. Silver's home address in Hamilton was in a modest

district not known for having a Jewish enclave. Being Jewish myself, I found it odd that he'd lived so far removed from the sections where other Jews lived. I knew Hamilton, having spent my summers there as a teenager with an uncle who was a fruit peddler at the old open market. As the city grew, the Jewish population shifted but remained intact. That conjured up a few possibilities. Betty Silver, the wife, had been informed of her husband's death by the local police and was on her way to Toronto to confirm that the body was indeed her husband's. It was always awkward dealing with the family of a victim. There was generally a sense of guilt, for whatever reason, that surrounded the last days of the deceased, a lot of tears, followed by anger and then the need for justice. Revenge is another word. In this case, I was mistaken about the tears.

The duty sergeant brought Betty Silver over to my desk. I shuffled papers around, trying to look busy. I stood. She was a good-looking woman, maybe not by Melrose Place standards, but she had a lovely face, was about five-ten, lean and tall, nice figure, with short blond hair like a boy's, soft brown eyes and sensuous lips that hid, I soon discovered, a sharp tongue. She looked older than her husband. I retrieved a chair from an empty desk and placed it behind her. She remained standing. She was all business. She had been to the morgue and made a positive identification. I had asked that she be brought to head-quarters to meet with me. I never found the morgue a place for conversation. Her eyes were dry, but her face was angry. "She did it," she said even before we were introduced.

"Who did it?" I said.

"His mother."

"I see," I said. "Why?"

"She didn't like me because I'm not Jewish."

Talk about guessing wrong. Not only no tears but already she knew who the killer was. I couldn't help noticing how well she was dressed. I'm not an expert on women's fashions, but I suspected she didn't buy her clothes at Wal-Mart. This was where Iris's expertise was needed, and she was nowhere near. "I don't understand," I said, and indicated that she take the seat. She seemed to hesitate as if sitting wasn't part of her agenda. I sat; reluctantly she did too. "My condolences, Mrs. Silver. I'm Homicide Detective Gabriel Garshowitz. Now, could you explain?"

"My mother-in-law forbade Solly to marry me. She threatened to disown him if he went through with the marriage, and when he did, she was furious. She told him in front of me that she would see him dead before he ever set foot in her house again with a *shiksa*." Anger showed in every line on her face. "*Shiksa!* That's me. It's an ugly word for a woman who's not Jewish. My mother-in-law is Orthodox or something like that."

"I'm familiar with the word," I said.

"You're Jewish?"

"Yes."

"Good! Then you'll understand what I mean when I say that she threatened to kill him if she saw him again. She did it. She murdered her own son."

"Well, Mrs. Silver, in all fairness to what you claim she said, it could have been more of a reaction than a real threat. I'm sure that's what she said, but that doesn't mean his mother killed him. Uh, what is his mother's name?"

"Sarah. She lives near all her friends at Glencairn and Bathurst."

Watching her face throughout the interview, I was having mixed reactions. I had the suspicion she wasn't telling me everything, but there wasn't anything I could put my finger on. I always watched the eyes when questioning a witness, but she was giving me nothing.

"May I ask how you met your husband? Considering his background, it appears the two of you wouldn't have been in the same circles. Your not being Jewish and his being Orthodox puts you worlds apart."

"Not true," she said, her voice showing her annoyance at the question. "Not true at all. We met at a computer conference."

"Really. You're a computer programmer or something like that?"

"Of course not!" She sat up straighter in her chair. "I was a model. I was hired to display a line of computer accessories, and I want you to know I was very much in demand as a model when I agreed to marry Solly. After we were married, he wouldn't hear of me working."

"It was a long courtship?"

"Why these questions? I can't be a suspect. It's his mother you should be questioning. You don't know what she's like," Betty Silver said emphatically. "If you did, you wouldn't be asking me these questions. She has to be in control. Has to be. She dominated Solly every single day of his life. You have no idea what it took for me to have him stand up to her and marry me. No idea. He was a computer genius and well thought of in his field, but a wimp whenever his mother was in the room with him. Control. That's her game. She killed him and I'll swear to it. And no, it wasn't a long courtship." She smiled sweetly at me; her white teeth and sultry lips said volumes without another sound being uttered. "We met and married in one week. He swept me off my feet." Her smile broadened.

I gazed at her, not saying anything, but thinking that if Solomon Silver swept her off her feet, she tripped him onto his back and ground him into submission.

"Do you know that Solly's father died under suspicious circumstances?" she said next. "You check that out and you'll find she had a hand in his death, too."

"How did he die?"

"Solly wouldn't talk about it. But once, when I was trying to get him to stand up to her, he said his mother killed his father for standing up to her. It slipped out."

She rose to her feet. "Solly came to Toronto three days ago to face her. He left me a note. I didn't know which hotel or I would have come after him. It said he wanted to be alone with her. He felt my presence would upset her, and he hoped he could reason with her when he gave her the good news."

"What good news?"

"I'm pregnant."

There was a pregnant pause while I digested this news. "Well, Mrs. Silver, you've been a great help. I'll keep you informed."

"When will you release my husband's body? As a Jew, you must know it is customary for the burial to be within twenty-four hours of death."

"Yes, I know, but under the circumstances that won't be possible. It will be necessary for us to perform an autopsy first."

"Oh! His mother won't like that. Solly once told me that an autopsy was a desecration of the body. Besides, if he was shot, you know how he died, so why examine his body? The only one with motive is his mother. Arrest her. Solly had no enemies, and I can't be a suspect – I'm pregnant with his child." She added hesitantly, "Anyway, how long will all this take?"

"Right now, I have no idea. I have one last question, Mrs. Silver. Do you own a gun?" I noticed the colour in her face deepen, her eyes widen slightly.

"What? Good grief, no. Why would I own a revolver? I wouldn't know what to do with one."

"Well, thank you for your co-operation. You've been a great help. Will you be going back to Hamilton immediately?"

"Yes. A friend drove me here and is waiting outside."

"I see. Well, then, I'll be in touch with you as soon as I have more information. My condolences again, Mrs. Silver." Without another word, she turned and left, passing Iris, who was approaching. "Did you see that woman?" I asked Iris.

"Nice clothes."

"That's Betty Silver, the victim's wife. Follow her outside and see who she came with and get the licence-plate number."

Iris did a quick about-face and left the room. She returned a few minutes later. "Okay," she said. She had scribbled the number on a piece of paper and held it in her hand. She sat in the chair recently occupied by Mrs. Silver.

"Did you get a look?"

"Yep. A hunk. Younger than her, I think."

"What was he wearing?"

"All I saw was a white shirt and a white pullover. Looked expensive. V-neck collar."

"Not mourning clothes?"

"Far from it."

"Mrs. Solomon Silver claims the mother-in-law did it because her son married her. She's not Jewish."

"If it's not the butler, it's the mother-in-law," Iris said matter-of-factly. "Hey. People marrying out of the faith happens every day. Is that a reason for murder?"

"It's a touchy subject. Yes, it can be a reason for murder. Not very rational. But most murders are spontaneous, the result of a sudden loss of control. Marrying out of the faith can be the worst thing anyone could do if the belief in it as a sin is strong. In my years on the force, I've seen people go berserk over something that to me was trivial, but to them was beyond acceptance. The mother being Orthodox, yes I believe it could happen. Unlikely but possible. Did you get Forensics' report?"

"Forensics says there was gunpowder on his hand as well as his temple. The fingerprints on the door handle are the housekeeper's. There was alcohol in his system, but not an excessive amount. He ate within two hours of his death but not at the hotel. Italian food. There is no Italian food served in the hotel, but there are Italian restaurants within walking distance."

I was staring into space.

"What?" Iris asked.

"I just had a thought. I asked Mrs. Silver if she owned a gun. She said, 'What would I want a revolver for?' I said gun – she said revolver. A .22 is a revolver. It has six cylinders and revolves when each shot is fired, unlike other types of hand-guns that eject shells. So how would she know the gun in question was a revolver? I'd say that yes, she owned a revolver."

"If she does, it's illegal."

"I know. But I think she owns one, or did. It's not that hard to purchase a weapon. Could have purchased it from someone who belonged to a shooting club. Could have brought it in from the States. Husband could have had one before they got married."

"Could have, should have, would have, but did she? Are you playing hunches or what?"

"It's a thought. Have you got any photos of the victim?"

"Yes, but they're pretty grim, with that hole in his head."

"What about asking his wife for some? I'd like for you to get to know her," I said. "How about driving to Hamilton and finding out more about her? Woman to woman. And while you're there, pick up a photograph of Solomon Silver. Tell her we're trying to track where he went and would like a recent snapshot. Who knows, you might smell gun powder."

"This smells like a hunch. I seem to recall a lecture about not letting hunches get in the way of deductions."

"Did you look at her? Did you see how she was built? That woman when she inhales causes male hormones to boil over. And him, a poster model for the computer nerd of the week. A whirlwind romance, she said. If it's a hunch you think I'm working on, how about this one? It was a growing affair. She made him a man and he made her his wife. But this story had an unhappy climax."

"And you figure she killed him?"

"I didn't say that. I said I think she has a revolver. That's my deduction."

Iris grinned. "It sounds more like her seduction and your testosterone."

"*Oy.* And you say my jokes are bad. Okay. You're going to Hamilton. Also drop into homicide headquarters and get a detective to accompany you for confirmation of whatever is said. Besides, you'll need a guide to get around."

"I don't need a guide, Gabe. I was born in Hamilton. Not everyone was born in Toronto, you know."

"I didn't know that. How come you came to Toronto?"

"I attended York University. And that was where I met Jeff."

"Your ex?"

"Yes. Let's get back to this case. And while I'm visiting the grieving widow, what are you doing?"

"Introducing myself to the mother-in-law. Who knows, she might be the killer."

THE BATHURST AND Glencairn area is heavily populated with Orthodox Jews, with dozens of small synagogues along Bathurst Street, kosher restaurants, bakeries and stores that cater to their needs. The men can usually be identified as orthodox by their distinctive black frock coats, wide-brimmed hats, beards and long *payes* – sideburns – while the women wear outfits with long skirts and long sleeves, and most keep their hair cut short, hidden under wigs to prevent their appearance from being a temptation to another man, or something like that. Mind you, some of the wigs are extremely attractive. Some don't follow the tradition so rigidly.

I pulled into Sarah Silver's driveway. Many of the original houses had been demolished and replaced by "monster homes." Hers was one, a large, oversized two-storey square-box structure that resembled a mausoleum more than a residence. Wealth was immediately evident. I climbed the concrete steps to the double doors and pressed the buzzer. I waited what I thought was a reasonable amount of time and pressed again. Finally I detected movement behind the peephole in the door before it opened slightly. A short stocky woman peered out at me. There's that old chestnut, that you only get one chance at making a first impression, so I smiled, hoping my white teeth and minty breath would put her at ease. One look at her eyes was enough to tell me that nothing I could do would impress her.

"My name is Detective Gabriel Garshowitz," I said, showing her my badge. "I'm investigating the death of Solomon Silver. Are you his mother?" It was a rhetorical question. If she was the maid, I was in for more trouble than I wanted. This woman's face was chiselled in stone, and her eyes were jackhammers drilling the stones apart. I could feel myself being mentally dissected and the pieces discarded.

"Yes," she answered. I don't think her lips moved.

"May I come in? There are some questions I need to ask you."

I had just said her son was dead. I knew she already knew this, but still, the reminder usually brought forth tears. Not in this case. Just as with the wife, nothing. And usually when a cop gets to the victim's home, there are people milling about to comfort the next of kin; when I stepped over the threshold here, there was no one in the house but Mrs. Silver. She locked the door after me and led me into the parlour.

On the outside, the house looked like a mausoleum; inside it was a museum. The hall and rooms I passed were decorated in Persian carpets, delicate European traditional furniture, and oil paintings with thick ornate frames, no prints. All the scenes were either abstract or landscapes, no portraits. Even the air smelled thick with money. Mrs. Sarah Silver looked me up and down before indicating which couch I should sit on, while she sat in an overstuffed chair. I noticed she didn't wear a wig, and her dress, although long, was fashionable rather than traditional; she did wear black, but I didn't think it was because of her son. Heavy people usually look better in black. A necklace of pearls hung around her neck, and she had rings on six of her fingers. I noticed a large decorative mirror when I came in. Even though tradition required that a human image should not be reflected during the first seven days after the death of a family member, the mirror wasn't covered. This woman, I concluded, was not in mourning. A cold heart and a sharp tongue were about to be unleashed.

"My sympathy for the untimely death of your son," I began.

"I appreciate your sentiment, but my son has been dead to me for two years. Your sympathy is not necessary. I regret this tragedy, but I expected something like this would happen. Have you arrested his wife yet?"

"Why?"

"Why? That, Mr. Garshowitz, should be obvious. Look around you. She thought by being Mrs. Solomon Silver, she would inherit my money. She will not. I disowned him. Whatever Solomon inherited when my dear husband died is all he was ever going to get. She more than likely took out large amounts of insurance on him when she realized my threat went beyond words, and then killed him for it. No, Mr. Garshowitz, without question, that woman murdered Solomon. When he married her two years ago, his life had no further meaning for me. His marriage was a disgrace. You arrest his wife, Mr. Garshowitz; she murdered him."

I had known cold women before, but this one was the ice queen. During all her measured words, she expressed no remorse and never lost her composure. She sat rigidly, as if her spine was a steel pole; her hands remained neatly folded on her lap, not once moving. That takes control for someone who is Jewish, I thought. Using one's hands is almost universal when talking: it's necessary to illustrate the words. I knew this. There were times at headquarters when my colleagues told me I looked as if I was conducting an orchestra.

The doorbell rang and Mrs. Silver stood. "If you'll excuse me, that will be the rabbi."

She left the room and returned in a moment with a tall, thin, elderly man dressed in black. He had a salt-and-pepper beard. "If there is nothing else, Mr. Garshowitz, I have to arrange for Solomon's burial," she said.

She didn't introduce me to the rabbi and I noticed she called me Mister, not Detective. "I'm not sure you can do that, Mrs. Silver. I believe that will be Betty Silver's responsibility," I said. "She is his wife."

"When you arrest her, she will be a criminal, and lose that responsibility. I believe it is my right as his mother. I have purchased a plot for him just outside Toronto."

"I'm not sure about the legality, Mrs. Silver. A lawyer would be better qualified to answer that. But there is one more thing – were you aware that your son's wife is pregnant and that your son was in Toronto to tell you this?"

Her lips tightened. "No, I wasn't. I have not heard from my son for more than a year. At that time I told him not to call me anymore. For the last three days I have been involved in organizing a cantorial concert with several synagogues, and I've kept some very late hours. It is a time-consuming project and I have immersed myself in it so that it will be a success. Besides, her being pregnant doesn't change anything."

The rabbi looked at Mrs. Silver and then at me. He smiled, but it didn't look genuine. "The marriage was consummated outside the orthodox protocol, sir. The woman is not Jewish, and as such, the child cannot be Jewish. I'm sure the authorities will make the necessary arrangements for the welfare of the child when Solomon's wife is incarcerated. It is regrettable that the innocent should suffer, but the responsibility is not ours to consider. Marrying out of the faith is forbidden. His tragic death requires that we forgive him. His life is over and his mistakes will be set aside. What matters now is that Solomon Silver is put to rest, and Mrs. Sarah Silver's life goes on." He should have quit when he was ahead, but he added, "Not being Orthodox, sir, I fear you wouldn't understand."

I smiled for the sake of smiling. "But I am Jewish," I said.

"Are you?" He looked at me more closely and offered me another form of smile, one that said I still wouldn't understand.

I thanked Sarah Silver and left the house. She didn't bother to show me out.

I LEFT WITH a nagging thought. Mrs. Silver said she had purchased a plot for her son outside of Toronto. It seemed to me that a family such as hers would have purchased plots for the family and generally on land owned by their synagogue. She didn't want him buried with the family. I found that odd. Why, if she was so anxious to bury him, would she not bury him where he belonged? Unless...

I had two interesting new angles to follow, and I didn't mean the two deceitful Mrs. Silvers. Mrs. Betty Silver was cheating on her husband, and Mrs. Sarah Silver was a liar. She knew her daughter-in-law was pregnant. She didn't miss a beat when I broke the news, and neither did the rabbi. What was gelling in my mind was so bizarre I could hardly believe it myself. I had two female suspects, both of whom would have been admitted into the room by the victim and both of whom might have had a motive for killing him. But maybe there was a third motive. And it was this that interested me.

I arrived at the station at the same time that Detective Munz was coming out. "Hi, Pop. How was your nap?"

"Restful. It's better than sleeping at your desk. Must be uncomfortable." I went to pass him, but Munz blocked my way.

"Don't think that Holloway will protect you forever, old man. You're shit and the day will come when I'll flush you out of this station."

"Munz, you're a bully. A bad cop. We don't like each other and that's fine with me. Don't threaten me. I don't need Holloway to protect me. Or Iris. So back off or take your best shot. Just get out of my face. I have a job and you're in my way."

Munz laughed. "Big man. I know you fucked up my promotion last year and I'll make sure you pay. It was none of your business."

"You beat that eighteen-year-old kid for no reason. You're

twice his size. He couldn't have touched you. I just told what I saw. You were lucky all you got was a suspension. You don't belong on the force."

"When I'm through, *you* won't." Munz moved aside and went to his car.

I took a couple of calming breaths and entered the station.

9

I**RIS RETURNED FROM** Hamilton with some of the information I needed; I had called her on her cellular to have her find one more piece of the puzzle. "What did you learn by talking to the widow?" I asked. We were in a coffee shop: I needed my caffeine and bagel. Iris was drinking boiled hot water. Each to his – or her – own. I never could figure out what the attraction of the hot water was.

"She's no grieving widow, that's for sure. She's very aggressive. I'm sure she was the boss in their marriage. The poor sucker went from a dominating mother, if what you told me is accurate, to a demanding wife with a lot of needs. She's also got it in for the mother-in-law. Wants desperately for her to be charged with her husband's death. She won't gain anything from that, because as you said, the mother-in-law disowned her son, which means Betty still gets nothing even if the older Mrs. Silver does get charged. It also means she's more pissed off with the mother-in-law than about her husband's death. She lives in a nice house. It's well furnished – she likes good stuff.

"I asked if I could use her bathroom. She told me there was a bathroom at the bottom of the stairs. I left Detective Sawyers with her, then went upstairs instead, as if I hadn't heard her right. The master bedroom was down the hall, so I went in and did a quick tour of the room and her bathroom. I'm sure she's got a lover."

I grinned. "I'm not surprised. A man drove her to Toronto. At a time like this, a grieving woman usually cries on another woman's shoulder. But what made you decide that?"

"Well, the toilet seat in the bathroom was up."

I started to laugh. "Really?"

"Yep. That's a guy thing, right? And whoever he was, he was probably in there that day. The shower had been recently used – there was moisture on the walls. She's seeing someone, and now that her husband's dead, he's right there servicing her."

Her cellular phone rang. "Iris Forester here," she said. "Yep. Yep. Right on. Thank you. If there is something we can do for you, let us know. Thanks again."

I listened to her one-way conversation with interest. Whatever was being revealed apparently was good news. "What?" I asked.

"That was Detective Sawyers. You were right. She gets nothing."

"Okay! Now we know why she's so keen to trot to have the mother-in-law convicted of murder. Now we have to confirm why the mother-in-law wants *her* convicted."

"Are you sure about your conclusions? They're far out," Iris said.

"Absolutely. I gave you all the details. Can you find a hole in my argument?"

"No. But they're based on something I don't know about."

"C'mon, let's go to Forensics and find the last piece of the puzzle."

THE LAST PIECE of the puzzle was to see if Forensics had come to the same conclusion I had. They had. I wondered if another detective had taken this case, would he have understood what had happened. Being Jewish was the key, and being Jewish, I understood the mentality of the son and the mother. The wife, of course, was another matter. The next thing to do was to accost the mother. I didn't care for her, but I understood where she came from.

Iris knocked on Mrs. Silver's door while I stood behind her. The door opened and Mrs. Silver greeted us with her grim face and gestured for us to enter. We were led to the same room I was in before, and again I sat on the couch; Iris stood. Mrs. Silver resumed her throne.

"Have you arrested her yet?" Mrs. Silver asked.

"No. She's not guilty, Mrs. Silver."

"Of course she is. She's a conniving, scheming woman who destroyed my son because of her greed."

"Well, possibly. What we would like to know is, what were you doing in the hotel after your son died?"

"I beg your pardon?" She looked very convincing in her indignation. She stood and glowered at us. "I resent what you're implying. I did not have anything to do with my son's death. I gave him everything he ever wanted. I would never have hurt –."

Iris interrupted. "Your son committed suicide, Mrs. Silver. You were there and found the body. We know. If we show your photograph around enough, we're bound to find someone who saw you, either in the hotel or in the parking lot. If you tell us the truth now, we can avoid making this more public than it already is. It's in your hands, Mrs. Silver."

The woman sank slowly back into her chair. Her face remained adamant, but we had put a crack in her wall. "The revolver, Mrs. Silver. What did you do with it?" I asked.

"I gave him everything. He lacked nothing. I gave him and my husband my life. I devoted myself to their needs, and this was how they repaid me. Both were selfish, thinking only of themselves."

"What did your husband do?" I asked.

"Took an overdose of his medication. To avoid the embarrassment of his actions, I lied about his mental health. I said he had memory lapses and in his confusion must have forgotten how many times he had taken his pills. But he knew what he was doing. He wanted to embarrass me. He did it to humiliate me. He was weak. It was me who pushed him. We became wealthy because of me. He wanted to retire and enjoy his wealth. That was ridiculous. We had the ability to make more money, and I showed him the error of his ways. My son was like his father. When he called me that afternoon from a restaurant, he asked if I would come to his room at the hotel at eight that evening. He had called two days earlier and we argued. He promised he would make everything right. I reluctantly agreed."

Throughout her statement, the expression on her face never changed. Her eyes remained hard and her hands didn't move. I glanced at Iris. She wore a look of disapproval.

"He said the door would be ajar, to just come in. I did. He was lying on the floor. The revolver lay a few feet away. He had shot himself in the head. He wanted to shock me. I found his actions disgusting. I, who had done everything for him, he wanted to hold up to ridicule just like his father tried to do. I saw the note. It said his wife was pregnant and he suspected he was not the father. He had nothing to live for, and he said it was my fault. Can you imagine? My fault! I took the note and the revolver. I tore the note to shreds and scattered the pieces over the Don Valley Parkway before returning home; the revolver I dropped into a sewer near the hotel. I gave him my life and he repaid me with humiliation."

There was silence. She had finished.

It was pretty much as I had deduced. A dominating woman, consumed by her own needs and status, had ruined the lives of the two men in her life. Even now, she felt that she was the aggrieved party. The Jewish-mother syndrome, some might have called it. The umbilical cord stretched forever, couldn't be severed. What was it I had read? "Death is free, but to attain it, you must give up your life." Solomon Silver wanted revenge and to get it, he gave up that which in his mind had no value.

Iris and I stood. "I would suggest that you remain home for the rest of the day, Mrs. Silver. I'm going to turn over our findings to my superintendent and see what he wants to do."

Mrs. Silver remained seated. We left on our own and drove away. Iris was silent for a good while. "She doesn't understand, does she?"

"Nope, she doesn't. And never will. Her kind are used to getting their own way and when they don't, they retaliate. Always retaliate. Forensics was convinced that Solomon Silver had committed suicide, but couldn't account for the missing revolver. The wife admitted he was depressed with the loss of his mother's affection, or what he perceived as affection. I'm sure his father's death must have played into his thoughts, too. Three days he sat in that room getting angrier and angrier. His wife was cheating on him, his mother had made him dependent on her, his life had no meaning. Domestic violence, Iris, is the number-one reason for murder. Money is a close second. Solomon Silver murdered himself to get even.

"The wife would have been the beneficiary of a $250,000 life insurance policy if he died from natural causes or was murdered.

You found that out from the call from Hamilton. She gets nothing if it's suicide. So she had to find another motive for his death. What she suspected, I don't know, but I'm sure while driving from Hamilton, she and her boyfriend concocted a story to try and make his death seem like a murder. Blame the mother and hope she gets convicted. There was no love lost between them."

"What do you think will happen to Solomon Silver's remains?"

"My guess is he'll be buried in some gentile cemetery in Hamilton, forgotten by all. Sarah Silver is very resourceful. She'll create a lie to fit her needs. Better he's buried away from her domain – out of sight, out of mind. In time, most will accept her story. For her, her son taking his life was worse than marrying out of the faith."

"What do you think will happen to her?"

"I don't think she'll be jailed. Tampering with evidence? There's a stronger case for being a bad mother. My guess – a deal will be made. We'll retrieve the revolver and get Betty Silver to admit ownership. I think now that we know the facts, she'll confess that she owned a .22 or at least knew her husband owned one, and that would mean Mrs. Sarah Silver couldn't have shot her son. Messy, but case over."

We drove in silence. "Are you all right? Is this case bothering you?" I asked.

"It's such a waste. All for what? I think I'll go home, soak in a tub and wash away the memory," Iris said.

"Really! Care to have company? I hate bathing alone."

Iris laughed. "I can solve that problem. I'll introduce you to my grandmother. She volunteers at Baycrest Home for the Aged. She's used to bathing old men."

I clutched my heart and sagged against the seat. "Just take me home. I'll take a cold shower."

She laughed.

Why is it when a man gets to a certain age, women no longer look upon him as a threat?

The Charlie Talbot Case

Donny Worth, his wife, Suzie, and his best friend, Charlie Talbot, sat in the kitchen of his two-storey house celebrating his recent promotion to district manager. On the table was a large bottle of Canadian Club rye, now a quarter full, three glasses and a bowl of fruit. "A toast," he said.

"A toast? To what?" Charlie's words were slightly slurred. "To what?" he repeated. They had been sitting at the table for more than an hour reminiscing, telling each other stories about things they had done together and feeling comfortable in their companionship.

"To us," Donny answered. "To the three of us. To our lasting *friendship! To our love for each other! And above all, to our charmed lives."*

"Charmed lives? How's that?" Charlie asked. Donny and he were the same age, but Charlie was built like an athlete, priding himself on keeping fit, while Donny had let himself get soft and overweight. "I'll tell you, guys, if I make it home like this, I will have a charmed life. I've had too much to drink."

"Hey, we're indestructible. You know that. Nothing can hurt us."

"You wish," Charlie said, flapping his hand disdainfully and taking another sip from his glass.

"I know," Donny answered. "We've been friends for most of our lives. We fell in love with the same woman, and when I married her, our friendship survived. That was an omen. Each of us has been involved in accidents where we should have wound up crippled or dead. I had a car accident, you a skiing accident, and Suzie, sweet Suzie, took that bad tumble down the stairs. We recovered without any permanent injuries. Doesn't that tell you something? We are protected. Charmed!"

"Lucky," Charlie said. "Plain dumb luck."

Suzie's head bobbed in agreement. "But I lost the baby, Donny. I lost the baby." Her glazed eyes were blinking hard as she tried to focus her thoughts on Donny's words. It didn't take much to make Suzie drunk. It didn't take much to make Suzie do anything. Danny poured another inch of the amber liquid into her glass.

"That, too, was a sign, baby. We're not the parent type. You know that. We got our own lives to live."

Suzie, barely five-five, brunette and quite pretty, wasn't known for being overly bright. "I guess," she said, taking a little sip from her glass.

"We're indestructible!" Donny's voice rose with drunken enthusiasm.

Charlie shook his head. "Lucky," he said again, "and maybe stoopid."

"Stupid! Never! Just indestructible. I'll prove it." Donny hauled his heavy body up out of the chair and staggered on his

skinny legs out of the kitchen, then thumped down the hall. Suzie and Charlie exchanged silly grins. When Donny returned he held a revolver in his hand, which he pointed at Charlie. "I'll prove it," he said as he circled the table.

Charlie paled; his mouth fell open. Suzie gazed stupidly at the erratic movement of the revolver.

Donny returned to his seat and rested the weapon on the table. "There's six bullets in this gun," he said. "Six. Did you know that?" He looked at the two of them smugly. They hadn't taken their eyes off the gun. "I'll show you." He ejected the bullets onto the table. "See? Six." He picked one up between two fingers and with much giggling and clumsiness inserted it into the chamber. He rolled the chamber three times, gripped the revolver in his left hand and rose unsteadily to his feet, his right hand gripping the table to steady his balance. He licked his lips, then grinned at Charlie and Suzie as he placed the gun against his temple and pulled the trigger.

His wife and friend gasped at the resounding click.

Donny roared with laughter. "I told you we're charmed. Nothin' can happen to us, nothin'." He pushed the revolver to Charlie. "Shoot me," he said. "Go ahead, shoot me!" He weaved unsteadily as he waited for Charlie to pick up the gun.

"You're nuts," Charlie whispered. "You were just lucky."

"No! None of us can be hurt. I proved it. Shoot me. Nothin'll happen."

"Forget it." Charlie rose unsteadily to his feet, staring at the gun. "This is dumb."

Donny grabbed the gun, twirled the chamber, placed it against his temple again and pulled the trigger. Click. He laughed so hard he lost his balance and fell behind the table. Charlie and Suzie stared down at him rolling on the floor. He pulled himself to his feet, a ridiculous grin on his face and shoved the gun towards Suzie. "Go ahead, Suzie, shoot Charlie. Nothin'll happen."

Suzie stared at the gun, then hesitantly, she raised it and swung it toward Charlie.

Charlie laughed nervously. "You gonna shoot me?" He pulled himself up to his full height.

Suzie closed one eye, swayed to one side and aimed just as Donny slumped against the table, one outstretched arm striking the bowl of fruit, tumbling its contents onto the floor. The gun exploded and a red stain erupted across Charlie's shirt. With a look of incredulous surprise, Charlie opened his mouth, but all that came out was a strange gurgling sound as he slid to the floor to join the fruit. Suzie looked dumbfounded at the gun in her hand, before she began to scream.

THE PHONE RANG I watched as Iris scrawled on her pad. When she hung up, I asked, "What?"

"Would you believe Russian roulette?"

"No shit!"

"There were three. Now there's two."

I stood slowly. My knees were killing me again today. Actually they were worse. I had an appointment with my doctor, not because I couldn't handle the pain but because I was concerned my stalling might result in whatever it was getting out of hand before it was diagnosed. Sometimes I could hardly move my left leg. "You drive. You know where to go."

Iris shook her head in mock sympathy as I hobbled by. "You sure you can make it? Shall I get you a walker?"

"Nice. What's next? Twisting the knife after it's imbedded to the hilt?"

She laughed.

I grinned. It wasn't a joke. Maybe I had gout? Considering the crap I was eating, that wouldn't have surprised me. Gout can be treated. Could be my high blood pressure. I've been thinking about getting a dog. I heard that dogs keep your blood pressure down and your mind off your problems. But I put in some crazy hours and I figured the dog would smell up my place before I got home to take him out. In the meantime, Iris had become more than a handful.

The house was in the north part of Toronto on a large

property with a manicured lawn, on a street that reeked of money – or big mortgages. Patrol cars blocked the intersections and yellow caution tape was strung around the property. The neighbours were watching from their doorsteps as if ready to bolt inside if something happened.

Constable Howard Claremont guarded the door. "Okay, Howard, what've you got?"

He ignored the question. "Good to see you again, Gabe." He looked appreciatively at Iris.

"Meet Iris Forester. Keep your eyes in your head, Howard. She won't marry a cop." Iris jabbed me in the ribs.

"Hello, Iris. I'm Howard Claremont. The old fart making your life miserable?"

Iris smiled. "Only on good days. The rest of the time, it's pure hell."

"He's a pussycat. He grows on you. I know."

"So does fungus."

"Talk to me, Howard," I broke in. "What's inside?"

Howard fished out his notebook. "Three adults – two men, one woman, apparently intoxicated. Celebrating. As near as the woman, Suzie Worth, can recall, there was some talk about being indestructible. Donny Worth, her husband, brought out a gun. She thinks he placed the gun to his head twice and pulled the trigger. She took the gun and pointed it at their friend, Charlie Talbot, but doesn't remember pulling the trigger. He got a bullet in the heart. Her husband passed out." Howard flipped the notebook shut. "End of story."

"For you," I said. Detective Stella Morgan from Forensics crossed the hall, and I waved to her to come to the door. "Hi, sweetie."

"I cringe every time you call me that, Gabe."

"That's why he calls us that," Iris said.

"Everyone's touchy tonight," I muttered. "It's been a long day, Stella, and I'm hungry."

"When aren't you? This is an easy one. Open and shut. Three

idiots – one's the shooter, one's the victim, and one's the instigator. Coroner's on the way, the body's in the kitchen, the booze is on the table, and the husband and wife are in drunken shock."

"Aren't *we* the lucky ones, Gabe," Iris said. "More paperwork."

"Get used to it."

"You in pain, Gabe?" Stella asked.

The grin on my face disappeared too quickly. "No. Why do you ask?"

Stella was giving me a hard stare, not a mean one, but like she was giving me an examination. "Your eyes, Gabe. They're tearing. Pain does that."

I put my grin back on as I moved over to the couple sitting on the couch. "Allergies," I said. "Could be your perfume."

"Not wearing any," she said to my back.

Donny and Suzie Worth sat at extreme ends of the couch, cups with the dregs of coffee in them on the small table in front of them. Suzie Worth clenched a handkerchief but was no longer shedding tears. Her face was ashen, pasty actually, her eyes red-rimmed. The tears were apparently real. Donny Worth stared down at his feet, his mouth gaping.

Maybe because I'm not a drinker, I cannot understand why anyone would want to consume alcohol to the point of stupidity. What's the attraction? If you no longer have the capacity to function, how are you able to enjoy what you've consumed? I stared at this sorry looking pair. Now I had to find out how much they remembered.

IT WAS AN open-and-shut case. A married couple and friend were celebrating. An excessive amount of alcohol takes the celebration from joy to horror. No motives, no arguments, no reason. Case over – or so I thought.

Iris disagreed.

"What's bothering you?" I asked after we finished arresting and charging Suzie Worth.

"I don't know. I have a feeling there's more to this than what we know. The husband starts the series of events, the wife shoots the friend, she goes to jail and the husband sleeps in his own bed. That stinks, don't you think? Let's keep it going."

"Why? She pulled the trigger. She admits it."

"The husband gave her a loaded gun."

"I repeat, she pulled the trigger. I could hand you the keys to my car. That doesn't give you permission to run anyone down."

"It does if I'm drunk."

I looked at her. "Okay. What do you suspect?"

"If I told you I don't like the husband, would that satisfy you?"

"Come again?"

"I don't like the husband, and I don't understand the gun."

"They were drunk. Drunk people do stupid things."

"But why bring out a gun?" she said more emphatically. "It doesn't make sense to me. If the conversation went the way she remembered, what's the gun got to do with being indestructible? What's he doing with a gun anyway?"

"He said he bought it more than ten years ago for protection when he had another job and was on the road late at night. He's going to bring us the permit. It's in his safety deposit box. An old gun and a foggy brain. It was a gesture. A symbol. Why does this have to be more complicated than that?"

"I want a couple more days to satisfy myself."

"How?"

"C'mon, Gabe. What's the hurry, a couple of days to check them out? There has to be more. Everything's too pat."

"You think he concocted this whole scheme?"

"Maybe. I'm not sure. Look. Suzie Worth is in jail until she gets a bail hearing. I want to talk to her again. Couldn't get two words out of her tonight without her breaking down. Maybe tomorrow, she'll be more coherent and we can get something. I just have this feeling."

"Sounds like a hunch. Hunches can be dangerous."

"It's more like an itch. I just want to get rid of it. I have this feeling that something's not right."

"Well, an itch I can understand." I grinned. "Maybe you would like me to scratch it?" I said, not expecting an answer.

"If I'm on a wild-goose chase, yes, I'll let you scratch it." Iris headed for the door. "But I won't tell you where the itch is unless I lose, though." She disappeared down the hall.

And I thought I was the tease.

I HAD NO bad feelings about this case. I'd seen dozens like it. When I worked in Traffic before I became a detective, a drunk driver hit a pedestrian. When asked why was he speeding, he said he noticed his gas gauge was almost empty and was hurrying to the nearest pump before he ran out. His answer sounded perfectly logical to him when he was drunk. After he sobered, he cried when his answer was played back, especially knowing that the pedestrian had died. People do stupid things when they're drunk, so I was satisfied this was an accidental shooting and knew that the Worths, who were now sober, regretted their actions. Charlie Talbot, unfortunately, had no say in the matter.

I was satisfied. Iris was not. No amount of persuasion on my part could make her change her mind. I figured I'd let her have her way. If she was wrong, and I was sure she was, then learning that hunches were not always right was a good lesson. Besides, if Iris was feeling sorry for Suzie Worth, the odds were her lawyer would plead that she was drunk as her defence. Leave it up to lawyers and they'll make Jack the Ripper look like a conscientious citizen getting rid of the unsavoury elements on the streets, deserving of a sanitation citation.

The next day we sat in the interview room when they brought Suzie Worth to us. She looked like hell. Her face was pale and her eyes were puffy and she moved like someone in a trance. If anyone was taking what happened badly, this woman was. I've seen some people fake emotions and you could bet the house they were sincere, but if you look at their eyes, their mouth, even their hands, you can tell it's an act. This woman looked for real.

Suzie sat opposite me. Iris sat to her left. I advised her that she didn't have to talk to us without her lawyer.

"I know," she said. "I have nothing to hide. What I did was stupid. I was too stewed to be aware of what I was doing." Her faced screwed up in pain. "I never would have harmed Charlie. Never." There was a softness in her tone, and tears began to trickle down her cheeks.

"We'll be recording this interview," I said.

"I understand."

"I pressed the start button on the tape recorder and Iris took charge, staring intently at the woman as she asked, "Do you and your husband have a good marriage? He's away a lot. Were you lonely? Were you and Charlie Talbot more than friends?"

That last question blew me away. I had picked up something in Suzie Worth's tone, but I would have circled the wagon for a while. Iris was attacking with her teeth on the bit and both guns firing. I turned to see how Suzie took to the question. She dried her eyes on her handkerchief – too deliberately, I thought – before answering.

"Why would you ask that?"

"The way you sounded when you mentioned Charlie Talbot. Did you and Charlie Talbot have something going on, Mrs. Worth?"

"What do you mean?"

"I think you know."

Suzie lowered her eyes.

"Did your husband know?"

Suzie shook her head.

"I'm sorry, Mrs. Worth. I need an answer for the recording."

"No, I don't think Donny knew."

"How long?" I asked.

"A while," she whispered. "It just happened," she added desperately. "It wasn't planned. I was lonely. Donny was always away. Charlie and I never met when Donny was home.

No, he couldn't have known."

"What if he did? How would he react?" Iris asked.

"I don't know. Angry, I suppose. Hurt."

"Could he have planned this?" Iris asked.

"Killing Charlie? How? He was drunk. I remember him falling down because he couldn't stand. No! They were best friends."

"Were you going to tell him about you and Charlie?" I asked. Iris was treading on shaky ground, putting suggestions in Suzie's mouth. I wanted to divert the questioning to another area.

"Charlie and I spoke of breaking it off many times, but we couldn't. We were in love. You have to understand, Charlie always loved me – it wasn't his fault, it was mine. I made the wrong choice. I should have married Charlie."

"Did Charlie want to break it off?" I asked. "You said you spoke of breaking it off. Who wanted to break it off?"

"I did. But Charlie convinced me that I shouldn't have to deny my feelings. He wanted me to tell Donny. I couldn't."

"Weren't you afraid of being caught, Mrs. Worth?"

"Yes. There was always that possibility. Not from Donny, but from the neighbours."

"You're sure your husband never knew?" I asked.

"How could he?"

"Maybe you wanted out and Charlie wouldn't cooperate," I said. "Maybe you saw this as the perfect way to get rid of him. Drunk, a foggy mind, then an accidental shooting. You were trapped and became desperate." I was asking the questions and Iris was watching.

"No, not true!" There was desperation in Suzie's eyes and panic in her voice.

Knowing she was off guard, I pushed harder. "You said neighbours might catch you. Where did you and Charlie Talbot meet? Apparently not in motels or hotels."

"No, at my house. Donny called every night. He liked to

speak with me before he went to bed. He said talking with me made the empty hotel room bearable. I never knew when he would call. Charlie would park his car around the corner and enter the house by the back door. I kept the house dark so he couldn't be seen through the windows. He was always gone by three in the morning."

"I noticed there's a chain lock on your front door. Did you use it?" Iris asked.

"Who'd come in? Donny was a thousand miles away. No one else had the key to our door."

"Could you have heard anyone entering if they did?"

Suzie shook her head. "We sometimes closed the bedroom door. And besides, we...you know...were preoccupied."

"Then Donny could have entered, seen the two of you involved and left without you ever being aware," Iris said.

"But he was out West. We were perfectly safe."

"Maybe you felt safe from your husband, but I wonder, how safe was Charlie from you?" I added.

Suzie Worth rose from her chair. "It was my fault, wasn't it? I should have told Donny. If I had we never would have been sitting in that room celebrating Donny's promotion. I killed him. I pulled the trigger. I committed adultery. No matter what, I'm to blame." She looked at us, her expression that of a person with regrets – and guilt. A lot of guilt. "I'm tired, Detectives. I would like to go back to my cell."

Iris nodded and opened the interrogation-room door. They both left me sitting at the table.

As I said, it was an open-and-shut case. I couldn't tell from Iris's expression when she left if she was now convinced as I was, but at least we had that Suzie was definitely the one who'd pulled the trigger. Even if the husband knew his wife was cheating on him, he didn't pull the trigger. Anything else was academic.

When Iris returned, she said, "Something about this case stinks."

N<small>O REAL CHARGES</small> could be laid against Donny Worth
except owning a gun without a permit, something thousands of
Canadians had. He said he was sick about what happened. Iris
still wasn't convinced. I thought it was a woman thing. Iris had
a bad marriage and apparently so did Suzie Worth. It wouldn't
have surprised me that Iris's hunch was no more than her wanting Donny to be the bad guy. Iris seemed to have bonded with
Suzie. Me, I saw a woman who forgot her vows. Mind you,
they used to say till death do you part.

Anyway, we were on our way to see Donny at his home.

We had some loose ends to tie up. During the night of the killing, it was apparent that Donny had drunk a lot and was having difficulty remembering. Several cups of coffee later, he still wasn't much help. When we left to have Suzie booked, we told him we'd see him the next day. During the ride over, Iris was quiet. I was getting to know her habits. She sat staring out the front window, her lips pursed tight enough to cut the circulation, and her eyes mere slits. If ever I saw a volcano about to erupt, this was it. The lava was perking. I knew as soon as I stopped the car, it would gush out. It did. I opened my door and looked to her, sitting like a rod. "Coming?" I asked.

"Somehow Donny set everything up," she said. "He found out about his wife and Charlie Talbot and set it up. I feel it."

"We've got no evidence against him, only against her. Charlie was his best friend. The evening was a celebration. They were drunk. People do stupid things when they're drunk. When are you going to accept that?"

"There's drunk and there's acting drunk. We tested her, but not him."

"He wasn't the shooter and he had no motive."

"He would if he knew about his wife and his pal."

"He placed the gun against his own head and pulled the trigger. Not once but twice. Is that the act of a sober person?"

"That's my point. Was he really drunk?"

"Let's be logical. They started with a full bottle of liquor. Three people consumed the amount of liquor not in the bottle. The alcohol level in Charlie was over the legal driving limit but not to the point that he couldn't drive. Suzie was plastered. Donny must have drunk the rest. If he didn't drink what he took, how did he stay sober?"

"I don't have all the answers – yet."

"Let's go. You're running in circles. Let it rest."

"Not yet."

I climbed out of the car and left her. When I got to the door, she was behind me. If looks could kill.

Donny Worth answered the door, unshaven and bleary-eyed. His clothes looked slept in. He waved us into the house. It smelled of neglect. Partly eaten food was strewn on the corner table by the couch, and a blanket lay crumpled on the floor. Donny sat on the couch and ran his fingers through his hair, trying to make himself more presentable. Iris and I sat in separate chairs facing him. He looked at us for a while before asking, "So how can I help you? What more can I tell you? I still don't remember too much."

Iris jumped in with both feet. "You're on the road quite a bit, I understand, Mr. Worth. How long are you away at one time, usually?" she asked.

He licked his lips before he replied. "You know, that was the problem. If I wanted to get ahead, I had to put in some crazy hours out of town. I excelled and they made me a district manager. Do you know what a DM does? I get a percentage of everyone's sales, but to do that I have to be on the road even more. I have to check my staff on location. If I hadn't made DM, we'd never have been celebrating. I should be the one going to jail, not Suzie. It's my fault."

"How long are you usually away, Mr. Worth?" Iris asked again. Her smile looked forced.

"Every second week for four days," he mumbled. "I always leave on Tuesday and return on Friday. Uh, I have two routes. One, I fly, the other by car. One week on the road, one week home. Twelve months a year."

"Where do you drive?" Iris asked.

"To Hamilton, Ottawa, Fredericton and Montreal. It's a triangle of sorts. I sell electronic accessories for computers." His voice got stronger as he spoke. "When I fly, I go to Winnipeg, Regina, Calgary and Edmonton. I need four days each to cover both routes."

"Ever come back early?" I asked.

"No, never. I follow the same sequence of cities each time. Why?"

"Being away so often, ever get lonely?" Iris asked.

"What are you implying?" Donny asked. The tone was not friendly any more.

"Trying to get a picture. "It happens, you know. Strange cities, needs and such, loneliness. Things happen."

"I don't like what you're implying."

"Just tying up loose ends," Iris said. "Questions will be asked of us, and we're making sure we have all the answers. How's your relationship with your wife?"

I swung my eyes to Iris and gritted my teeth. I'd hate to have her in the jungle behind me swinging a machete when she's pissed off. She was going in for the kill and didn't care what she hit. I looked to Donny to see how he was taking the question. It took only a second for his reaction. He was on his feet.

"My relationship!" he said angrily. "I don't have a relationship with my wife – I love my wife. I blame myself for what happened. I'm not denying what I started. As for your question if I ever came back early, no, never, not possible. My appointment in Edmonton is in the afternoon on Thursday. Sometimes early, sometimes at the end of the day. My plane ticket is purchased with air miles, and those tickets are not exchangeable. I have to take a flight that I can make, that's why I leave on Friday. I even have receipts from the taxis that pick me up at the airport."

"Where do you accumulate the air miles for so many flights?" I asked.

"Hotels, gasoline, food; everything on MasterCard. I make some bulk purchases for the company when I see suppliers, as well as clients, and use my card. I get the miles, the company pays me back. I use the system and pocket what I don't spend. Everyone does it."

I wasn't sure if he was taunting me or just mad enough not to care. "Can you give us your travel vouchers for the last six months?" I asked.

"Especially the week prior to Mr. Talbot's death," Iris said.

My eyes went from her to him to her to see if any weapons were being drawn.

Donny stood. "No problem. Give me a few minutes and I'll get them." He left the room.

I stood. "He doesn't look like he's scared. You've pissed him off. Looks like he's taking this hard – but you don't buy it, do you?"

"No."

"Aren't you just being stubborn? Listen, I've had hunches, too, and been wrong many times."

Iris stood when Donny Worth returned. He carried an accordion file and handed it to her. "That's everything. It goes beyond six months. Please return it intact – I need them for my income tax at the end of the year."

"Thank you for your cooperation, Mr. Worth. We'll take care of them and make sure they're returned as quickly as possible." I nodded to him and gently pushed Iris out before she said anything else.

I drove. Not that I wanted to, but there was something in her expression that told me Mount St. Iris was about to erupt, and the last thing I wanted was her behind the wheel.

"There was no bullet in the gun!" she said. Her words were thrown out with so much energy I knew she had been mulling that over for a while.

"Come again?" I said.

"There was no bullet in the gun. He made like he'd put it in the gun. They were too drunk to know what he really did. There was no bullet in the gun when he pulled the trigger those two times."

Ahead was a strip plaza. I turned into the lot and parked. I faced her. "How did the bullet get back in the gun?"

"He put it in."

"When?"

"You're my partner, can't you think of a way?"

"It's your itch, remember?"

"You're a big help," she said indignantly.

"Sorry. What's next?"

"Follow up on his trips out of town. If we can prove he knew about his wife's adultery, then that's all we need to give him a motive. If there's any time gap that can't be accounted for, that might give us a clue to the day he returned."

"And if there isn't and you can't?"

Iris stared out the window of the car before answering. "Then I'll back off."

"Okay. Let's check him out."

IT TOOK TWO more weeks of checking until Iris finally threw in the towel. Suzie Worth pleaded guilty and was sentenced to three years for manslaughter. Our judicial system was at work again. Donny stood by her right to the bitter end, even when Suzie told him about her affair with Charlie. He changed jobs to one that kept him home and would be waiting for her when released, which should be in about a year.

The car angle proved a no-brainer. He had chits, gas vouchers, food bills and hotel receipts that made it impossible to get from one destination to another any sooner than he did.

His order book for the business calls out west showed orders at every city every time he was there. His client in Edmonton confirmed he'd been there every Thursday for more than two months prior. We even checked the other airlines going back two months to see if he had bought a ticket and returned earlier. No tickets were found in his name. Unless he knew about his wife and Charlie before, there would be no reason to buy tickets in another name. Besides, most people pay by credit card or cheque. If he paid cash, a red flag would have gone up. There was nothing like that. Zip.

A few months later, Iris and I were sitting at a table at Kiva's having breakfast on a Sunday morning. The place was noisy. It's always noisy on Sunday. The Worth case was still an ongoing subject with Iris. She still believed that Donny had masterminded the shooting. The tables are so close to each other, it was no problem reaching over to another table and taking the bottle of ketchup off without getting up. There were several patrons at the next table telling jokes and it was impossible not to eavesdrop. One man told a story.

"At the beginning of summer a customs officer at the U.S.-Mexican border stopped a young boy crossing on his red bicycle with a burlap sack tied over his rear fender. "What's inside?" he asked. "Sand," he was told. "Sand?" He examined the contents and discovered that it was sand. Every week for the entire summer, that same boy crossed the border on a red bicycle with a bag of sand. The guard knew the kid was smuggling, but what? All he ever found was sand. At the end of the summer, the boy never returned. Many years later, the guard, now retired, was vacationing in the Canary Islands when he saw a young man he recognized as the lad he thought was smuggling. He approached, identified himself as a retired civil servant and pleaded with him to tell him what it was he smuggled. The man denied he had done anything illegal. The guard could not make him change his mind. The young man said he had to go, but as he passed, he uttered one word – bicycles."

Iris turned to me. She had that look again. "How do we know Donny Worth actually was on the airplane?"

"His ticket was used. You can't get on an airplane without a ticket."

"Maybe someone else used the ticket. He could have sold it or given it away. It was no good to him if he decided to come home a day early. We've been looking in the bag of sand, not at the bike, or plane, in this case."

"What you're saying is he exchanged tickets with someone who was leaving earlier. Man, that's a stretch. And if he did, how are you going to prove that?"

"At least you admit it's possible."

I didn't have an answer since neither of us had tried to identify the holder as someone other than Donny Worth. It was assumed he was. "Is that itch back?"

"It never went away."

"I never got to find out where the last one was."

"He's guilty. I just couldn't prove it."

"You'll have trouble reopening the case."

"The wrong Worth is in jail."

"Shit, woman, she confessed!"

"In effect, her husband pulled the trigger. If we can prove he arrived earlier, caught them in the act, that's motive."

Exasperated, I asked, "Who's going to remember Donny Worth after all these months if he got on another plane?"

"The cab driver who picked him up might. He wouldn't have covered his tracks because he had no reason to. There has to be a record of someone dropping him off a night before he was expected. That would be Thursday. If I'm right, we got him."

"Okay, I'll tell the superintendent on Monday, and if he says to follow it up, we'll do the rounds of the cab and limo companies."

IT TOOK FOUR days and nights of checking, but we finally

found the cab that delivered a man to the Worth address on a Thursday night not long after a flight from Edmonton had landed. A further check with Donny's account in Edmonton revealed that the order he received was given to him on Thursday before noon. It was a big order. We had checked every cab and limo company's records that worked the airport on a Thursday for two months before the killing to make sure, and found him the week before the shooting. The cabbie remembered him as the man who told him that he was coming home early to celebrate with his wife. Won't she be surprised? he had said. Unfortunately, yes.

It was circumstantial, but the Crown Attorney thought there was enough information to quietly reopen the case. The fact that Donny hadn't revealed that he had come home earlier was in itself suspicious. Iris and I checked the motels in the vicinity. He had to sleep somewhere that night. We hit pay dirt on Highway 7 and Dufferin; a male occupant had booked a room about the time it would take to get there from Donny's place by car, allowing for initial drop off, entering the house, seeing the two involved and getting another cab blocks away to the motel. What led us to this registration was the occupant had no car-licence number listed and paid with cash in advance for the one night. The motel was central but awkward to get to without a car. A further check of the cab drivers that worked the north section of the city gave us a driver. He made Donny Worth's photo. We had him in Toronto.

The only missing piece was how he got here from Edmonton on a fixed ticket. Iris flew to Edmonton. Never in a million years would Holloway have approved that if she hadn't been his niece. Something about blood being thicker than water. When she returned, the grin on her face was so wide that, if it got any wider, she would need reconstructive surgery. There'd been a convention at the same Edmonton hotel he stayed at that week, with a lot of delegates coming from Toronto. It was not practical to find who might have switched tickets with him, but the scenario we had created was possible. We had reconstructed what had happened. In the morning Donny Worth left the motel and took a taxi to the airport, waited for his regular flight to arrive, then took another taxi home as if nothing had happened. We spent a lot of time in cab offices, but a hundred coffees and as many donuts for me later, we had the whole picture.

Iris made the arrest.

The last piece of the puzzle fell into place when Donny confessed. On the night of the murder, he had deliberately eaten a large meal of pasta before he came home. Then the three went out for dinner where he ate another big meal. His wife ate like a bird, which he knew, and he had deliberately taken them to a restaurant where the selection was not to Charlie's taste. With his bulk and the amount of food in him, he knew he could absorb the alcohol better than his companions. He made his move when he thought he was too close to losing his motor abilities. He was afraid he might be too clumsy to be able to stick a bullet back into the chamber.

If the word *itch* ever comes up again, I'm keeping quiet.

And I thought *I* was stubborn.

The Harvey Shulman Case

14

The full moon cast an almost eerie glow on the parkland. The air was crisp and penetrating. Tall bare trees stood like sentinels, their branches rustling ever so slightly, heavily weighted with age, crusted in thick coats of bark. Metal striking the hardened earth, followed by a human grunt, broke the silence. Over and over it occurred, more insistently now. A flashlight shone for a brief moment, then the earth was again struck repeatedly. Each successive blow widened and deepened the elongated hole.

The digger stopped when he heard the sounds of an oncoming vehicle. He lay down in the opening, concealing himself, and waited.

He saw a thin beam of light shine from the window of a moving car. It was the police scanning the grounds for intruders. The vehicle inched nearer, the beam swinging in several directions, then the vehicle passed the cluster of trees and disappeared around the bend in the park road. A few minutes later it returned, moving faster, and continued back to the entrance.

The first sprinkling of snow began to fall as the digger pulled himself out of the hole and dragged forward a large tube-like shape. With much effort, he laid it alongside the opening. Pausing only a moment to catch his laboured breath, he rolled the tube into the hole, then replaced the disturbed earth until the ground appeared smooth. He stomped on the freshly dug earth and then shovelled more into place and stomped it flat. Whatever soil was left he spread over a wider area. The snow was falling faster and soon would cover the churned ground. With luck, time would remove all traces of what he had buried.

With axe and shovel in hand, he exited the park and headed to his car in the parking lot of the large grocery store across the street. The balaclava insulated his head, and his heavy work clothes kept out the cold, but still, when he reached the car, he was shivering and it wasn't from the cold. He unlocked the trunk and threw the tools inside. Snow had already covered the surface of the road, and according to the weather forecast, would be centimetres deep by daylight. He drove away.

IRIS AND I entered the homicide office after spending the morning in court waiting to be called in as witnesses in a murder case. It was a waste of time. The accused changed his plea from not guilty to guilty. His lawyer had worked out a plea bargain. By saving the province money, the Crown agreed to a lesser charge. It wasn't the first time and I guess it won't be the last. Our courts were so bogged down that economics played a big role in determining punishment. The stats said there were fewer violent crimes. I didn't believe it. Because of plea bargaining to expedite the backlog in the courts, too many criminals were sentenced for less-serious crimes than they actually committed.

I was tired. Not the usual tiredness from long hours and short sleep, but the weariness that comes from living with constant pain. The initial diagnosis was not arthritis, which I thought I had, but a baker's cyst under my left knee. What's a baker's cyst? I asked. An inflammation between the joints that contracts and expands as I use my leg, brought on by normal wear and tear, overweight and a sudden move from a sitting or kneeling position. The doctor was telling me I was old, fat and sedentary. I'd discovered that doctors were beginning to talk like lawyers. No amount of aspirin was any help. I was onto Tyenol 3 now and that only brought temporary relief. I was told to see a therapist and exercise to see if the cyst would break off and dissolve on its own. I love the way specialists tell people what to do but never how. Did he think I had a desk job? Whatever the problem, it wasn't going away. I threw myself into my chair and suppressed a groan. Or thought I had.

"Have you seen a doctor, Gabe?"

I gave Iris my blank look that said what are you talking about? "For what?"

"Your knees."

I looked at my knees and tried to say something funny. "I'm quite attached to them."

"You got something wrong, Gabe. You're in pain. I watched you in court. You were always rubbing your knees and you walk like a lumbering truck. Why aren't you seeing a doctor?"

"There's nothing wrong. I twisted my knee somehow. It'll go away."

"I told Howard about you."

"Howard? Howard Claremont? You seeing the patrol cop?"

"Yeah, I'm seeing him. I described the way you walk and he thinks you got arthritis. That can cripple you if not treated."

"Shit! Did you tell your uncle, too?"

"No, Gabe. Go see a doctor."

Superintendent Holloway entered the room and headed our way. I looked at Iris and she gave me a defiant stare.

"And lose some weight," she hissed as Holloway stopped at her desk.

"Good idea, Gabe," he said. "You're putting on the pounds. At your age it's harder to lose. If you're not careful, you could end up with arthritis. And that hurts."

"You're not giving us another case, are you?" I asked.

"Yep. Just came in. A patrol answered a call from a woman who was complaining about a barking dog. Apparently the woman went to the house next door to ask the owner to make his dog stop barking when she noticed what looked like blood between the front door and the screen door. She knocked and rang the bell, but there was no answer, only the dog still barking. The patrol went over to see what's what. They rang the bell, but no answer. They called it in just in case. Here's the address. Have fun."

"C'mon, Greg," I pleaded. "Send Munz. Iris and I got enough going on, and now you want us to waste time on one that might be a snoop and scoop for a dog that's been left inside too long. This is ideal for Munz. He's a real shithead."

Greg laughed. "Gabe, you should have been a stand-up comedian. Stop complaining. You're getting to sound like an old man."

"Sixty is not old," I said. I gave him my best dirty look, while Iris grinned. I turned to her. "What's so funny? Your uncle made a bad joke and you think it's funny? Well, it's not sweetie, maybe you want to go by yourself – Uncle Greg won't mind – and let me know what happens. I'll work on finishing these files alone."

Her face lost its grin quickly. "Don't call me sweetie." She stood and peered down at me. "Maybe you should go with Munz. The way you two bark at each other, this sounds like the ideal case for the two of you."

"Ha-ha."

"Let's go, Gabe. You could use the exercise."

I got to my feet slowly. "I exercise every day."

"Yes, I know, when you push yourself away from the food."

I ignored this and headed for the door.

Toronto is not like New York, Chicago or Los Angeles; the city only gets about sixty homicides a year, with the murderers in a good number of the cases identified and arrested. In any event, getting another case while already working on one was one more case than I wanted. Last week a Jamaican was shot dead in the north part of the city and the lead indicated drugs were involved. Someone we thought was trying to muscle into their territory. And besides my damn knees were killing me.

Outside, I waited by the car for Iris. "You drive." We got in the car and pulled away.

"You've been to a doctor, haven't you?" she said.

"You're pushing."

"Are you taking any pills?"

I didn't respond.

"What did he say?"

"I maybe got a cyst," I said in frustration. "Watch where you're driving – that white stuff on the road isn't dandruff, you know." It was still snowing. Had been off and on since last night. "Do you know where you're going?" I had the slip of paper.

"Yes. Do you know what you're doing?"

For the rest of the trip there was silence.

THE GAWKERS WERE already out in droves. The house was a two-storey with a bedroom over the garage. A couple of scout cars were waiting for us. One of the cops took us to the door and showed us the rust-coloured stains between the door and the screen. I was pretty sure it was blood. I rang the bell a few times. The dog answered. I told the cop to radio for a search warrant and to call Forensics.

I turned to Iris. "You walk around the property and see if everything's kosher."

"You coming?" she asked. I could see she was still pissed off at me.

"Uh, I'll wait out here."

She cast a look around and must have seen what I saw. Her face smoothed out and she smiled. "Good idea." I watched her trudge into the drifts that were piled next to the house, taking huge exaggerated steps as she made her way around the back.

It was cold. I went to the car and waited. Iris showed up ten minutes later, snow clinging to her hips. "Anything?" I asked.

"Yes. Suspicious tracks around the tool shed. Two sets. I figured they were squirrels."

The dog continued to make a racket. He had better tonsils than a baritone – I assumed it was a he. The woman who had made the call came to the car. She was concerned. She told us the dog, named Mystic, might be part collie, part this and part that; a pure all-Canadian mutt. It was not like Mr. Shulman, the owner, to leave his dog unattended. They were inseparable. I told Iris I would canvass the other neighbours, while she went to a justice of the peace and got a search warrant. Just then, a truck from the Humane Society pulled up. Someone must have called. It never fails to amaze me about people and the way they react. A dog barks, and almost everyone within earshot comes to the rescue. A man or woman is on the ground, and almost everyone walks around the person, not wanting to get involved.

I did a quick tour of the neighbourhood and was satisfied that the dog barking his head off was out of character. I told the guy from the Humane Society to stay in his truck until I needed him – if I needed him. I notified Forensics to stand by, just in case, and waited for Iris to return. When she did, I broke the panel of glass in the door, reached in and unlocked it, letting it swing all the way open. There was no dog in sight and no smell. Which at least meant that no body was decomposing. The owner of the house was about sixty, his neighbour had said. A widower, no kids, lived alone. Alone, unless you counted the dog.

The barking was coming from the second floor.

"I think that's the master bedroom," Iris said. "It's over the garage."

I told one of the cops to stay by the door. Iris went ahead of me, her hand on her holster, the revolver still inside. I don't know what she was expecting. Never heard of a dog packing a gun. We stood outside the bedroom door: Iris, me, and behind, three patrol cops. Iris quickly opened the door and jumped aside. The dog bounded out and raced down the stairs.

"Close the front door!" I yelled.

I heard the door shut. The dog skidded to a stop, turned and raced down the hall. Two of the cops chased him, while Iris and I entered the bedroom, with the remaining cop staying by the door. It was a two-room bedroom. There was no one in the room with the bed, but it was a mess. While the furniture seemed intact, small items were scattered about the floor; fragile decorations lay in disarray, some broken, others cracked. The bed was made, but rumpled. The second room was a sitting room: roll top desk, swivel chair, long L-shaped couch and a low glass table in front of a television. A closer inspection of the table showed blood on the edge; some had run onto the floor. I went back to the stairs and shouted, "Did someone catch the dog?"

"Yes," came the answer.

"Put a leash on him and take him out to the backyard. He needs to poop. Don't let go of the leash," I shouted. I turned to the cop at the bedroom door. "Nobody in until Forensics gets here."

He nodded.

"Where do I find a leash?" the cop downstairs shouted.

"Look in the closet by the front door," I answered.

"Got it," he shouted back.

"You know something about dogs," Iris said. "I'm impressed. I thought you were only an expert on food."

I smiled. "Being a woman, you wouldn't understand. As a man, it's a dog's life we sometimes have to live."

"Shit!"

"Exactly what he's doing."

"God help me," Iris lamented.

"He did. He brought me into your life."

Iris shook her head. "Yeah, I'm really blessed."

FORENSICS WAS CALLED, and Iris and I waited downstairs. When they came, we let them do their thing while we questioned the neighbours more intensively to get an idea about the owner and what might have happened. The owner's name was Harvey Shulman, wife died eight years earlier of cancer; no kids. An electrician by trade, he had his own company until he became sick with a heart ailment about five years ago and sold it about a year afterwards. Retired. Good neighbour. Puttered in his garden in the summer, took long walks with his dog. Bought the dog about a year after his wife died.

"The perfect way to pass the years," Iris said.

"That's what I would do if I had to retire: get a dog and make a lasting friend. Dogs are the ideal companions, loyal, devoted, sincere and sympathetic. They can sense their master's pain and somehow are able to share it. Having a pet has been known to lower the owner's blood pressure and combat depression."

"Well, this is a side of you I've never seen," Iris said. "There's actually more to the man than I suspected."

I grimaced. "Let's see what Forensics has found out. We still don't know if there's been a murder. An absent owner is not a crime."

"How about the blood?"

"Could have had an accident, maybe drove himself to the hospital."

"No tire tracks leading into or away from the garage, unless he went before the snowfall last night. He obviously did not leave since."

"I figured that out already. I just wanted to see if you picked it up," I said.

Iris grinned at me. "You'll never change. You know, it's a big house for only one person."

I nodded. "Could have stayed to be with the memories. If he did, he must have had a happy marriage."

Stella Morgan was handling the forensics team. We went up to her as she was writing something on her clipboard.

"Hi, guys," Stella said. "This won't take that long. I'll have the whole report for you later tonight."

"Whaddaya got?"

"Someone must have spilled a lot of blood."

"A lot? Where?" I asked.

"On the carpet," Stella answered with a grin.

"What carpet?" I asked.

"The one that's gone. Those three white circles on the floor near the table edge are around spots of blood. There's a large gap and the blood appears again ten feet away."

"How d'you know there was a carpet?" Iris asked.

Stella pointed to the floor. "Hardwood floor usually means a scatter rug or centre carpet. The floor, according to my measurements, is unscarred for an area that measures five feet by five feet. This is a big bedroom. There's lots of dead space. No pun intended."

I looked at the floor that had been marked off and saw the unmarred surface as compared to the area near the table and television. "You figure a body was rolled in the carpet and taken out."

"That's my guess."

"What about the mess in here?" Iris asked.

"The dog," Stella answered. "Must have been locked in after the fact and went into a frenzy trying to get out. Ran all over the room. Some of the furniture was moved, but I don't believe because of a fight. My guess is, it was deliberately moved. Both rooms are a mess. It's unlikely a fight would cover that wide an area, especially when one of the opponents is a guy sixty years old with a bad heart."

"How bad?" Iris asked.

"Medicine cabinet in the bathroom indicates bad enough. Nitro patches, blood pressure pills, water pills, cholesterol pills. I'd say he had a congestive heart condition."

"Anything else?" I asked.

"I'll get you his blood type later, otherwise you got the best of it."

"Thanks," I said. I turned to Iris. "Let's go back to head-quarters and see if there's any next of kin." We went downstairs. The dog was facing the front door and pulling on his leash; the cop was obviously having a hard time restraining him. "This dog wants out," he said.

"Did he do his business?" I asked.

"Yeah, but he still wants out."

"Did you wipe off his paws when he came back in?"

"You're kidding me, right?"

I bent down and held one of his paws in my hand. They were wet. "Should wipe his paws dry," I said. I left them and went into the kitchen, picked up a dish towel lying beside the sink and returned with it to wipe his paws. The dog looked at me, but still pulled on his leash.

"What we going to do with him?" Iris asked.

"Guy from the Humane Society is outside. He can take him, I guess," I answered.

"Can we keep him?"

"Where?"

"Headquarters. Until we find a next of kin."

"It's not our jurisdiction."

"We're talking about a dog," she said. "You're a cop. Give the Humane Society guy a reason to leave him with you."

"You going to take care of him?" I asked.

"Who me? Nope. You!"

"Got no time."

"Bull! I saw the way you looked at him. Couldn't you take him home at least until we can give him to a member of

Shulman's family?"

"Maybe they won't want him."

"Stop with the excuses. You gonna have him put in a cage until someone claims him? Haven't you got a heart?"

"I ain't got time," I replied. "You take him."

"I know nothing about dogs. You do."

With that she strode out of the house, leaving me with the officer – and Mystic. I looked at the dog and he gazed up at me dolefully. I ground my teeth and grabbed the leash.

HARVEY SHULMAN HAD one living relative – a younger brother. Further checking showed they'd been partners until their electrical company was dissolved. They contracted their services to developers to wire commercial and residential buildings under construction. According to the records, Melville was three years Harvey's junior. Iris called him and told him that his brother, Harvey, was missing.

She hung up the telephone and gave me a look that said something was fishy.

"They don't talk to each other, right?" I said.

"How'd you know?"

"Don't have any brothers or sisters, do you."

"No. What's that got to do with it?"

"There's hardly a family that doesn't have someone not talking to someone. The reason brothers and sisters fight is simple – it's too easy to get mad. Often it's petty jealousy that magnifies into justification by one and resentment by the other. I've seen my share. If it wasn't for the business, the two more than likely would be at each other's throats. They saw each other almost every day for most of their lives and built a relationship between them around their business, and when the business was dissolved, there was nothing to tie them together. The question is, which one was the bad guy? My guess is Melville. Good guys like dogs. Mind you, Adolf Hitler liked dogs."

"Did you just make this up?"

"I have a brother who lives in the States. I see him two, three times a year. I'm a cop, he's a salesman; no common ground and no friction. He's happily married, two kids, a nice house, large mortgage, works long hours and has a boring life that pleases him. I'd die before I'd imitate him. When I visit, my nephews call me Uncle Gabe. To them I'm just the screwball Canadian uncle who lives with Eskimos in a cold country, and to me they're nice kids as long as I only see them a couple times a year. Thank God for differences. All right, sweetie, what did Melville Shulman say?"

Iris picked up the telephone and feigned throwing it at me. She scowled fiercely.

"Put it down – it's attached to the floor. Okay, okay, I forgot. I won't call you sweetie any more…today." I grinned.

Iris rolled her eyes.

"It's only a word."

"It's demeaning and patronizing."

"*Oy!* What did Melville say?" I repeated.

She put the telephone down and pecked on her computer,

ignoring me.

"Are you giving me the silent treatment? I don't believe it. See how easy it is to get mad?"

Iris gave in. "He said, 'I hope he's not dead. He owes me money. After he pays me, he can drop dead.'"

"Affectionate."

"Mean-spirited."

"Okay, let's find out what happened between them."

Stella approached. "Hello, guys. I can hear you two fighting again. Someone who doesn't know any better might think you were married."

"Whose side are you on?" Iris asked.

Stella chuckled. "You guys goofed."

"How?" I asked.

"There's no car in the garage, and Harvey Shulman owns a car."

"Aw shit! We got on about the dog and I forgot to check," I said.

"What happened to the dog?" Stella asked.

"He's in a jail cell at the Provincial Court building. Gabe booked him for disturbing the peace."

"Taking the dog home, Gabe?" Stella asked.

"I'm not sure."

"Well, dogs make good company. Doesn't anyone want him?"

"I have a feeling the answer might be no. We'll find out soon. Iris and I are going to see the only immediate relative, a younger brother. From what Iris said, I have a feeling all he wants is some money that the missing Mr. Shulman owes him. While we look into Melville Shulman, I'll put out an APB on the car."

Stella put her report into my hands. "My advice, you two, is to stop fighting and learn to accept. It makes for a reasonable life. Not perfect, mind you, but reasonable." She chuckled again as she walked away.

Iris looked at me. "She's right. Let's call a truce."

"I'm with you."

"Good. Go find your walker and let's go."

"*Oy veh!*" I muttered.

I KNOCKED ON Melville Shulman's door. A tall, thin, cantankerous-looking man, whose smile was upside down, opened the door. We showed him our badges, and before I had a chance to say anything, Melville blurted, "What more do you want?"

"Mr. Shulman, I'm Detective Garshowitz and my partner is Detective Forester. We're investigating your brother's disappearance. There's an indication of foul play. We do need to talk to you. If you please, sir, let's go inside so we can get our information. This won't take long."

There appeared to be a battle going on inside Melville's head, and from the look of his eyes, I wasn't sure which side would win. Finally Melville stepped aside. His reverse smile got bigger. "Make it quick. I don't have anything good to say about him. Everyone knows he and I don't talk. He cheated me out of my share of the company when he wound it down, and that makes him a crook in my eyes. And a bastard! Brother or not, he should rot in hell."

I looked at Iris and she made a face. We followed Melville into the living room. I sat on the couch. Melville sat opposite me, while Iris stood, just in case Melville's anger went from words to deeds. Looking at him, I didn't think he was a fighter, even if he was thin and wiry.

I pulled out my notebook. "When was the last time you saw your brother?"

"Do you think he's dead?"

"We don't know. We've checked all the hospitals and he's not in any of them. When did you last see him?"

"Over two weeks ago. We had a fight."

"Fight?"

"Words. I demanded my money."

"Why the confrontation?"

"He stole my money, that's why. That son of a bitch stole my money."

"Why didn't you sue him?" Iris asked.

Melville gave Iris a dirty look. "I tried, but my lawyer said I had no case."

"I don't understand. Why not?"

"Don't you know anything?" He was shouting now.

"Sir, we're trying to determine if there was a crime, and at the same time, learn something about your brother. Why couldn't you sue him?"

"I wasn't his partner. We shared the responsibilities, me more than him. When he got sick, the ungrateful bastard, I kept the company going. And when he sold everything, I got nothing!" He rose to his feet. "Over twenty years with him. Twenty years! He owed me. I worked harder than him. I worked outside. Do you know what it's like to work in the cold? You freeze your ass. He was the inside man, the so-called brains. He had the connections. He wore a shirt and tie. I wore coveralls and dirt. He could have made me an inside man. But he didn't. Big man, my brother! Anyway, what difference is it if I didn't put money into the fuckin' company? I worked long hours and got nothing for it. He got it all." Melville towered over me, his anger all-consuming. Spittle foamed at the side of his mouth and his face became red.

"Weren't you paid for your work?"

"Paid? Yeah, peanuts! The value was in the company's equity. I was entitled to a part. Any more questions?" he demanded. "Go find him and get me my money."

"Do you own a car, Mr. Shulman?"

"A car? No, I don't own a car. When my brother sold everything, he never renewed the lease on my car. No, I don't own a car!"

I rose to my feet. "Do you have any idea who might want to harm your brother?"

Melville looked at me in disgust. "Don't play that stupid game with me. I didn't do anything to my brother except curse the day he was born. I'm the last one who wants him dead. I want my money. I want it now. I'm not a well person either, you know." He stalked toward the front door and we followed.

"You had a job for twenty years, Mr. Shulman," Iris said.

He glared at Iris, the colour on his face deepening. "A job! I didn't have a job. I had a position. I made that company. Without me, he had nothing."

"His dog, Mr. Shulman," Iris asked. "Do you want to take care of him?"

"No!" Without another word he slammed the door behind us.

"Pleasant fellow," I said.

"For a minute there, I thought he was going to slug you." She reached into her bag and retrieved a photograph of Melville Shulman. "I had him pegged as a nice, quiet guy who was ornery and lonely."

"Isn't that a bit of a contradiction?"

"Yep. That's what men are – a contradiction. Also, he was never married."

I stared at the photograph. "How do you know that?"

"When I looked through his brother's photograph albums, there were a couple of Melville and Harvey, and Harvey getting married, but none of Melville getting married or with a woman. But pictures can be deceiving."

"How'd you know it was Melville in the wedding photos?"

"He was the best man. Some of the other shots had him under the tent, and I figured that's a place of honour."

"It's called a *chupa*."

Iris looked at me, not sure I was making with the mouth again. I smiled to show my sincerity. "The tent's called a *chupa*. It's the roof that symbolizes many things to those being married in the Jewish faith."

She nodded. "Okay. Anyway, I was right, right?"

I climbed into the car without answering. I had also forgotten to check the photo albums, and Iris knew it. The goddamn pain in my knees was screwing up my thinking.

THAT NIGHT I took Mystic home with me. The dog seemed resigned to my authority because he made no effort to run away. He also appeared to be well trained. God, he looked sad. On the way home, I had dropped into Wal-Mart and bought a brush, dog food and a bowl. I pulled a large Hudson Bay blanket out of the closet and placed it on the kitchen floor for him to lie on. After I made myself dinner, I went into the den and switched on the television. My routine hardly varied. Being a widower has its bad moments; coming home to an empty apartment was the worst. Having nothing to do after dinner ranked second. The dog had followed me into the den and flopped on the broadloom. I watched him lying in the middle of the floor and wondered what I was going to do with him. Mystic faced the window, head between his paws, eyes glued on the darkness beyond the pane, never making a sound. Heaving a sigh I was sure could be heard outside my apartment, I got to my feet and retrieved the brush. "Come here, Mystic," I called softly.

The animal turned his head and stared at me for a moment, then returned to his previous pose.

"Come here, Mystic," I tried again.

The dog looked at me again, then slowly rose to his feet, ambled over and placed his head between my legs.

"Talking's good for the soul," I said. "Want to talk?" Mystic's woeful eyes held mine as his tongue kept beat with his heart. I gently stroked the brush over his head, and Mystic closed his eyes and mouth. Using small gentle strokes, I worked the brush over his back and down his side. The eyes stayed close, but the tongue flipped out and played its heartfelt tune. "What am I going to do with you? I don't even know if my lease allows me to have a pet. Mind you, I've seen a few cats around."

Mystic licked my face.

"Thanks, it's been years since anyone kissed me. Ever been in love, Mystic? It's like nothing you'll ever experience. You can tell when a person's in love – the kiss gives it away. I know." I continued to drag the brush across Mystic's back. "Yes, it's the kiss, soft and moist. My wife's were like that. When her lips became dry and hard, I should have noticed. But I was too busy to see the change. Too busy about what? I can't even remember why I was too busy. To lose someone you love is to lose the will to live sometimes. I can tell you loved your master, and he loved you, but not his brother. Any ideas where your master might be?"

Mystic raised his head and stared into my face.

"Got nothing to say? Well, you think about it." I kept on with my grooming. "Should have got a dog years ago. Would have kept Edith company when I wasn't around. Do you know that loneliness is a killer? Too much time to think."

After twenty minutes, I put the brush down and Mystic gave me another lick. Obviously the dog's owner had been gentle. Not the picture Melville gave. Mystic flopped on the floor by my feet and closed his eyes. "Whenever you feel like it, you can talk to me," I said. "You and me have a lot in common." Mystic looked at me a second, then closed his eyes. His breathing became regular and I figured he'd fallen asleep. "What do you know?" I whispered. "What do you know?" I got up carefully. The movement shot pain behind my knees. I hobbled to the couch and took off my clothes. It was going to be another toss-and-turn night. Before getting into bed, I took two Tylenol 3s and made a note to call my doctor. The pain was getting worse.

T HE NEXT DAY I was in before Iris and received a report that
the missing car had been found in a plaza parking lot in the east
end, miles from Harvey Shulman's house. It had been towed
away by one of the city's friendly tow trucks that prowled the
streets lifting cars from plaza parking lots after the 2:00 a.m.
deadline and impounding them for fees that made the aver-
age motorist choke. A few minutes later Iris walked in. She was
wearing a black windbreaker with a belt and black slacks. She
knew how to dress. She also looked good enough to eat.
Figuratively speaking, that is. "Let's go," I said. "I got a report

the car's at a pound."

I drove. I had purchased a tensor bandage at a drug store and wrapped it around my left knee. The druggist said it would reduce the swelling. I had had trouble getting my foot into my shoe that morning.

"I checked with the Ministry of Transportation, and Melville Shulman does not own a car. I also got his bank records and he has enough money stashed away to buy a dozen cars. So why no car?" Iris asked.

"For the most obvious reason – to feel his pain. Every time he needs a car and knows he hasn't one, it fuels his hate."

"Something else's been bothering me. The dog," Iris said. "Why didn't the dog attack the person who must have been struggling with his master?"

"I don't think the dog was in the room."

"He was when we got there."

"I know."

"Any ideas?"

"I think the dog was downstairs during the fight and let in after it was finished," I said. "Harvey Shulman let someone into the house and they went upstairs. The fact that they went upstairs interests me."

"Why don't you figure someone broke in?"

"You don't take a stranger into your bedroom. Also, the desk in that room had an assortment of business papers stacked on top. Whoever he took up there had to do with his business. Nothing else in that room was connected to his business."

"Why not a woman? There was a bed in there and although he's sixty, he's not necessarily sexually dead. Are you?"

I laughed, a bit uncomfortably. "That information is on a need-to-know basis. How interested are you?"

Iris grinned. "Listen, Gabe. Girls my age don't go to bed with guys old enough to be their grandfather."

"I'm not that old."

Iris chuckled. "You are to me. Let's get back to business. Why not a woman?"

I offered an exaggerated sigh. "You think about it and tell me."

We drove a few more blocks. "You're right," she said. No food, nothing to show he was entertaining, and the bed was made. Messed up, but made. More than likely the messing-up was thanks to the dog. You're right. If he had a woman, there would have been a sense of preparation and there wasn't. Most guys don't bring hookers home. The last thing they want is to have the hooker know who they are and where they live. It can get complicated. How about same sex?"

"Remote. Remember he was married for over thirty-eight years."

"Okay, not likely. His brother?"

"Good possibility, but they don't talk to each other unless it's through a lawyer. There might be other people who had grievances against him. After we dig some more, we'll know better. In the meantime, we have his car and we'll see what that reveals." We pulled up to the car pound used by the towing service, and I recognized the place from a previous visit. "This might be awkward," I said. "The owner doesn't like me."

"You've had a run-in with him?"

"You could say that."

"What about?"

I made a face. "Greg and I were on a stake-out about three in the morning. It was raining. We were parked in this little strip plaza for hours. Our suspect was across the street in an office building. Greg had gone for some coffee, and I had to take a leak. I left the car and hurried into an alley. When I got back, a tow truck was pulling my car out of the plaza. I yelled at him to stop as he approached me. The driver gave me the finger and laughed. I was so mad I picked up a metal garbage pail by the curb and heaved it into his windshield. When he stormed out at me, I showed him my badge and made him uncouple my car. My suspect was leaving the building at that moment and drove away before I could follow. I was so pissed off I arrested the driver of the truck and impounded his vehicle. Then I made sure the owner paid a hefty fee before it was released. The owner of the towing company was fit to be tied when it was all over."

"You busted the guy's windshield? You can't do that. What happened to you?"

I grinned. "Your uncle smoothed the ruffled feathers; Greg's a good guy. I got a reprimand. You and he don't talk. How come?"

"Personal."

"I see. Well, if you ever want to talk, I'm a good listener. Ask Mystic. Anyway, this took place about eight years ago. If the owner recognizes me, we'll be in for some trouble."

"You're so exciting to be with," Iris said, smiling. "Come on, I'll protect you."

I rolled my eyes and left the car.

Inside the dingy office sat big Charlie G. The G was for a Polish name that no one could pronounce. I entered first. Charlie G was working on some papers on his desk. He looked up and recognized me in an instant. His face turned redder than the inside of a watermelon. In fact with all the pock-marks on his face, a watermelon was a good description. He got to his feet so fast his chair fell backwards with a thud and ended up sideways at his feet. "What the fuck do you want?"

"It's nice to see you, too," I said. "I'm here about the 1999 red Honda Civic Sedan that your friendly driver picked up abandoned in a plaza on Danforth Avenue near Main."

"That'll cost you three hundred bucks. It was a legit job." He stood in front of me, his eyes boring into mine, his smirk indicating he was enjoying himself. "No money, no car."

"This is police business. I could get a court order and seize the car."

He grinned; his bad breath closed the gap between us

quickly. "No money, no car," he repeated slowly. "I'm an honest dealer and you can't deny me what is mine. No car."

"Can we look at it? It may not be the one we want," Iris asked.

Charlie G noticed Iris for the first time, standing by the door. His grin turned into a leer. "Hello, sweetie," he said. "You with the bozo?"

I cringed. Charlie G had just made a big mistake.

"We'll get you your money," she said. "You look like an honest guy. Right now we want to look at the car just to make sure it's the one we're looking for. Be nice and cooperate."

"You can't go in it. Not until I get paid."

"Just want to look."

He walked past me and stood in front of Iris. I turned to watch. She had been talking between clenched teeth, but she was smiling.

"Okay, sweetie, for you anything. Maybe we could have dinner sometime."

Iris still smiled. Charlie G should be looking at her eyes, not her breasts, I thought.

Charlie G left the office and headed for the pound in back, Iris right behind him, and I behind her. I could tell that Iris was going to explode lava if their escort said sweetie one more time. Charlie G stopped in front of a car and pointed. His eyes were on Iris, his thoughts doubtless in the gutter. I walked around the vehicle and peered into the windows. Iris kept her eye on Charlie G. When I was finished, I approached him. "Where are the original tires?"

"What d'you mean?" he said.

"You swapped the tires for baldies. Those tires on the car are so smooth they couldn't grab shit. You changed the tires. No one drives on anything that bald. So where're the original tires? We need them."

Charlie G's look turned ugly. "What you see is what you get."

"I think not. You're impeding an investigation. I want the originals and I want the keys. This car is being impounded."

"Up yours."

"Trouble, boss?"

Charlie G's clone, Big and Ugly, had appeared. "Police business. Back off," I said.

"You a cop?" Big and Ugly snorted. "Coulda fooled me. Boy, you got me scared." He turned to Charlie G. "Want me to toss them out?"

"Him. Leave the little lady for me."

"I'm also a cop," Iris said, approaching Big and Ugly. "Want to toss me out?"

His grin widened, showing no bottom teeth in front. "The boss wants to toss you." He laughed at his supposed joke, pushed her aside and came for me.

Iris swung a fist into his kidney. Big and Ugly's face went red, his mouth opened as the oxygen gushed from between his lips and he let go one big fart. The smell staggered Iris. She backed away momentarily, holding her breath. He swung around and faced her, his fists clenched. Growling like an enraged bear, he charged. Before I had a chance to interfere, Iris smoothly avoided his rush, dropped to one knee and rammed her fist into his testicles. A squeal of pain emerged from his mouth, his eyes popped and he farted again as he fell to the floor like a train falling off a trestle, his hands clutching between his legs.

"Son of a bitch!" Charlie G screamed, charging Iris. He swung his fist. Iris diverted the blow over her shoulder, grabbed his outstretched arm and threw him over her body, letting his momentum carry him over her shoulders to land on Big and Ugly's face.

I raced over and handcuffed both their hands together. "Good teamwork," I said.

Iris glared at me.

"Just kidding," I said. "I'll call headquarters and get a truck down here to take the car away. Sit down, you look tired."

"Jeezus, did you smell him?"

"Smell what?" The air was still ripe. I stuck out my tongue and gagged.

AFTER FORENSICS TOOK the car away, the original tires were located and examined. We spent the day checking into Shulman's background while waiting for Forensics to give us some insight on where the car might have been. I went home that night and walked Mystic. The dog tugged on his leash straining to go somewhere but not where I intended. I wasn't used to walking. After all, what was the point? Where do you walk when you're alone? I'd seen old men strolling in malls trying to fill time, and it was a sad sight. Sitting home alone, clicking the remote on my television from channel to channel, trying to fill the void of doing nothing was my method of hiding my loneliness. Mystic's presence was having an effect on me. He shared my loneliness and was a good listener. I didn't call the doctor either. I don't know whether the tensor bandage was responsible, but the pain seemed to have subsided. I popped a couple of Tylenol 3s throughout the day and I guess that helped. Maybe I'll call the doctor tomorrow.

The night air was not biting; cool but not cold, street lamps illuminated the area and vehicular traffic was light. I sat on one of the benches positioned outside the park by my apartment and watched life pass. Mystic sat in front of me, eyes focused on the road. "Ever wonder about life, Mystic? Its purpose? Why you are born, why you are alone, why you're loved by your parents? You find love, marry and make a life. Death enters and loneliness returns, but this time it's accompanied by pain. You're born, you live, you die, for what?" I looked to Mystic watching the cars for an answer. "That, too, is life. Passing by so quickly, each day an eternity, yet each year a breath, every neglected moment a memory that never dies, stored one on top of the other."

Mystic turned his head and fixed his gaze on me.

"Ready to go back?" I stood, bent down and ruffled the fur on Mystic's head. "I hope my problems don't weigh on you as they do on me. I'm afraid of getting old, Mystic. I had it all and wasted it. Do you know I have a kid? Don't even know where she is. I made a mess of her life by not being there when she needed a father. I had my priorities mixed up. That's what life is all about. Priorities." My pace was slow as we made our way back to the apartment. The pain in my knees had returned. I wondered if it was the weather.

I moved Mystic's blanket from the kitchen to my bedroom. I was getting ready for bed when Mystic came over and nudged me with his nose. I wasn't sure what that meant, so I gently stroked his head. The brush I had used the day before was on my dresser. I picked it up and started brushing. Mystic's tongue beat a fast tempo, his body pushed against the brush as he absorbed each stroke with silent contentment. After a while, I told him it was time to go to bed. The dog looked at me with eyes that said thank you, then flopped onto the blanket. "You're a good dog, Mystic. You had a good owner."

WHEN I SHOWED up at my desk the next day, Iris had the forensic report. "Forensics found gravel in the tire treads and the trunk had a few drops of blood and some loose earth."

"Harvey Shulman's buried somewhere," I said.

"Brilliant. Where?"

"In the ground."

"What's eating you?"

"Nothing."

"Well, get a handle on nothing and come to grips with it. Why the terse answers?"

I plopped into my seat and stared out the window, trying to understand what was eating me. Iris waited for my answer, which was unlike her. "Did you see a doctor yesterday?"

"No, that's not it."

"You're a *shmuck!* It's the dog. He's getting to you."

"He's a good dog, Iris. He was well treated, I can tell. That tells me Harvey Shulman was a good man. Good men don't lie buried in anonymity. I think his brother's responsible in some way. I can't figure out if it was premeditated or an accident, but my gut tells me Melville Shulman's the bad guy."

"You're gut is sticking over your belt. Remember about hunches?"

"This is no itch. I know it's him."

"Then bring him in," she said.

"A waste of time. That cantankerous old SOB is enjoying the situation. Why kill someone and not profit? That's not Melville. He wants money. The question is, where does an cantankerous old man bury a sick old man?"

Iris was sitting opposite me as I gazed at the forensic report. "Close to the house. The body would be too heavy for him to lug too far. I'd say someplace not far, and close enough that a car can get to the place where he dumps the body," she said.

"Makes sense. Gravel, you said. A dirt road or a gravel pit, or north of the city where the side roads are gravel. How far is close?"

"How about a park?"

"Too public."

"I'm not so sure."

"Maybe a conservation park, just outside of Toronto. Boyd, maybe," I answered.

"Roads are closed at night. They have barriers blocking the entrance. No, wrong kind of park."

"We can sit here all day and not come up with the right answer. What's Forensics doing?"

"Checking the soil samples and vegetation ground into the stones. They might be able to narrow the location."

"I'll go see Harvey Shulman's lawyer, you see his doctor. Get his blood type just to be sure. In the meantime, let's figure out where Melville buried his brother."

Iris went to Dr. Marvin Gelkopf, Harvey Shulman's doctor, while I went to Sheldon Berg, his lawyer. At the end of the day, we met at headquarters and compared notes.

"The doctor wouldn't say much about Harvey Shulman's medical history, but he did tell me that what he was being treated for was hereditary, and both brothers had similar health problems," Iris said. "And the blood in the trunk is his type. I'm waiting for a DNA confirmation, which I expect."

"Are you saying Melville has the same condition?"

"He treats them both. Melville never had a heart attack. It affects people differently."

"Did the doctor tell you when Harvey was last there for an examination?" I asked.

"Yes. A few days before he disappeared."

"And?"

"He said he was fine, considering."

"Considering what? Doesn't he realize we're trying to help?"

"Yes. He wasn't being difficult, Gabe. He didn't know if Mr. Shulman would want his medical records revealed. Harvey also had a thing about his brother, and didn't want his brother to know anything about his health. As I was leaving, the doctor handed me a brochure on congestive heart failure. One of the symptoms is dizziness and light-headedness from low blood pressure."

"That's interesting."

"What did you find?" Iris asked.

I smiled. "A whole bunch. Harvey started the company. After three years he offered Melville an equal share. He wanted the book value at the time, but Melville wanted to pay what Harvey started with. Start-up was $10,000. By this time, the company was worth about $25,000. So Harvey wanted $12,500, but Melville wanted to pay $5,000. They couldn't come to terms, so Harvey withdrew the offer and began paying him a salary equal to what he was paying himself, and that was how the company existed for the next twenty-four years.

When Harvey had a heart attack five years ago, he gave Melville signing power. He was away for two months. When he came back, he found that Melville had taken twice his normal pay. When Harvey asked why, Melville claimed he was doing the work of two and was therefore entitled to twice the wages. A few months later, Harvey sold the company for $500,000 and gave his brother the difference between what he had taken from a $50,000 severance pay. That started the final argument. Apparently they argued about everything."

"Who was right?"

"Sometimes one, sometimes the other. The lawyer became the referee. He said Harvey was a good man, but when it came to his brother, he was a different person."

"Sounds like Melville's a *putz*," Iris said.

"Not according to Melville."

"He could have had $250,000 if he had paid his brother $7,500 more than he offered. That's a *putz!*"

"The question is, is that reason enough to kill his brother?"

"Are you referring to the $50,000 or the $250,000?" Iris said. "Who knows what someone with that kind of tunnel vision would do? I'd say it's not impossible."

"You're right, it's not impossible. Let's talk to Melville Shulman again."

WITHOUT A BODY, the evidence indicated too many options. Blood on a table, spots on the floor, missing carpet, blood in the trunk of a car…It would appear a violent crime had been committed, and yet nothing was missing from the house as near as we could tell, no break-and-enter and no body. Kidnapping was a possibility, but nobody was making any demands. Harvey Shulman didn't appear to have any real enemies, except his brother, and although they'd been known to argue, the arguments were never violent. Loud, but not physical. The problem was, was Harvey dead? Had he injured himself? Did he take himself to a hospital and lose his memory?

If so, why was the car found where it was?

Melville let us into his apartment and was his usual charming self as we sat in his living room. "Why are you badgering me? Am I being accused of something?"

"No, Mr. Shulman," I answered. "We're trying to figure out what happened to your brother. You are his only living relative. We're trying to understand what your brother was like and whether his disappearance was by choice or by force."

"Do you think he's dead?"

"You've asked me that before. At this point, I can't say."

"If he's not dead, what do you want from me? He owes me money. If he pays, I don't care what happens to him. If he's dead, I won't get my money. I'm not in his will."

"How do you know?"

"I am not a fool, Detective. Why would my brother put me in his will? Why give me money after his death if he won't give it to me before? I'll tell you this, if you can't find his body, no one gets his money for seven years. Not even the charities he more than likely left it to. He even left money to the dog. The dog! As his only living relative, I'll claim a share. I'll make it so tough that the charities will compromise. By then the damn dog will be dead. They'll give me his share. As long as the body's not found, I'll get my money – eventually."

"How do you know the dog's in the will?" I asked.

"My brother told me!" he shouted, glaring at me like I was stupid. "If I killed him, it's for damn sure you're too stupid to catch me."

"Are you challenging me, Mr. Shulman?"

Melville stood up, smirking. "No. I'm telling you my brother cheated me of my share of the company. I'm entitled to half of what he got when he sold it. He used his heart attack as an excuse. You think I did something? Prove it. Find his goddamn body." For the first time, a look of sheer pleasure crossed Melville Shulman's face. "If you can. If not, leave me alone."

"I'll find the body if there is one, Mr. Shulman," I said.

"No, you won't," he said in a quiet voice, still grinning. "You'll walk all over it, but never find it." As he led us to the front door, he never stopped grinning.

Iris and I left his apartment knowing the answer to the big question. The arrogant son of a bitch had done it.

As we drove away, Iris asked the question I was asking myself. "You want the dog, don't you?"

"It's not my dog," I said.

"If the dog's in the will, you have a conflict of interest."

"We don't know that for sure. Anyway, I'm taking what we know to the Crown Attorney. We got us enough to see what they want us to do."

FOR THREE DAYS, Iris and I went over every lead, but nothing new turned up. Melville Shulman did in his brother, of that we were sure. The Crown Attorney told us to keep on it and get more evidence. We figured Melville must have come to Harvey's house for a showdown, they go upstairs to where Harvey keeps his business papers, argued, maybe Melville pushes him, Harvey loses his balance, falls and strikes his head, and dies. I figured it was an accident. Melville panics and covers up what he'd done by burying the body. There's a tool shed in back with all the necessary tools. He doesn't have a car, so he doesn't have to go back and get it. Dumps his brother's car, ditches the tools and goes home. It sounded a bit farfetched, but that was our conclusion. We were convinced he was responsible for Harvey's death, even though we didn't have a body. What we didn't know was if it was accidental or deliberate.

I finally went back to my doctor. Now he thought I might have a torn meniscus. "A torn what?"

"Soft tissue behind the knee. It has a tendency to weaken in older, overweight people."

"So how did I tear it?"

"Something as simple as getting off a chair or standing from a crouched position. Any number of ways." He asked if I had trouble tying my shoelaces.

I said no, and he seemed surprised. "I wear loafers," I said. Boy would he make a terrible cop.

The doctor made me an appointment for an MRI – four months from now.

The look on my face must have given him a clue that I couldn't believe what he said.

"You can always go to Buffalo and pay for it," he said.

I thanked him and left his office. Asshole. It was time to find another doctor. I called my brother in the States and told him my problem. He let me know how much it would cost if I went to Buffalo. I decided I'd rather wait the four months. I get a cop's wage, not the premier of Ontario's. The tensor bandage had stopped working. I discovered that pain could be very personal. Except for the occasional toothache, this was the only time I could recall having lingering pain. I awoke to it, lived with it all day and went to bed with it. It was mine, all mine, and it wasn't going to go away or jump onto someone else. Growing old were just words to me until I realized that my body was telling me it was running on low octane. The engine needed fine-tuning and the wheels were getting bald. I needed a good mechanic not just a mechanic. I was getting to appreciate those words I'd heard often but never paid attention to, that getting old sucks – but the alternative was worst.

It snowed again. December was going to be difficult for the old, a pleasure for the sports-minded and a pain in the ass for my knees and me. On the third day, I came home to Mystic and asked him the sixty-four-dollar question. "What happened? You were there. Say something." That was when I realized that Mystic had not barked since the first day. Hadn't made a sound since being led away from the house. When we went walking, he always strained at the leash, but was obedient to my commands. Silent obedience. Even dogs feel pain, I thought.

Other cases were taking our time away from the Shulman case. Time seemed to be working in favour of Melville. It was no secret among the cops at the station that I wanted to solve the disappearance. It was also no secret that I seemed to be less confrontational. That's what Iris called me. I never figured I was confrontational. She referred to my change as "Mysticpower."

HOLLOWAY APPROACHED IRIS sitting at her desk. "Where's Gabe?"

"He had an errand."

Holloway sat opposite her. "Uh, I was wondering if everything is okay."

"Sure. Why wouldn't it be?" She looked down at her hands.

"Where is he?"

She raised her head. "Took Mystic to be groomed. Only appointment he could get."

"I see. Uh, how are you getting along?"

"Fine. Why wouldn't we?"

"He's a good man, Iris. And you're a good cop. You know, you're his daughter's age."

"No, I didn't know. Is that why you teamed us?"

"That, and another reason. I wanted to make sure you learned from the best." He paused. "About your father and me…"

"I've decided not to be involved. It's between you two. I'm discovering that not everything is as it seems."

"I'm glad. There's something else. What's the matter with Gabe?"

"What do you mean?"

"The way he walks. He has a problem, a serious problem he hasn't told me about. Should I be concerned?"

"No."

"That's it? No?"

"It's under control. He's seeing someone."

He looked at her, his face showing he was sympathetic. "He's a good friend, you know that. You'll keep me in touch if I should be concerned, won't you?"

"It's under control."

"I heard you the first time."

"Uncle Greg…About Gabe…I like him, too. I like him a lot. He's a good guy as well as a good cop. He doesn't fool me with his sexist talk. He's lonely and I feel for him."

"He's older than your father."

Iris shook her head. "No, not that way. I think I can fill some of that loneliness by being his friend. I ask we be partners until he retires. But don't tell him I said that."

Greg stood. "I think you two are a great match. Okay, It's a deal," he said. "I'll tell you something. He's said the same thing."

IRIS AND I were busy. We had our hands full with what looked like a lovers' spat that ended in murder. The suspect was hiding out in the city, we figured, and we were hunting down the leads. That meant a lot of walking. When the knees are concerned, the simple act of walking becomes tantamount to climbing a mountain. I was having trouble and still had two months before my MRI appointment. I didn't know too many doctors personally. The ones I did were the hack and chop guys at the coroner's office. I asked Iris about hers. I didn't think a gynacologist and I were made for each other. I couldn't picture myself standing naked before her asking me to cough. Besides, her squinting would destroy the image I had created about myself. Iris suggested Dr. Gelkopf. She said she got good vibes from him. He suspected arthritis, didn't think it was baker's cyst, but it could also be a torn meniscus. I was learning that medicine was not a perfect science and a lot about degenerative illnesses.

One day, Iris greeted me with some good news. "Your appointment for an MRI has been bumped to one o'clock tomorrow morning at another hospital," she said.

"How come?"

"I was able to pull some strings."

"Who do you know that has that kind of influence?"

"My ex."

"Really. What's he do?"

"He's a sports doctor. I had dinner with him last night, and this morning he called with the appointment."

"You just had dinner with him?"

"Yes, just dinner."

"Did you have to give away the family jewels?"

"They aren't jewels anymore."

"Thank him for me," I said.

"He got his reward."

F OUR MONTHS LATER, Holloway called us into his office. "Melville Shulman has had a heart attack. He's asked for you. He's at Toronto General."

I had trouble holding back my smile. "So maybe we finally hear what happened," I said.

At the hospital, we met Dr. Gelkopf leaving Melville's room. He offered us a tired smile. "Not too long." He started to walk away, but stopped. "Are you taking the pills I prescribed?" he asked me.

I nodded.

I saw Iris flash me a look before she asked Gelkopf the question. "What happened to Melville?"

"Threw a tantrum with his brother's lawyer. He went ballistic."

We went into the room. Melville had more gadgets on him than a ten-pin bowler. Machines were pinging, tubes in his nose, I.V. in his arms, wires running from one machine or another, and he was breathing like a steam engine. He looked terrible. As we stood over him, his eyes opened.

"Want to find my brother?" he wheezed.

"Sure," I said. "You realize that anything you say can and will be used against you."

Melville closed his eyes and his lips moved, but I couldn't hear anything. "What?"

Melville forced his eyes open. "Fuck you!"

The machines hit high notes, and the heart monitor flattened out. The nurse ran in and told us to leave. We did.

A few minutes later, Dr. Gelkopf rushed in.

"What do you think?" I asked Iris.

"Stubborn bastard. When it came to his brother, he had total tunnel vision. They both did." She shook her head. "Am I glad I have no brothers and sisters."

The doctor came out.

"What's the verdict, doc?" I asked.

"We lost him. Sorry, there was nothing I could do." He continued down the hall.

"It looks like he took the secret to the grave with him," Iris said.

BEFORE RETURNING TO headquarters, we drove over to the lawyer's office to find out what had triggered Melville's tantrum. Mr. Berg greeted us in his foyer and walked us into his office. "A few minutes ago, Melville Shulman died at Toronto General," I said.

"That's unfortunate, but I'm not sorry. I never liked him."

"You and he had an argument, I understand."

"What? No, not at all! He asked me about Harvey's will. I knew I could prevent him from knowing for a while, but I wanted he should know."

"What did it say?" Iris asked.

"Well, Harvey left money for the dog, an allowance, so to speak, in the event that he died before the dog did, to be used by whomever took care of him until he died."

"Really? How much?" I asked.

"Five thousand a year for ten years. The dog being about eight, Harvey estimated the dog might live to about eighteen. Any money not spent on the dog from the allowance would go to the person who cared for him. I was to invest fifty thousand and give five out every year. With interest there should be a tidy sum left over for the caregiver."

I shook my head at Iris to say nothing. "And the rest?"

"A hundred thousand to the Heart and Stroke Foundation because of his condition, and a hundred thousand to the Canadian Cancer Society because of his wife. The rest, about a million dollars after selling his assets, home and such, would go to Melville."

"No shit!" I exclaimed.

Berg smiled. "No shit. Unfortunately, since we don't have a body, he would have had to wait at least seven years to collect, or until such time as there was definite evidence that Harvey Shulman was dead. That was when he blew a gasket."

I felt my mouth drop.

"Yep," Iris said. "I call that justice."

BACK AT HEADQUARTERS, Iris showed me a small article from *The Toronto Star.*

DOG TRACKS OWNER TO GRAVE
A border collie has tracked down his former owner's grave despite never having been there before. The dog escaped from his new

owner's home more than six kilometres from where his former owner was buried, crossing busy roads before lying down on the grave of his 78-year-old previous owner.

"Do you have any idea what you're implying? Do you realize how big Toronto is?"

"No! Tell me. No, never mind. Let me tell you."

"Where?"

"Remember Melville said, 'You'll walk all over him, but never find him'?"

I thought a minute. "Okay. Let's say a park. Which one? The city has a thousand parks."

"One that has a road into it. Remember what we're dealing with here. Melville wasn't strong enough to carry something as heavy as a body very far; a big park with a road, and my guess probably not too far from Harvey's house."

"Why not High Park?"

Iris shook her head. "Too far. That bastard was cunning. He dumped the car in the east part of the city and close to downtown. That's a false clue. From the Danforth he hopped a subway home. My guess he'd already dumped the body else-where. Where? When you think about it, in one of two parks: Earl Bales or G. Ross Lord would fit the description. I say G. Ross Lord Park. Earl Bales has a short road off Bathurst. It's in a residential area. The grounds are too open. It used to be a golf course, rolling hills and flat, very few trees. Now G. Ross Lord is a different kind of park, a conservation park, several roads, twists and turns, and trees, lots of trees and thick bushes, and lots of ravines. There's a dozen ways to get into the park on foot, but only one by car. Across from the Dufferin entrance are a lot of parking spaces from the commercial busi-nesses – even a huge food store with a massive parking lot and that's open until midnight. A car sitting there late would not be suspicious. Drive into the park, dump the body some-where, drive out, park the car, return on foot, bury the body, then back to the car, dump the car, then home. Get rid of the tools, drive it away from the area and come back by public transit. G. Ross Lord Park is where I figure the body is. Now, could Mystic locate it?"

I stood, grinning. "My dog can do anything,"

"Your dog?"

"Yes, my dog. And I don't want the money. It can go to the Humane Society."

WE DROVE TO my apartment, got Mystic, went to Iris's, and then to G. Ross Lord Park, to a parking section near the trees. Iris put on her running shoes. Mystic sat down while I unhooked the leash. Free of restraint, Mystic looked at me, but made no effort to leave. "Go find Harvey," I said. Mystic turned his head and looked at the park. "Go find Harvey," I said more loudly. Mystic rose to his feet and glanced at me and then out at the park. "Go!"

And he went.

Iris took off after the dog at a run.

I walked. I'd been taking an anti-inflammatory pill. It made a world of difference. I still had pain but nowhere near the intensity. I was told to get used to it. My walking was steadier and not so exaggerated. At home, I used a cane, though. I never brought it to work or outside the apartment.

Iris and Mystic were gone from sight within seconds. Down a hill or around a bend, I didn't know. I stuck to the road. Then I heard Mystic barking. I followed the sound into the trees. It took me a while to get there, and when I did, I saw Mystic digging away like mad. Iris was panting and grinning like a Cheshire cat. "What do you think?" she said.

Mystic barked.

"Harvey's here."

And he was.

HARVEY SHULMAN WAS buried ceremoniously next to his brother Melville. It seemed ironic that the two who had never gotten along with each other in life should be buried on the same day, side by side. We stayed until both graves were covered and everyone had left. Mystic sat obediently beside me and watched it all. Dogs aren't stupid; Mystic had to sense what was happening. I didn't even have him on a leash – didn't need it. It wasn't that I was his owner as much as Mystic had agreed to be my dog. Iris and I headed for the car when I realized that Mystic wasn't beside me. I turned to see where he was and saw him doing his business on Melville's grave.

Iris laughed. "Did you bring a bag?"

"For what?" I answered as I continued to the car. "You know, what just happened was illegal."

"That's why I asked if you had a plastic bag," Iris answered.

"No. I don't mean that." I gestured at the grave. "What just happened was double jeopardy. You can't punish a criminal twice for the same crime."

Mystic ran ahead of us, barking.

"Wanna bet?" Iris said, laughing.

I smiled. I was feeling good. All the bad in my life was behind me. I had a good partner and a good dog. It had been a long time coming. I opened the door to my car and Mystic bounded in. Iris got into the passenger side, and I climbed in behind the wheel.

"Remember," Iris said calmly, "you must turn the key clockwise for the car to start."

I snorted. "Don't you ever let up?"

"In your case, never. Let's go. Another day, another case."

The Solly Solinus Case

19

The large storage door opened and the green Toyota Camry drove into the warehouse. The beams from the headlights broke the darkness as it edged into the building. It stopped, its engine idling. The warehouse doors closed and overhead lights were turned on, exposing the inside of the building. The engine of the car was turned off.

From behind several large packing cases, two men approached the car from the front, both with shotguns. From the rear, the two men who had opened the warehouse door also approached the vehicle. They, too, carried shotguns. The four stopped and stood *watching the vehicle, the firearms by their sides. The driver's door opened and a man removed himself from the vehicle, his coat open, fingers spread to show they were empty. He backed slowly to the passenger door and opened it. A Spanish dark-skinned man wearing a turtleneck shirt and slacks stepped out carrying a black attaché case. He placed the case on the hood of the vehicle and stepped away from the car. No one moved.*

Several minutes passed before a huge man appeared, thick neck, muscular arms and torso, head shaved bald, eyes that bore into the two men standing by the car. He was holding a long, thin knife. He approached the attaché case and opened it, removed a large white bag from inside among many other such bags and stabbed a hole into it. He licked the tip of his knife and seemed to savour the contents. Apparently satisfied, he returned the bag to the case and closed it.

Another man appeared, middle-aged, dressed in a full well-cut suit, clean shaved with a thin pencil-style moustache under his Roman nose, a smile on his face and his hand outstretched ready for a shake. "You must be the Matador," he said, "I'm Harry Greco."

IRIS AND I ran from our car to where Detective Simon Munz and his partner, Jack Elman, were crouched. We were responding to a call for backup. We didn't know who or what – we just happened to be in the neighbourhood and closest to the location when the call for assistance was made. When I realized it was Munz who made the call I knew we were in for trouble.

"Took your sweet time getting here," Munz snarled when he realized it was me coming to his help. "Don't you fuck up my bust."

Iris and I exchanged looks of disgust. "What have you got, Simon?" she asked.

"What I got is the drug bust." There was no affection in his words. "My snitch told me that Harry Greco was going to be at this meet. If he shows, we got us the main guy."

"What's going on? This is not our jurisdiction," I said.

"Greco's responsible for selling shit that's already killed two. I happened to hear he's going to be here tonight. If we can get him off the street, what difference does it make for what?"

"Does Holloway know what you're doing?"

"I know what I'm doing."

"This doesn't make sense to me. Why would Greco risk showing up to a drug buy?" I asked. "He has stooges for that."

Munz stuck his face into mine. "Listen, old man, this is my bust. Are you my backup? Do what I ask and everything will go down right. I got me the big man and that's all I care about. When I called for backup, you were the last one I wanted. You take the back of the warehouse so you won't get in the way. Jack and I got the front. Iris goes to the roof by the fire escape, just in case. The roofs connect with all the buildings on the block. Greco's a smart cookie. I figure he came in by the roof and his car is parked somewhere in the vicinity. Only one car went inside and it was too cheap for Greco to be seen in. The man's got himself a big ego. I'm going in fast. When we enter, they'll scatter. I want Greco. I don't give a fuck about the others."

"You need more men," Iris said. "The warehouse's too big for the four of us."

Munz turned to face her. "I can't wait for more men. These guys ain't gonna wait around for long. It's now. What's the matter, sweetie, scared?"

Iris glared at Munz.

"Okay, let's move. Give me five minutes to get in place. Then be prepared for the rats to run for their lives." The only thing missing from the expression on his face was a rat dangling from his lips. "Okay, Jack, let's go." Munz sprinted for the door.

I grabbed Elman's arm. "What's with him?"

Detective Jack Elman rolled his eyes. "Personally, I think he's flipped," he said. He chased after Munz.

"C'mon," Iris said.

Reluctantly, I followed.

"Bastard," Iris muttered. "Who does he think he is, Clint

Eastwood?"

"More than likely Dirty Simon. I don't like this. This is wrong."

"The man's really got it in for you."

"I know. He thinks I fucked up his promotion because I reported he beat up a kid who wasn't resisting arrest. He likes being physical."

"Did you?"

"Yes. You be careful. You don't have anyone to cover your back."

"Yes, I do – the vest I'm wearing."

"Just be careful. He's got you out on a limb and I don't like the look of the branch."

We stopped at the fire escape, and Iris leaped for the bottom rung and pulled it down. The ladder rebelled at being moved, screeching its disapproval. "Shit! They'd have to be deaf not to hear that." She grabbed the rung above her and pulled herself up, then worked her way to the first platform and disappeared into the darkness.

I made my way to the back door, hid behind several barrels and waited. Four cops covering a building this size was stupid. Munz was known for taking risks. He'd already had two partners quit him. They knew as far as he was concerned they were expendable. Suddenly I heard several rapid gunshots and shotgun blasts from inside the building, a lull, then more shots. The back door never opened. Then I heard shots on the roof.

I ran to the fire escape intending to bring down the ladder, but I couldn't push off with my leg. My knee wouldn't take the exertion and collapsed under my weight. Anti-inflammatory or not, the pain was intense. I wasted precious seconds making several attempts before I realized it was futile. I couldn't jump. I could hardly move without the pain cutting into my knee. I rolled a barrel over to the fire escape and crawled on top, then reached for the ladder and climbed to the roof as fast as I could. It was a moonless night and the roof was pitch-black. I crouched low, using whatever obstacles I could find for cover, scanning the flat surface for Iris. It was too dark to see. Police sirens wailed, and cars screeched to a stop below. Excited voices shouted. I strained through the cacophony to hear any sound of human distress on the roof. At last I heard a low moan. I determined where it came from, worked my way to the ledge separating this building from the next and saw Iris, slouched against the wall, almost ready to topple over. I hobbled the last few feet to her just as police emerged from the adjacent roof entrance. "Get an ambulance!" I shouted. "Officer down! Get an ambulance!"

I shone my flashlight on her and saw the blood on her shoulder. I pulled her off the ledge, ripped the velcro from her bullet-proof vest and exposed her collar. A bullet had crazed her neck. I cradled her head in my lap and pressed my fingers directly on the wound to stop the flow of blood. Her eyes closed and her head fell lifelessly to the side. Other officers came to my aid. More flashlights brightened the area. A few minutes later I was pushed aside, and an ambulance medic took my place. I stepped back, my hands and clothes covered in blood, fear in my heart, as I watched the medic working on my partner's unconscious body.

Munz rushed onto the roof. "Did she get him?" he demanded. "Did she get him? The bastard ran for the stairs as soon as I yelled 'Police!' and had the metal door barricaded from the inside." He saw the medic working on someone and approached. "Fuck! The dumb bitch let him get away." He saw Gabe and shook his fist at him. "You two screwed up! As soon as I saw you, I knew you'd –"

I stepped forward and smashed him in the face. Munz staggered backwards a few steps, recovered, then lunged at me. Several cops jumped between the two of us before the fight escalated. As they held us apart, I could see the hate in his eyes.

SOLLY SOLINUS WOULD never have earned a second glance. A clean-cut kid, eighteen, thin, too thin for his six-foot height, hair cut short, jeans with torn knees, jersey and white runners, a look seen on any street, on thousands of kids. Behind his back, he was referred to as "Beanpole," and it wasn't said with any affection. Beanpole was a drug pusher, but not your usual drug pusher. He didn't hang around with a gang, had no tattoos, no nose rings or earrings, didn't use foul language, but he was part of Harry Greco's operation. He bought, sold, but never consumed. His was a cash-and-carry business. Although some of the buyers always tried getting credit, Solly never changed his rules – no dough, no blow, and no amount of pleading would change his mind. He was a kid who knew what he wanted.

He stood across the street from the neighbourhood high school during lunch break, his usual spot, leaning against the lamppost almost in front of the main entrance. The school side of the street was a no smoking zone, so many kids crossed over to light up. Backpack at his feet, hands in his pocket, he waited for his clients to approach. They knew where to find him, and over the past few months since he started working for Greco's group, he made it a rule that all his selling was done before the school day ended. Always. He had another rule – never telephone or come to his house to buy. It was the school and nowhere else. The few who broke the rule at the beginning got roughed up. Very shortly the message became clear – you don't screw with Beanpole.

Julie Lipton approached; a grade ten student, a sloppy dresser, but clean, a small rose tattooed on her shoulder, rings on all her fingers, none on the thumbs, a middle-class teenager with a home life that, according to her, sucked, who found solace in a heroin snort and used her body to pay for her habit.

"Still got?" she asked.

"What you want?"

"Three, pay for one now and the others Monday."

Beanpole shook his head. "You look strung out."

"Could use a couple more for the weekend."

"No. Don't ask again. Pay and move. Or just move."

Her eyes pleaded with him to reconsider. He never did. And he wasn't interested in trading what she had for what he had. She slipped him a folded bill and he palmed a package the size of half a teabag into her hand. Julie put it into her purse and left much faster than she'd approached.

Beanpole's gaze followed her as she entered the washroom in the corner gas station. No emotion showed on his face. He was also smart enough to know that other eyes could have been watching him, and he never forgot that what he was doing was illegal – and dangerous.

HARRY GRECO'S ANGER erupted in a terrible tirade. He glared at the half-dozen men around the room after he had vented ten minutes of non-stop verbal abuse. Their gazes followed him as he paced the floor and muttered obscenities under his breath. "We've got us a snitch," he finally said. "It's either one of you or one of you talked to the wrong person and almost got me caught." He stopped and slowly panned the faces, looking for a sign that would reveal which of his men was responsible. "Only you knew, and that wasn't until I told you that morning. My mistake. My mistake!" he yelled. He glared around the room. "Do you know what happens when you shoot a cop? We're hot. I got enough heat from a bunch of Jamaicans trying to muscle in and now cops too. Someone here talked too much. So who was it?"

No one said anything.

"I'm giving you all two days to come up with the snitch. I want every pusher checked and rechecked until someone comes up with a name. Find the snitch. I ain't putting any deals together until I knows it's safe. After that…" He let the threat hang and scanned their faces once more, then turned and marched out the door with his bodyguards behind.

Gregory Synes left the room. He had nine pushers working for him. He remembered saying something to one of them, Solly Solinus. He couldn't remember exactly what he said, but he was friendly with Solly because he'd known his father. Synes had a feeling he might have been the one who screwed up.

I SAT BESIDE Iris's bed in the hospital, gazing at her pale, inert form, angry with myself for not getting to the roof faster, for not backing her up instead of crouching behind a stupid barrel. I shouldn't have let her go up alone. I hadn't wanted to cause an argument with Munz, was my excuse. I had exercised bad judgement. I was the senior cop and I should have known better. I peered at the heart monitor and followed the pattern of Iris's breathing as the graph peeked and plunged, peeked and plunged. My gaze returned to her face. The pillow and her complexion were almost the same shade. I leaned back in the chair and closed my eyes, trying to pull my thoughts elsewhere. I'd fucked up my marriage, alienated my daughter and now jeopardized my partner's life. Enough was enough! My body had been sending me signals that I wasn't what I used to be. My knees were a constant reminder. I was a liability to anyone who worked with me. I wasn't mobile enough. I would have liked to stick it out until I hit sixty-five, but after a mistake like this, maybe I was better off retiring sooner. I had the years.

"This business sucks," a voice whispered.

I flung myself forward. "Hi, kid," I answered.

"What, am I dead, no 'sweetie'?"

I grinned. "How you feeling?"

"Did you get the number of the truck?"

"No jokes. You had me worried."

"Ever been in this situation?"

"No."

"I don't recommend it." Iris groaned in pain when she

moved her head.

"What happened?" I asked.

Iris shook her head. "Don't know. Saw two flashes from two directions." She closed her eyes as a surge of pain crossed her face.

I went out to the nurses' station to tell them Iris was awake. I followed the nurse partway back into the room, before she turned and stopped me. "Stay here," she said.

The nurse bent down and examined Iris's bandage and took her pulse. Smiled, tucked her blanket around her and came back to me as I watched, concern written all over my face.

"You should go. She's weak. Lost a lot of blood and needs her rest."

"Is she going to be okay?"

"Looks good. Say goodbye and let her rest."

I nodded. "Gotta go, Iris. I'll be back tomorrow."

Iris offered a weak smile and flapped her hand at me, her eyes closed.

I left with the nurse. "Friend?" the nurse asked.

"Something like that. Partner. She's a good kid. She's got balls."

"I don't think so," the nurse said with a smile, "but I know what you mean."

SOLLY SOLINUS RECEIVED a telephone call from Gregory Synes asking for a meeting. Solly wasn't pleased. Synes promised he would never call him at his apartment. That was the deal. Solly wanted no links from the trafficking organization to him except when he picked the stuff up and paid for it. He should have known they wouldn't keep their word. Solly was the man of the house. His father disappeared a couple of years ago, and his mother sweated over a sewing machine in one of the garment houses downtown, earning barely enough to make ends meet. So he had found a way to make life easier.

He didn't mess with the drugs. To him, the kids that bought were stupid. Drugs were never an answer. But for him, selling them was a necessity.

His old man had been a pusher. Spent what he made gambling, and the odds were his disappearance was not voluntary. Solly figured his father finally did something with his life that had meaning, like mixing with the cement that went into some of the high-rises going up all over the city. Too bad Solly didn't know which one. He would have liked to know how big a monument the old man got.

Solly had few friends. He didn't need them – he needed money. He had hoped to sell the stuff for another six or seven months and then quit. That was his original plan, but his plans changed. Fuck Synes. He didn't scare him – a small man in a big pond. Greco scared him. That man was heartless. Solly had seen him beat a guy senseless for shorting him on a pay-off. Greco knew the guy hadn't done it deliberately, but he wanted everyone to know what happened when he didn't get what belonged to him. The last thing Solly wanted was to bring himself to Greco's attention. Synes was waiting for him when he stepped out of his house. His car was running and he signalled for Solly to enter. The car pulled away as soon as Solly was inside. "Strap up," Synes said. "Don't want a cop stopping us."

They drove in silence, and quickly, since the traffic going north was light and the signals cooperated. They left the city and were far enough north to be on a dark stretch of road where there were no streetlights. Synes pulled over to the shoulder, stopped the car and let it idle as he faced Solly. "I got a problem, kid."

"The answer is no. I'm not working longer hours. That was our deal, remember?"

"Different problem. I said something to you yesterday I shouldn't have. Now I got me a peck of trouble. I mentioned that Greco was going to make a big buy last night. I might have said where. I can't remember, but I do remember I told you that."

"I think so," Solly said. "But I didn't tell anyone, if that's what you're asking."

"Someone told someone, kid. The cops showed. Someone talked, I don't know who. What I do know is you knew."

"Wasn't me, Mr. Synes. I didn't tell anyone, honest."

Synes gazed at Solly in the dark interior of the car. "Okay, kid. I just wanted to hear you say that."

"Really, Mr. Synes, it wasn't me."

Synes put the car in drive, made a U-turn and headed back to the city. No further words were said. Back at the house, Solly got out and Synes sped away.

Solly stared after the receding taillights, his pupils dilated with fear.

I WAS AT my computer at the office. Now that I knew Iris was all right, I wanted to check on some things. That bust was a bad scene. It wasn't our scene. Besides it was poorly planned, which, considering Munz's track record, didn't surprise me. Harry Greco had become the focus of police attention. Whoever brought him down would be commended. Munz knew that. Greco was the big drug distributor in the north part of Toronto. He'd carved himself a large territory and muscled the small fries out. A Jamaican gang had a piece of the action before Greco. Now there were three dead Jamaicans and Greco running the show. We had expected a war, but it didn't materialize. To make matters worse, the garbage Greco sold wasn't good. A couple of kids had OD'd on his drugs recently, and catching him had become a priority – a top priority. We wanted him for the deaths, the feds for trafficking.

When Iris got to the roof, his goons were there. Was Greco being smart by covering an escape route or were they there for other reasons? Iris said there were flashes from two different locations. It sounded like a trap. The Jamaican gang was still around. Was this buy a means of getting them to come out and pop them? Did Greco know that Munz was coming? If so, why go for a hit? Kill a cop and the city comes down on you. Or was Greco just lucky or stupid? The possibilities were endless. One thing for sure, Munz trying to get Greco was like driving a Mack truck with a trailer on a nature trail. He might get him, but how many would die first?

The phone rang. It was a call I was expecting. I went to Holloway's office, and Munz and Elman were already there.

"I want to know what the fuck was going on!" Holloway shouted from behind his desk. "What the fuck were you two thinking? Who gave you the authority to mix in federal business? I want answers and I want them now! I got me a cop that's been shot and shit coming at me from the top to the bottom of the chain of command. Who authorized this? Who?"

I looked at Munz, but he said nothing.

"Who was lead cop?" Holloway bellowed.

"Me."

Holloway glared at Munz. "Okay. What happened?"

Munz jerked his chin at me. "That asshole screwed the bust. Him and his dumb partner. They're the ones that fucked this up. I had Greco dead to rights. I had him locked tight and they let him get away."

"What were you doing there? What the fuck were you doing there? Why wasn't I aware what was going down?"

"I didn't have time. I had to get the place covered or I'd lose him. I called for backup and this old fart and his papoose showed up. I warned them not to fuck up. But they did."

Holloway came around his desk and stuck his face right into Munz's. "You have a dirty mouth, Munz. This cop has done more in five years on the force than you'll ever do until you get kicked off. I know what you are and I know how you operate. You think you're the Lone Ranger. Well, let me tell you something. I don't like the Lone Ranger 'cause he gave the dirty work to his partner and took all the credit. That's you. You've blown more partners than a hooker."

I couldn't help smiling at that line, but I shouldn't have.

Holloway turned to face me. "What the fuck you smiling at? You risked your partner's life. You could have got her killed and that's not a laughing matter. You have a responsibility to her and you blew it. You were senior officer. I expect you to exercise good judgement. You didn't. This guy's an asshole, but it's obvious I gave you more credit than you deserve. I understand you belted Munz. I won't tolerate that. We are a unit, not a bunch of street hooligans. I'll suspend you both if I hear that either one of you are at each other again. That's a promise." He went back to his desk and stared at the three of us. "I want a written report on my desk tomorrow from all of you, and God help the one who lies if they don't match up. Now get the fuck out of my office."

Munz snarled and stormed out. Elman waited for Munz to be gone before heading for the door. "Get me a another partner," he said as he left.

I waited until Holloway and I were alone. "I'm sorry, Greg. I hold myself responsible."

"How's Iris?"

"She'll be fine."

"I don't like the look on your face, Gabe. I meant what I said."

"My partner got hurt, Greg. I made a big mistake letting Munz do what he did. You should have seen him. He was a kamikaze pilot. All he saw was Greco and he didn't give a fuck who or what got in his way." Gabe's voice had risen.

"Wow, you must be really pissed off. It's not like you to lose your cool two days in a row. That fight would make front page news if it gets out."

"Didn't mean to get anyone in trouble. Tunnel vision, that's what he had, fuckin' tunnel vision."

"What you going to do?"

"I'm not walking away. I need to know what Munz knows."

"Munz won't give that information to you. I don't want

you crossing paths with him. Iris is my niece, but she's also a cop. She knew the risks. You're only a few years away from retirement. He can mess you up, and you know he plays dirty."

"So can I," I said. "And I will if I have to."

JANET POTTS APPROACHED Solly. A black student who loved wearing tight black jeans and a black jersey so moulded to her body that her nipples looked like they would penetrate the fabric. "How ya doin' Solly?"

"When they let you out of jail?"

"This morning, the stupid pricks. The judge was a fucking bitch. She had my sheet. Called me a liar. Got thirty days for prostitution. Asshole."

"Is that the way you talked to the judge? Every second word is fuck or shit or asshole. Why don't you drop the crap and talk English?"

"Fuck you!"

"Not even if I was dying. No credit, Janet. I've told you before."

She edged closer. "I lost my job, Solly."

"Forget it, Janet. I'm not interested."

"My friends tell me I'm good. C'mon Solly, a couple of bags for a good time."

"Forget it. I pay for the bags. I'm not paying for yours."

"I think you're a faggot," Janet spat at him. "No one turns me down unless he's queer."

Solly grabbed her by her neck. "Get lost. No credit. Don't get me mad and don't fuck up my business." He gave her a shove. Janet glared at him and moved away.

Alvin Frost, a white student in Solly's class, came over. "Hey, man, you're making a lot of enemies doing that. Don't you want the money?"

"She don't have any."

"But you know she'll get it. She makes the bread with her ass, not her head."

"If they don't have the money now, let them find another habit." Solly looked at Alvin with suspicion. "I've been to your house, Alvin. Your parents got lots of money. They got money for you for a university education. You were born with it all. If I had what you had, I wouldn't be doing this. This is my shortcut to university. Yeah, I want the money, but I just want enough – not all."

"You're a funny guy, Solly. If I had this, I know what I'd be doing."

"Well, you ain't got this, Alvin. And why would you want it?"

Alvin shrugged and walked away.

"HOW ARE YOU doing?" I asked as I hovered over Iris, covered in a white sheet. "You're looking good for someone who's been shot."

She made a weak smile. "I owe you," she whispered.

"For what?"

"They told me I would be dead if you hadn't showed up as fast as you did."

"I shoulda been there quicker. I couldn't get the knee to jump."

"It wasn't your fault. I got shot before you came up the ladder."

"I shouldn't've let you go up alone. I made a bad mistake."

I could see Iris was getting angry. "Do you know what you're doing? You're making me the scapegoat."

"What are you talking about?"

"You're using what happened to me as the excuse to blame yourself so you can justify quitting."

"I'm a liability."

"You may not have the legs to chase a ball, but you got the brains to still hit one."

"What?"

She raised her head off the pillow. "You do follow baseball, don't you?"

"When did we get off the subject?"

"We didn't. Sometimes when an older baseball player can't do what he used to do, he still has the ability to contribute by playing the game in a different position. I'll be your legs. I need your brains to make me a better player. You ain't quitting."

"Calm down! Shit, look at your heart monitor. We'll talk about this later."

Iris fell back onto the pillow. A grin appeared on her face. "I heard you belted Munz."

"I lost my head."

"Watch out for him. He's an animal."

"I will. Right now I'm watching you. I'm trying to figure what it was that we were part of. The whole scene was surreal. Greco's not stupid. He has to know he was under surveillance. Why chance getting caught with his hand in the cookie jar?"

"Who were his tails?"

"Nesbitt and Petersen. He took them for a ride, then lost them at the Golden Mile Plaza. He was driving through the lot when two cars blocked them. The drivers in both cars were part of Greco's gang. He had led them into a maze and only he got out. Something else must have been going down that night and he had to be there. But what?"

"What's Munz say?"

"A lot of colourful words, none relevant."

"What are you going to do? It's not your case."

"You got shot because I didn't insist on waiting for backup. It's me who owes you. I've decided to do some checking on my own. How did Munz know that Greco was going to be there? Who's his snitch? Whoever told him didn't give him much time to get ready, otherwise why the hurried set-up? I'm looking for answers."

"Without me?"

I smiled. "This can't wait. Besides, you're due for a rest when you get out."

"When I get out, I want to get the sons of bitches who

shot me. Then I'll rest."

I laughed. "Yesterday you had me worried because I was afraid you might die. Today you're giving me a headache. I can hardly wait for tomorrow. Until you get on your feet, I'm on my own. I'll keep you in the loop."

"Watch your back."

The nurse brought in a bouquet of flowers and placed them in an empty vase by the window. She handed Iris a card.

Iris read the words and smiled.

"From Howard?" I asked.

"Yes."

"This serious?"

"Don't know yet."

"He's a good man," I said.

Iris smiled.

"I gotta go. Got work to do."

"Stay away from the bagels," Iris said.

"If you stay away from bullets." I waved and left the room. There were feelings in me that I wasn't accustomed to. Is this what a father feels for his daughter?

"WHATCHA WANNA SEE me about?" Greco asked Synes. He was sitting in his favourite booth in Tony's Bar and Grill, a Heineken and a plate of bruschetta in front of him.

"Uh, about the snitch," Synes mumbled.

Greco stopped eating and stared at Synes. "Yeah? Do you know who?"

"Not exactly. But I got this kid working for me. Solly Solinus…"

"Solinus? Buddy's kid?"

"Yeah, him. I talked him into taking a corner. Part-time, like. The kid's got ambitions to go to university. I heard he needed money, so I made him a deal. My guy who did his school got picked up last month on a break-and-enter, and I needed someone. I didn't want to lose the action to the

Jamaicans. Anyway, the kid said he was interested."

"Cut to the chase. What about it?"

"I might have said something to him."

"You asshole! I figured you for a smart guy. Loose mouths mean trouble."

"Look, I'm sorry. I figured I screwed up. I think the kid was using me."

"His old man got concrete for doing that. How sure are you?"

"Not very, but I know I never said nothin' to anyone else."

Greco picked up a bruschetta and crammed it into his mouth. "You made the problem. You fix it," he said between chews.

IT WAS AFTER two in the morning. I was driving home when I heard my name on the police band. "Garshowitz," I answered.

"Someone's just found a body behind the arena on Steeles, near the mausoleum. Holloway says for you to take it." The dispatcher paused. "You live nearby, he said."

"Am I the only cop in Toronto? I'm beat."

"Holloway said if you complained to remind you that he has a desk job for you." There was laughter in the background.

"Funny," I mumbled.

As I approached the yellow tape, I recognized Detective Munz. His small eyes followed me as I neared.

"Lose something?" I asked.

"On the way home, thought I'd see what's going on."

"I'll tell you what's going on. You. I don't want you here. Get lost." With those words I turned and walked toward Detective Stella Morgan.

"Hi, Gabe. How's Iris?"

"She's doing fine. Everything looks good. What you got?"

"A kid was beaten to death with a blunt instrument."

"A blunt instrument or several?"

"My guess, one."

"I noticed our mutual friend and you had words just now. I've never known anyone to work as hard as he does at being obnoxious with such a limited vocabulary."

"I try not to let him get to me."

"The way I heard it, he got to you when Iris was shot."

"I reacted. I was out of line."

"You telling me you're sorry?"

"No. It felt good."

She snorted.

"Was this a local kid?"

"Yes. I.D. in his wallet had the name of a school near here. His name was Solly Solinus."

AFTER A FEW hours' sleep I was at my desk typing out what I knew so far about the Solinus case. Solly Solinus's father had been a drug pusher. Maybe the kid was too. His mother was notified late last night, and I would see her later in the day. I was musing about what else to put down when my phone rang.

"Gabe, my office, please."

I entered Holloway's office and approached his desk. "Close the door, Gabe."

I gave him a curious look, returned to the door and closed it. I sat in the only chair in the room for visitors and waited for the bad news. It was always bad news when Holloway asked me to close the door.

"I need your help, Gabe."

"For what?"

"Jack Elman, Munz's partner, reported in sick. He was playing racquetball last night, he claims, hit the floor badly, pulled his collarbone. He's out for a while."

"I hope you're not going to ask what I think you are."

"Yes, but I got reasons."

"Find someone else."

"He's got no partner and you've got no partner. It's a logical fit."

"Do you know how many partners Munz has had?"

"Yes. That's the reason I'm asking you. Another won't look suspicious, especially since he asked for you before Iris. Jack told me something last week that's not to leave this office, Gabe. You're the only one I trust to get to the bottom of what Jack suspects."

"What do you mean?"

"Jack says Munz has been acting strange. He's involved in some way. I need you to find out what's going on. As his temporary partner, it's ideal."

"Munz won't go for it."

"He's got no choice. I give the orders."

"Are you saying Munz is dirty?"

"No. Jack suspects that Munz has a stake in Greco – somehow. As his partner, you'll be able to monitor what's happening."

"This is a case for Internal Affairs, not me."

"There's no love lost between Elman and Munz. Elman's a good cop. When his partner quit the force, I tagged him with Munz. He didn't want it, but there was no one else. When he comes back, he's going to ask for a new partner or a transfer. No one knows yet. While he's recovering, you can get close. I know Munz will ride you, but that will only make what I'm asking you to do easier. He'll never suspect you're spying on him."

"Christ, Greg!"

"Munz is a bad cop. Whether he's dirty or not, he's a bad cop. We all know that. I'm hoping you'll find him dirty. I want him out."

"It doesn't sit well with me, Greg. I don't like him, either, but what you're asking me to do sucks."

"Like almost getting Iris killed doesn't?"

I scowled. "That's a low blow."

"She's my niece. I won't let anyone put her life in jeopardy, and she's your partner, Gabe. Find out what really happened. If you won't volunteer, then it's an order."

THE NEXT DAY when I entered the station, Munz was already at his desk. I could feel the hair on the back of my neck rise. The sight of him invoked a response in me that was foreign. I was never one to hate anyone. Even when tracking down a murderer, I didn't hate, I pursued. I took a deep breath and approached him. "This is temporary. Don't get comfortable," I said.

"You're the boss."

I stared at him, trying to see if he was playing with me. I knew this man. He was no one's friend, not even his own. His type manipulate, not cooperate. "Okay, then."

"Whaddaya on?" Munz asked.

"The Solinus Case. Know anything?"

"Never met the kid, but I busted his old man a few times." Munz stood. "Where to first?"

I was puzzled. This wasn't going the way I'd figured.

We went to Munz's car. "I'd like to check out the school, then see Mrs. Solinus," I said. Munz drove like he owned the road, as if he wasn't aware of the speed limit and with complete indifference to road conditions. I gripped the armrest. "In a hurry?" I asked.

Munz said nothing. He continued to drive like he was at the Indy 500, crossing intersections just as the lights turned red, not slowing down for a second. Finally he was forced to stop behind a line of cars waiting for the light to change. He faced me. "There's just you and me here, so let me put it to you nice and simple. Right now, I need you. As long as I know we're headed in the same direction, I'll work with you. Change directions on me and I'm history. I'm interested in anything that has to do with Greco, and I don't care what I do to get him."

"Why this obsession with Greco?"

"That's my business. I won't let anyone fuck up my chances of getting him. Especially you. You do, and it'll be the last thing you'll *ever* do. Understood?"

Now this was the man I knew. He must have tried like hell to be what he wasn't and couldn't last longer than it took to get into a car. I wondered if I should tell the scientific world that I'd found the missing link between the ape and man and he was still alive. We drove the rest of the way in silence.

I KNOCKED ON Mrs. Solinus's door; the house was a narrow semi that had seen better days. I was alone. After talking to the school principal, Munz said he had something to finish from his own caseload and returned me to my car. We agreed to meet at the office later. That was my suggestion. He just grunted, which I figured meant agreement. During the interview, Munz hadn't said a word. Just listened. It didn't take long to figure out why. Today, everyone uses a Pentium. Even when thinking, their brain is in a Pentium mode. Watching him from the corner of my eye, I figured he was struggling with a Commodore 64 when it came to storing or retrieving.

I knocked again. I tried the door handle and the door opened. "Hello," I shouted. "Anyone here?" There was no answer. I entered the dimly lit hall, peering into the rooms as I passed, and made my way to the kitchen. Mrs. Solinus was sitting alone by the table, staring at nothing. "Mrs. Solinus?"

She slowly looked up at me. Her eyes were red from crying, skin blotchy, and her hands gripped and twisted a handkerchief until it looked like a short piece of rope. "Mrs. Solinus, my name is Detective Garshowitz. I'd like to talk to you about your son."

"He's dead," she said woodenly.

"Yes, I know. I'm sorry."

"And so is my husband. Both because of drugs."

"May I sit, Mrs. Solinus?"

She shrugged.

I lowered myself into a chair. "Mrs. Solinus, I need your help."

She made a derisive sound. "I've heard that before. When my husband never came home, the police told me they thought he had been killed. Word was he skimmed from Greco and gambled the money away. I wouldn't doubt it. I was married to him, but we weren't living together. He had himself another woman. A kid. He had her performing his sick brand of sex for the drugs he had."

"Who was she?"

"I dunno. The other cop might know."

"What other cop?"

"The one who investigated when my husband disappeared. Detective Munz. He never found my husband's body, you know." She stood. "Can I get you a cup a tea?" she asked.

"No, thank you."

She went to the sink and filled the kettle with water, but didn't plug it in. She returned to her seat. "I asked him not to be like his father," she said. "I begged him. He said he wouldn't. I wanted him to go to college. We talked about it often. He was going to be someone important and have an education. He promised and I believed him. Why?"

"I don't know, Mrs. Solinus."

"You got kids, detective?"

The conversation wasn't going in the direction I wanted, but I saw the pain on her face and knew I was in a position to maybe help – a little. "A daughter. My wife is dead."

"Parents should never know from their children's death," she said. Tears welled up in her eyes. "How did you lose your wife?" she asked.

"Neglect." The word came out of my mouth before I realized what I had said.

"I'm sorry. She didn't take care of herself?" She used her handkerchief to wipe away more tears.

She hadn't gotten my reference. "It's a long story, Mrs. Solinus."

"There isn't much I can tell you. I never knew he was selling drugs until Detective Munz showed up and told me."

That caught me off guard. "When?"

"Last night. It was late. At the time I said I didn't know anything. He told me Solly's body was at the morgue."

"He take you there to identify him?"

"No. Just told me."

"I'll arrange for someone to take you, to identify him."

"I know it's him," she said.

"How's that?"

"He didn't come back last night. My Solly never even stays out late. He's a good boy. Always sleeps at home. Last night, he didn't."

"Why are you sure now he was into drugs?" I asked.

"Afterwards, I searched his room. I found a locked metal box. I broke it open and it had bags in it and lots of money. I knew what those bags were. My husband had them." She stood. "Let me get them. I don't want them in the house."

I watched her leave the room and a few minutes later return with a metal box, which she handed to me. I opened the box and saw the bags. The money was gone. I closed the box and said nothing.

"Who were his friends?"

"I don't know. He never brought anyone here. Hardly anyone ever called him. He did a lot of studying for school. I know he wanted to go to college."

"Anything else that might be helpful?"

Mrs. Solinus pulled on her handkerchief. "A girl called here the night he died. When Solly came home, I gave him dinner. I told him a girl called. He went to the telephone and a little while later went out. I think she was black – you know, her accent. I took down her name. I think the paper is still by the telephone." She got up again and went into the hall, then returned with a sheet of paper. There were several names and numbers on it. "That one," Mrs. Solinus said. "Janet Potts."

"There's no telephone number."

"She didn't give one."

I stood. "Thank you, Mrs. Solinus. You've been a great help."

"Do you think you'll catch the person who killed my Solly?"

"It won't be for lack of trying." I walked to the door.

"Detective Garshowitz?"

I stopped and faced her.

"Does the guilt go away?"

I looked at her in the half-light and shook my head.

HARRY GRECO APPEARED pleased when he shook Synes's hand. "That was quick," he said. "Been away a few days, and I find you took care of that matter."

Synes looked puzzled. "What matter?"

"The kid. You know, Buddy's kid. I'm told he's dead. You whacked him, didn't you?"

"No. I thought you did."

"Me? Why the fuck would I do that? I told you it was your mess and you clean it up."

Synes shook his head. "Well, it wasn't me."

The look on Greco's face turned ugly. "Well, find out who did it. If it's the Jamaicans making a run at us, I gotta know. Fuck! I just made the biggest purchase ever and I ain't gonna lose it. He glared at Synes. "All because you got a big mouth.

Who you got replacing the kid?"

"Someone from the school. A girl."

"A what! Are you nuts? A girl?"

Synes took a step back. "She's okay, boss. I knew her for a couple of years. She gave me two thousand and I gave her enough bags to cover her payment. She sold them in the afternoon and bought more. That night, she bought more after getting rid of what I gave her."

Suspicion replaced the anger in Greco's face. "Who's this kid? What do you know about her?"

"Janet Potts. The broad Buddy Solinus was shacked up with. She asked for the spot. I told her what I wanted sold and she said she could do it."

"How's she doing?"

"Good. Real good."

"Watch her. And you find out who whacked the kid. Soon."

MUNZ NEVER CAME to work the next day. Three more days passed and still no sign of him. I had a lot of unanswered questions and Munz was in every one of them. What was Munz doing talking to the kid's mother before he was even involved in the case? Cops don't go looking for work. They have enough of a caseload without voluntarily getting involved in another. Did he have something going with the kid? Was Munz so gung-ho to get Greco that he was just looking into other aspects that might get him closer to his quarry? Or was something else going on? One way to find answers was to ask him, and that was what I intended – when I found him.

I didn't tell Holloway that Munz was not in the picture. During the first two days, I conducted my own investigation. The kid's father being a dealer was interesting. On the surface, the kid had looked clean. That is, until I talked to his mother. After seeing the mother, I went to Forensics to find out what they had. Stella Morgan had left me a message that she had enough to get me started. At least I would get an idea of time and method. I knew the kid had been beaten to death. That, too, was a Munz question. The act was a Munz trademark.

I went over to the Centre of Forensic Sciences and entered the room where Stella was hunched over a microscope.

"Hi, sweetie," I said.

"Hi, sweetie, yourself. You haven't got Iris so you pick on me."

"I only torment the ones I love."

She smiled. "I'll take that as a compliment." She reached for a folder and handed it to me. "This what you want?"

I skimmed the contents. "You figure a baseball bat?"

"Wood slivers embedded in his scalp. Lacquer and grain says baseball bat."

I stuck my nose back into the folder. "Ribs broken, nose and cheekbones smashed and blows to his spine. Front and back?"

"I figure the first blow came from behind. He pulled around and then the bat worked him from the front. I figure at least twenty blows. Blows were angled down. That makes the killer taller than the victim; more likely a male. Death was between eight and nine in the evening. No wallet and no watch. I figured a watch because of the lighter skin around his left wrist. There was powder residue in his jacket, so I sent it to the feds. It was heroine. Fair grade."

"One person did this?"

"Yes, that's my guess. No fingerprints, lots of shoe prints. My guess the killer wore wool mittens. I found traces of wool fibres on the clothes, like where maybe the hands had swung around and brushed the body. I found that strange, being summer. I'm trying to trace the wool."

"Are you finished with everything?"

"Just about. I'm still checking the clothes. Should have all the answers by tomorrow. I told Munz that, too, this morning."

I looked up from the folder. "Munz's been here?"

"Bright and early. Thought you knew."

"No, I didn't. What did you tell him?"

"The same."

I moved to the door, holding the folder. "I'll get back to you when you finish the report."

I went to my car and drove to the school. Why was Munz still playing the Lone Ranger? Everywhere I went Munz had been there before me. We were supposed to work together. Was Munz trying to solve the case or hide evidence to prevent something being uncovered? Whatever was going down, I decided I'd better stop playing catch-up and move my own ass to whatever had to be done. If Solly Solinus was dealing drugs, it was at the school. When Munz and I had seen the principal, he told us he was aware that drugs were being sold outside the school grounds during school hours. He'd notified the police. He actually wanted to have the feds bring in a drug-sniffing dog but got flack from some parents who said that anything that happened off school property was not his jurisdiction. They said they didn't want no Big Brother telling them what they could or couldn't do. He went as far as he could, he said. He even got threatening calls. I thought I'd talk to the guidance counsellor now. I called headquarters to find out if Munz had come in. The answer was no. No one had seen him. I stepped on the gas. Maybe if I hurried, I would get there ahead of Munz, but I had a feeling Munz had been and gone.

I was right.

By the time I finished talking to the guidance counsellor it was noon. She said she'd seen Janet Potts that morning when she stood hall watch. The girl lived with her mother, a single parent, who worked as a cleaning woman. Father had returned to Trinidad. No other family. Talked tough. Swear words were as common for her as good words were from a minister. Rumour was she slept around. There were times she appeared spaced out. Drugs were suspected. No one on staff knew who might be peddling them. When told that Solly Solinus was suspected of selling drugs, the guidance counsellor was genuinely surprised. And no, she hadn't talked to Munz, but from my description, thought she had seen him in the hall that morning.

When I left her office, the kids had been out of class for least half an hour. I noticed they congregated on both sides of the street. On the south side was a donut shop in a gas bar where a lot of them seemed to hang out. I watched the activity and realized that the smokers were on the south side, too. There were pockets of activity everywhere I looked. Some wore weird clothes and the haircuts were from outer space. I glanced at the photo of Janet Potts the guidance counsellor had given me and scanned the vicinity. No sign of her.

When I returned to the station I would find out if she had an arrest record. Chances were she did. For now, I hung around the school, hoping to spot her. I didn't. I continued to watch the students from the main door. A number of them stared at me. Maybe they recognized me as a cop. That would be encouraging, considering I'd been feeling as if I was a fugitive from a seniors' home. Several of the groups across the street were breaking up and returning to the school. No one looked like Janet. Next step was to go to her class. She was a no show. At two, I left and decided to see how Iris was doing. Afterwards I would try to track down Munz.

SYNES DROVE OUT of the city. He always found it helpful to resolve problems away from where he lived. The soft purr of the engine, the feeling of power in his hands as he steered the large, expensive automobile along the highway always made him feel in control. The black girl beside him never spoke. She chewed gum. He glanced at her to see how she was responding to his pulling her off the street the way he did and ordering her into the car. He had a problem now, and if he didn't resolve it, and soon, everything he had would be lost, including his life. Greco was not forgiving.

Synes suspected she might be stoned. Another stupid mistake he'd made. Never work with those who take the product – it could compromise them. She'd told him she was clean, but now he doubted it. He got off the highway and drove north. He pulled into a flea market parking lot and stopped the car. "Who's your partner?" he asked.

Janet looked at Synes. "What partner? I ain't got no fuckin' partner."

"Where'd you get the original money?"

"Tricks."

Synes laughed. "Tricks? Look, kid, to make two grand, you'd have to fuck the whole school twice. Who you kidding?" His face twisted in anger. "Who's bankrolling you?" he grabbed her by the neck.

"No one," she choked out. "I made the money. I'm good at what I do. Buddy always said I was the best he ever had."

"Buddy Solinus was a moron. You're a user. You told me you weren't." He pressed himself against her. "I can smell it."

"I've doubled your take since I took over."

"You've doubled the risk, too." He fell back on his seat. "I figure you killed Solly."

"What? You're nuts!"

"If you didn't, you know who did. Everything points to you, kid. It was too smooth what happened. One minute Solly's here, then bang, he's not and you pop up. You're bring-ing heat. Greco don't want heat. We got us enough problems without this."

Janet gave Synes a sly look. "You had a snitch."

Synes gave her a hard stare. "What you know about a snitch?"

"I know who your snitch was. It was Solly. Him and this big cop were partners."

"What're you saying?"

"I'm saying the cop could have killed Solly."

22

W HEN I ENTERED Iris's room she was sitting up reading a newspaper. "Hi, sweetie," I said as I plunked down on the chair beside her bed.

"You're lucky they took my revolver away." She folded the paper and placed it on the table that held a telephone. "I've read the newspaper and I figured most of what is written isn't worth reading. So, what's been happening?"

"You're looking good."

"I feel like shit."

"At least you can feel."

She smiled. "It only hurts when I breathe."

"You're still ahead. Mine hurts when I move."

Iris sank lower on the mattress and pulled the sheet up to her chin. "You're staring, Gabe."

"There's more to you than meets the eye. If I'd known I was gonna see so much of you, I'd have taken a valium."

Iris broke out laughing while clutching her neck. "Oh, that hurts. Enough of your foreplay, what's been going on? Where were you yesterday?"

"Investigating. You okay?"

Iris removed her hand from her neck. "I'm okay. Talk to me."

"It's a puzzle..." For the next thirty minutes I told her what I had learned. When I was finished, I asked, "Any ideas?"

"Could the Solinus kid have been Munz's snitch?"

I thought about that a minute. "Could be. Munz knew the father. Maybe was aware the kid would go into the same business. All right, that's a possibility. Anything else?"

"If the kid was his snitch, why kill him?"

"He didn't," I answered.

"How come?"

"The bat."

"The bat?"

"I need to talk to Stella again to make sure I'm right. I'll tell you why later." I stood. "I gotta go. Uh, the reason I wasn't here yesterday was I was here, but could only stay for a minute. They wouldn't let me in. They told me you were being bathed. I offered to help." I smiled.

"I'll bet."

"Howard been here?"

"Yes. I'm consoling him. He's going through a bad scene."

"Why? What happened?"

"He got a call last night about someone sitting on the third-floor ledge of a hotel. He was the first to arrive. He went to the room and tried to talk the guy off. Apparently the jumper was gay and had had a fight with his lover. After ten, fifteen minutes, Howard was getting nowhere. The jumper got to his feet. Howard tried to reason with him. He said that he was too low to kill himself. There was grass below the room. He'd break an arm or a leg or, worse his spine, and survive. The guy looked down, realized Howard was right and climbed up to the sixth floor using the blocks that jut out, then jumped from there before Howard could get to him. The guy died and Howard holds himself responsible."

I was nodding my head when she finished her story. "Tell Howard it's not his fault. The unexpected always happens. He did his job and it wasn't meant to be. People are unpredictable. Sometimes the right way is the wrong way. He'll have to learn to trust his instincts. It's part of the learning experience." I looked down at her and saw she had a curious look on her face. "I gotta go." I bent down to give her a kiss.

"You gonna kiss me?"

"Yes."

"No tongue."

She was a character. I barked out a laugh. "Another time," I said and left.

"THAT'S IT SO far," I said to Holloway. "Munz has been one step ahead of me all the way. He's involved, but I don't know how."

"You're thinking he killed the kid?"

I got up from the chair and headed for the door. "I'm thinking he's involved. Beyond that I don't know – yet."

"What are you going to do now?"

I turned to look at the superintendent. "I don't like Munz – you know that. This department would be better off without him – you know that, too. Is he capable of killing the kid? I hate to say yes, but yes. I went to see Iris before I came here and we talked about what's been happening. She had some good thoughts. One was that Solly Solinus was Munz's snitch.

If that's the case, who would want to kill him?"

"Greco," Holloway replied.

"How about Janet Potts?"

"Who?"

"She called Solly the night he died. Potts has a rap sheet that says she'll go to any lengths to get what she wants. Born in Trinidad. Came to Canada with father and mother several years ago. Old man went back, wife refused to go. She's a cleaning woman. Guidance counsellor at the school says the old man sexually abused his daughter and fled home because the mother was going to the cops if he didn't. The girl's on drugs, been to rehab a couple of times. Picked up servicing guys for drug money. Foul-mouthed, unrepentant and indifferent to anything but what she wants. Another good suspect. That makes three. Munz, Greco and Potts. Are there more? Until I know conclusively, I'm not judging what I see until I have proof. Personally, I'm hoping it's Munz." I turned and left the office.

"So am I," I heard Holloway say.

I HAD POTTS'S address and drove directly to her place. I'd learned years ago, don't push evidence in the direction you want. The way I felt about Munz made me consider the asshole guilty and look at his actions as those of someone trying to cover up evidence. But Munz apparently hadn't done anything to cover up, just gone solo in the investigation. He never intimidated Solly Solinus's mother, didn't ask if there were drugs or money in the house – which would have been a logical question if he was after that – made inquiries at the school without doing anything that was suspiciously self-concealing. Whatever Munz's motives, they obviously put him smack in the middle of the investigation. What I hadn't determined, was he involved as a criminal or as a cop? Did Munz learn about Janet Potts and was that why he was at the school? And why was he avoiding me?

I got out of the car and made my way through the town-house court. I knocked on number forty-two. The face of a middle-aged black woman peered out when the door opened only as far as a chain would allow.

"What you want?" she demanded.

I showed her my badge. "I'm Detective Garshowitz. Are you Mrs. Hilda Potts?"

"What you want?" she demanded again. "Why you people coming around here today?"

I moved closer. "Was there another detective here?" I asked.

"About thirty minutes ago. Scared my daughter so much she ran out the back door. Like I told the other cop, I dunno nothin'. I ain't responsible for anything she's done. I've tried, but she don't listen. She's bad, that's all I know."

The door slammed shut in my face. "Damn you, Munz!" I mouthed. "What the fuck are you doing?"

GRECO LISTENED TO Synes explain what he had been told by Janet Potts. When he was finished, Greco stood and quietly walked around the room. Synes followed him with his eyes, not sure if Greco was thinking or about to explode.

"Now everything makes sense," Greco said at last. "We got us a dirty cop. Somehow he found out the Solinus kid was dealing and cut himself in for a piece of the action. That was how we almost got busted. Almost. The kid told him I was coming out and so the cop faked the bust to let me know there was another player around. According to the newspaper, there were only four cops involved. Four cops trying to cover the whole building. That was too stupid to be real. Okay, so he's a player, but why kill his source?" Greco turned to Synes. "Can you answer that? Why kill the source?"

"Maybe he didn't do it."

"Does that mean there's another player we don't know about?"

Synes studied Greco as he stood in front of him pondering the question. "Do you think the girl is involved?"

Greco smiled. "I think everyone's involved. Even you."

THE NEXT DAY, I called Stella to see if Forensics had anything new to add. Casts of several footprints had been made in the vicinity of the body. The ground where the Solinus kid had been found was a no-man's land between the crematorium and the hydro towers. Whether the footprints taken were significant wasn't known, but none appeared small enough to have been made by a female. There was no trace of the baseball bat. So far Forensics had revealed two things that told me the killer was not Munz.

I went to Munz's desk to see what I could find. There was nothing there that was relevant. Three days with Munz always one step ahead of me was getting on my nerves. When I telephoned his house, all I got was his answering machine. Last night before going home, I had gone to Munz's modest two-storey townhouse, where he lived alone, and sat in my car out front. The place had remained dark. The newspapers for the past two days were still on the small porch. The front yard was no bigger than a cemetery plot; a dog wouldn't have room to turn around to take a shit. If Munz was pocketing drug money, it hadn't been used on his house. Or his car. I knew Munz drove an old Sunbird, one that no self-respecting car thief would look at even on a dry day.

I gave up after an hour. Munz could be sleeping in a motel if he wanted to stay loose. Unless I caught up with him, I wouldn't have all the answers I was looking for. Somehow I had to get ahead of Munz if I wanted to catch him – but how?

And as I stood at Munz's desk, it came to me. If the right way isn't working, then try the wrong way.

THE RESTAURANT DIDN'T open until mid-afternoon. It was an evening-out type Greek restaurant that catered to the after-theatre crowd. I knocked on the door after trying it and found it locked. I knocked again – harder. The curtain was pulled back and a guy with a boxer's smashed nose and cauliflower ear peered at me. I showed my badge and the face disappeared. I waited a few more minutes and knocked again. Finally the door opened, and I stepped over the threshold into the small alcove where patrons confirmed their reservation.

Cauliflower blocked my way. "We is closed," he said.

"We is? Then what are you doing here?"

Cauliflower's lips curled. "You got a smart mouth."

"I like your ears."

"The boss wants to know what you want."

"To see him."

Cauliflower's breathing was audible, no doubt the result of the broken nose. "He don't want to see you," he said.

"Tell him it's about Munz," I answered.

Cauliflower glared down at me before sticking a finger in my chest. "Stay here," he ordered, then turned and went into the dining room.

I watched the bodyguard deliver the message. I could see Greco sitting by himself in a corner, his meal spread on the table. Another bodyguard stood to one side, and what I took to be the owner stood a few feet away. Greco looked up and saw me approaching. Cauliflower intercepted. "I told you to stay put," he snarled.

"I did," I answered. "But you didn't say for how long." I looked past him into Greco's smirking face.

"It's okay, Boris. Let him come."

Boris grunted his disapproval and lumbered aside.

"Who are you?" Greco asked.

"Detective Gabriel Garshowitz."

"Who's Munz?" Greco asked as he spooned the mashed potatoes and gravy into his mouth.

"Detective Simon Munz," I said.

"Who's he?"

"A cop who'd like to stick a knife in your back, unless I miss my guess."

"Never met him."

"He knows you."

"A lot of people know me. You know me and I don't know you." He cut his steak with his knife and shoved it into his mouth, closed his eyes and savored the taste. He looked at the owner with approval. "Excellent, Papi. Exceptional." The owner beamed his pleasure and scurried away. Greco turned back to me. "What can I do for you?" The knife and fork continued to dissect the meat, then his fork speared small pieces and deposited them in succession into his mouth until it was filled.

I watched him as he swallowed. He looked orgasmic. "You like food, I see."

"I like good-tasting food. What is it you like?"

"Bagel, lox and cream cheese. A good coffee afterwards."

Greco laughed. "At Kiva's, no doubt."

I smiled.

"I had me a Jew for a partner years ago," Greco said as he continued to eat. "You remind me of him. He had *chutzpah*. You got *chutzpah* coming here. I like that." He laughed again as he scooped up some vegetables. "Sit down, Garshowitz, sit down. Want something to eat?"

I sat opposite him. "Coffee will be fine."

Greco waved to Boris to come over. "Boris, get Detective Garshowitz a cup of coffee."

Boris glared at me, but he turned and stomped toward the kitchen.

"What happened to your Jewish partner?" I asked.

"Oh. We had a disagreement on a deal. I bought him out."

"What's he doing now?"

Greco grinned. "Let's see, that was seven years ago. I'd say he was pushing flowers up by now." He laughed again. "So tell me, Garshowitz, what do you want?"

"Solly Solinus's killer."

"Why me?"

"Why not?"

Greco put his fork and knife down on the table. He leaned back on his chair, a smile on his lips and a twinkle in his eyes. "You and Izzy would have gotten along great. Ask a question, get a question for an answer." He pulled himself forward and stared hard into my face. "That wasn't my doing."

"The kid worked for you."

"A lot of kids work for me. I'm an investor."

"We both know what you are. That doesn't interest me. If you didn't, who did?"

"How about the cop, Munz?" Greco answered.

"Why?"

"Why not?" Greco burst out laughing. He composed himself before he added, "Why should I help you? And don't say why not."

"I don't think you did it, and I don't think Munz did it."

"Sounds like cop loyalty. Solly Solinus was Munz's snitch."

"Munz is an ape. Him and Boris would make identical bookends. It took a dozen whacks to kill Solinus with a baseball bat. How many would Boris need to do the job?"

Greco sat straight, a frown wrinkling his forehead. "Interesting," he whispered. "Very interesting."

"Also, why would Boris use a baseball bat? With hands like his, a hard blow to the head would kill someone as thin as Solly Solinus. Munz is a cop with a reputation for using his hands. Why would he carry a baseball bat?" I stared back at Greco. "I'm told you're smart. But someone will get you sooner or later – it doesn't have to be me. Right now, I think you know something I don't that will help me make this go away. Tell me what you know and get rid of the heat. At least for now."

Greco pushed his plate away, pulled out a cigar and clipped the end. "Garshowitz, you got more balls than Izzy ever had." He started to laugh. Really laugh.

I watched him, thinking the guy was nuts. As long as I could see his hands, I didn't have to worry about him. Boris was taking a long time with the coffee. Was he watching and waiting for a signal? I smiled at Greco as if I was enjoying whatever he was laughing about, but for the life of me, I couldn't figure out what was so funny.

Greco pulled out his handkerchief and wiped his eyes. "Do you know what gets me about this?" he asked. "Meyer Lansky. You know who Meyer Lansky was?"

I nodded.

"He was someone to admire. When the Second World War broke out, the U.S. feds came and enlisted his support to keep the New York waterfront free of Nazis. The biggest crook in the States became their policeman while the war was on. A Jewish crook and a government known for corruption went to bed together for the greater good of all. And here you are, a Jew, trying to make a deal with an alleged gangster for the good of the community – too funny to be believed. Garshowitz, how would you like to work for me?"

"No thanks. I'm about to retire and I'm not into pushing up flowers."

Greco burst out in laughter again. When he stopped, he said, "This is hypothetical. If I was who you say, how would I respond? Better still, what might I know? Solinus is gone but business is still there. Someone has taken over. Maybe, and I say again maybe whoever took over has a secret partner."

"Who?"

"Maybe a cop? Think about that. Maybe someone from the school? A young girl who has unexpected money? There's a couple of good possibilities. My guess would be the cop. There is another possibility – the Jamaicans that used to work this area. Maybe them."

Boris showed up with a mug of coffee and placed it in front of me, spilling some onto the tablecloth. I took a sip and found it lukewarm. I stood. "I'll consider your hypothetical possibilities. My advice to you is to stay clear of the investigation. Too many feet, so to speak, might tread on each other. And thanks for the time."

Greco nodded.

I smiled at Boris, placed my hand in my trouser pocket, removed a loonie and flipped it into the cup of coffee. "Your tip. Good service." We glared at each other for a few seconds before I strode out of the restaurant.

MUNZ SAT OUTSIDE the school in the morning waiting for Janet Potts to arrive. That is, if she did. The school had a number of entrances, so he positioned himself where he could see at least three. He was unshaved and in need of a shower. He knew his breath reeked. Several empty cups of coffee lay scattered throughout the car, along with chocolate bar wrappings and a pizza box. Bleary-eyed, tired and in an ugly disposition from sleeping in his car, he flicked his gaze from door to door looking for a black girl fitting Janet's description. He was in trouble and he knew it. What was supposed to be a perfect catapult to detective sergeant became more like the spectre of a potential jail sentence if he couldn't prove his intent. His anger was not directed at himself, but at everyone and everything that fouled up his plan to bring in Harry Greco and shut down his drug ring. It could have all been his. When he grilled a kid on a break-and-enter charge, the kid said he was buying drugs from someone and for a lighter sentence he would cough up the name. Munz told the kid he had a deal, and the kid fingered Synes. Synes was Greco's number-one man. When Munz got the name, he told the kid to fuck himself.

There was no lawyer present when he offered the deal. Stupid kid thought he could screw around with him. He would even make a better superintendent than Holloway. Holloway was a soft prick. Good for only pissing. What was needed was someone strong and direct. Synes was easy to follow. That led him to Solly Solinus, a schmuck of a kid who thought he could go to college by selling drugs. Munz reached for the coffee he'd bought on his way here and realized the cup was empty. He rummaged on the floor looking for the bottle of water he knew was somewhere, taking his eyes off the street for a minute as he groped under the seat. That was when the door opened and Gabe Garshowitz threw himself into the seat beside him.

JANET POTTS APPROACHED the school with trepidation. She wore black jeans and her usual tight black jersey. Her cell phone was stuffed into her back pocket. It had rung dozens of times and she knew who was calling. For two whole days she hadn't been doing what she was supposed to be doing, and her partner must be furious. Not only hadn't she been at school, she'd been using. She was strung out. What was supposed to be a lark had turned into shit. She had no part in killing Solly. She thought when she was offered the deal that her partner was just going to injure him so he couldn't work the school. When Solly didn't report for school because he was in the hospital, she was to approach Synes and make the offer. She'd known Synes when Buddy Solinus was shacked up with her.

Solly's father was a pig. He liked young girls and she liked what he had – drugs. The old fart was one of the worst lays she'd ever had, but she made him think he was great. A real tiger. For six months she gave and she got. Then he disappeared. In the meantime she had met Synes several times and knew he was Buddy's connection. That was why her partner needed her. She was someone that Synes knew and possibly could trust. If her partner tried to go around her, odds were he would be turned down. She was offered a piece of the action for her part. Now she wanted out. That was why she was returning to school – she had a stash of drugs in the locker opposite hers. She needed it to get cash because she was catching a plane to Trinidad. Fuck her partner. He had killed Solly when the plan had been only to put him in the hospital. She owed him nothing.

She stood behind a car and gazed across the street at the school. She was looking for the big ugly cop, the one that had come to her place. She couldn't see anyone that was built like him and breathed a sigh of relief. She let her gaze slowly pan her side of the street, but there were no other cars parked and no one looked like the cop. She didn't know what the cops knew, but it didn't matter. Screw them. Screw everyone. There was enough in the locker to buy her a ticket and keep her away for weeks. She stepped out from behind the car and started toward the side entrance nearest her locker, but froze when she saw Julie Lipton by the door. Fuck! She stepped back quickly. She retraced her steps keeping to the north side where a few of the kids still lingered. School was already in session. She headed for the far entrance door, saw Alvin Frost, the last person she wanted to see, leaning against a lamppost on the south side, and bolted through the centre door instead and directly for the locker. She froze in horror when she realized the lock had been sawed. She reached to the upper shelf for the cosmetic bag with the stuff inside. Nothing. She pushed deeper into the shelf. Still nothing.

"Fuckin' cock-sucker!" she screamed.

"Looking for this?" I asked as I emerged from a classroom door.

One glance was enough for Janet. She turned and ran the other way – right into the arms of Munz. "Let go, you fuckin' prick!" she shrieked. Take your hands off me." She struggled, but to no avail. Munz had her arms locked behind her and was gripping the back of her neck. "Let go, asshole," she shrieked. "You're hurting me."

Munz turned her around and pushed her to me.

"You must be the elusive Janet Potts," I said. "It's nice to finally meet you."

"He's hurting me! He's breakin' my arm."

"Ease off her," I told Munz. "Where's she gonna go?"

Munz shoved her against the locker. "Who's your partner?" he asked, pushing his face into hers.

Janet screwed her face into a mask of disgust. "Yuk! Don't you ever brush your teeth?"

Munz put a chokehold on her neck with one hand, making her gag for breath.

"Smartmouth me and you'll have my handprint on your neck for life," Munz said.

"Back off," I told Munz. He released his hold. "Who's your partner?" I tried.

"Jesus Christ."

I shook my head. "Wrong answer. Listen, kid, this isn't your usual good cop, bad cop scenario. He –" I pointed to Munz "– really is a bad cop. I'm a pussycat compared to him. If I don't get the answer, he will. I'll give you two seconds to think that over." I waited a couple of beats. "Okay, who's your partner?"

Janet eyed Munz warily. "What's in it for me?" she asked. "You got nothing on me."

"I got this bag of goodies." I raised the bag for her to see.

"It ain't mine, and that ain't my locker."

"Your fingerprints are all over it."

"You put it there."

"It was the principal who had the janitor cut the lock. It was the principal who found the bag. If you notice, other lockers have broken locks. We've been busy. The principal supplied me with a list of all the registered lockers and then he opened all the ones that had locks that should have been empty. It was only a matter of elimination. Odds are your prints are not only all over the bag but inside the locker as well. Who's your partner?"

Munz took a step forward.

Janet cringed. "Keep that asshole away," she said.

"Who's your partner?" I asked again.

"I want immunity."

I smiled. "You watch too much *Law and Order.* You got

two choices. Go to jail as an accomplice to murder, or for possession for the purpose of trafficking. Take your pick."

Janet sagged visibly. "His name's Alvin."

"Alvin what?" Munz said, his voice brimming with fury. He lunged at her again to get a hold of her neck, but Janet threw herself against me and knocked me off balance. I reached out to grab her for support and instead grabbed her back pocket as she was twisting to get away from me. Her cell phone tumbled to the floor and so did I, crashing into Munz on my way down. My knees can hold me up, but don't have the strength to support me if I'm on an angle. We both hit the floor at the same time. Janet Potts was gone before I could get back on my feet. Munz was up in a second and charged after her, while I retrieved the cell phone. Munz returned, his face red, hands balled into fists. "I knew trusting you was a bad idea, Garshowitz. She's gone and so is the proof that I wasn't involved. Damn you!"

"Damn yourself for being a lone wolf. You got yourself into this mess. I know you didn't do it. And you just proved it – you're too stupid. All you think about using are your fists. You created the problem, you aggravated this situation, and it was you who gave her the opportunity to run. Not me, you."

"Fuck you!" Munz spat.

I raised the cell phone to show Munz. "Here's your proof. We'll get her later. Now let's get Alvin."

Munz stared at the phone, a puzzled look on his face. "Alvin who? You know the guy?"

"Alvin Frost. While you chased the girl, I checked on the calls. Alvin's been calling her for two days. Let's ask the principal what he knows about Alvin Frost, then find the guy and arrest him. Or do you want to go find the girl?"

I made my way down the corridor alone, but I could hear Munz muttering behind me. "Asshole," I said under my breath.

IT TOOK THE rest of the night for me to wrap everything into a neat package and peck the story into my computer. I was tired. Dead tired. When I thought about it, I realized I wasn't hungry even. That was a novelty. It was nine in the morning and I needed to go home. As I pushed myself away from my desk, I heard a commotion in the corridor. The sounds of voices grew louder, and I stood to see what was happening. Iris entered, followed by a dozen cops, all talking at the same time. I grinned as she approached.

"Move," she said to me. "I need to sit before I fall." She peered up at everyone. "I'm fine. I'm not coming back for two weeks. I just came in to say hello."

The hubbub continued until everyone got in their two cents and then scattered to their own areas, leaving Iris with me. "You have to sit down," she said to me. "My neck hurts looking up. If you don't sit, I gotta stand. Make a move."

"Welcome back," I said. "I knew there was something missing in my life. It's that tongue of yours." I got a chair from another desk and sat opposite her. "How are you? Really," I asked, eyeing the bandage on her neck.

"I'll be all right. Really. I need some rest. After that I'll be okay. The doctor says I'll have a scar. Don't you have a scar?"

"Yeah. It's in an area that requires us being more intimate if I show it to you."

"I'll pass."

I chuckled and she went on.

"My uncle came to take me home from the hospital a little while ago. He said it was standard procedure." Iris grinned. "He has difficulty separating his job from his relationship with me. Anyway, I was worried about you since I haven't heard from you in two days. I asked him to bring me here first. He told me you wrapped up the case. Fill me in."

"It's a long story."

"Make it short."

"Okay." When I told her about going to Greco's restaurant, her mouth fell open. "After I left Greco," I continued, "I figured Munz wanted to get his hands on the girl, so I staked out the school. I saw him in his car and got in. Munz got verbally abusive – nothing new there. I told him I didn't think he'd done anything wrong and believed I could prove it."

"Could you?"

"No. But I didn't want to spend my time tripping over him. I needed him to work with me. He calmed down. I learned he found the Solinus kid and convinced him to be his snitch or he'd put him in jail. A couple of times I think Munz acted as his enforcer when some of the kids might have blown Solly's cover. I can't prove that, but it's the only explanation considering. Some of the kids I'm told got beat up by a big guy. The only big guys I know in this case are Munz and Boris. For sure it wasn't Boris. And Solinus was a beanpole. Munz learned about the buy and tried to get Greco. If I'd told him he'd blown it himself by not keeping everyone tuned in, he woulda clammed up on me. So I kept quiet as he talked. I told him to park his car in the lot and we would stake out her locker. If she came to the school, that was where I figured she'd go. When we got inside, I decided to ask the principal to open her locker. I couldn't because I didn't have a warrant, but he could. He cooperated, while Munz kept an eye out for her. There was nothing in her locker and I asked could she have another he didn't know about. The principal had a list of who had what locker and realized some of the so-called empty ones had locks. He got the janitor and a lock cutter. That's when we found a bag in what was supposed to be an empty locker. The principal removed the bag and opened it. Inside was dope. No cash.

We staked out the corridor until she showed. She coughed up the name Alvin. Munz got impatient and made a move for her. She knocked me into him. In the scuffle her cell phone fell out of her back pocket. She fled with Munz behind her. I retrieved the telephone and checked on her calls. Discovered an Alvin Frost had been trying to reach her."

"Who is Alvin Frost?"

"The partner. A white kid who was selling drugs for some Jamaicans that wanted to encroach on Greco's turf. Solly didn't know he was the competition."

"I gather this Alvin confessed."

"The feds told him if he cooperated, they would let him plead to a lesser charge and get a lighter sentence. Gave us the names of the Jamaicans and their locations. Alvin claims Janet gave him the idea. I don't think so. She's too primitive to have thought this out. He said that when she couldn't buy drugs on credit from Solly, she went to him with her idea. Get rid of Solly and put her in as his front. She didn't know about the Jamaicans. If the plan worked, he had the whole area. He'd work both ends and make more money being his own competition. Alvin was a smart kid but his plan was dumb. Everything went wrong. He struck Solly from behind intending to knock him out, then was supposed to break his legs. But Solly turned around and recognized him, so Alvin killed him, and Janet was unreliable."

"How do you know it wasn't premeditated?"

"The mittens bothered me. Why wear mittens in the summer? The answer had to be to cushion the impact of the blow. He's not a strong kid. Tall, but had weak wrists. He actually thought the mittens would soften the impact. He never intended to kill Solly, just put him out of circulation."

"What made Solly come out and meet Alvin?"

"Janet Potts. She said she knew where his father was buried. She was going to show him that night. Apparently she claimed it was on the Hydro land. Alvin was waiting for him."

"Let me get this straight. She calls him, talks to Solly's mother, then talks to Solly to tell him to meet her. She's part of the plan to beat Solly and put him out of commission, but she's not going to be there. After Solly gets beaten, he knows she led him into a trap. He could tell Synes and the whole deal goes kaput."

"She'll claim to have been scared off by this guy she saw in the dark."

"Why doesn't she warn him?"

"She tries and goes to his house, but doesn't go in because Solly told her never come to his house."

Iris had a look of skepticism on her face. "This is a plan?"

"Two stupid kids trying to be smart."

"And Munz?"

"I guess that's in Holloway's hands. When you come back in two weeks, I'll have all the answers. There's still Janet Potts and Harry Greco to attend to."

Iris stood slowly. "I think you should go home as well. You look like hell."

"Your place or mine?"

"Gabe, I've got your number. You make like you're a hard case, but the only thing hard about you is your arteries."

I took her arm. "You have a way with words, Iris. C'mon, I'll take you home."

MORE THAN TWO weeks passed before Iris returned to work. She looked good. She would have a scar on her neck, and that was good. It would remind her to be more than careful. She convinced me to stick it out. We sat in a coffee shop as I filled her in. "Munz is on thirty days' suspension without pay and a warning. He'll never get any kind of promotion. When he comes back, I figure he'll come after me again as being responsible, because I got the credit for the bust."

"I didn't hear anything about Greco. I gather he's still doing business."

"Yes. Gregory Synes's body was found in a ditch on Highway 407. His neck was broken. Looks like Boris's work."

"That leaves Janet Potts."

I grinned. "Oh, she's in jail in Trinidad."

"No shit!"

"That's thirty days."

"What is?"

"Swearing or obscene language offensive to the public is a criminal offence and subject to jail in Trinidad."

"Fuck no!"

"That's six months. That kid can't say anything without at least one four-letter word in it. On a long shot I sent a notice to the police in Port of Spain in Trinidad and they found her. Inspector Carlos Kirk was very receptive to my plight. To extradite her would be costly and a long-drawn-out affair. I figured if convicted, she'd get five or six years for dealing in drugs, with good behaviour, three and a half. Inspector Kirk said he could offer a better solution. A complaint was made against her for swearing in public, and before the magistrate was through listening to her foul mouth, he gave her four years." I sat back, grinning. "So, I got you for thirty days and for six months. Care to make it a year?"

The Miriam Garshowitz Case

23

The night was silent. The city had gone to sleep and the streets were deserted. A woman stood by the entrance to the Sheraton Hotel and inhaled the mild summer air. An empty streetcar rumbled by and she watched it until it reached the intersection. The silence returned and she glanced at her watch. It was twelve-ten. After more than twenty hours in flight, she was too tired to sleep. Ten hours on Qantas Airways from Sydney to Honolulu and ten more on Air Canada to Toronto had screwed up her body clock. She'd crossed so many time zones her body didn't know whether to rest or run. She had stepped outside after leaving her luggage in her room, wanting to inhale real air.

Tomorrow was going to be a difficult day and she wasn't eager to start it. She was returning home to see her father, a father she blamed for her mother's death. She had been seeing a psychiatrist and it all came down to closure. She needed to face him for the answers she didn't have; her reluctance to face him was the reason she had left. A police car slowly drove by and the cop smiled at her. They had called Toronto a friendly city when she was last here, and it appeared the cops were just as friendly.

She decided to walk around the hotel and re-enter from York Street, giving her at least fifteen minutes of fresh air, maybe enough for her body to want to sleep. She tucked her purse under her arm and proceeded walking briskly, turned down Bay Street with its wide boulevards and bright lights for one block, then turned onto Richmond, which was narrower and darker. The illumination from the streetlights did not extend much beyond their bases. The street appeared empty. She hastened her steps. An unexpected sound caused her heart to quicken and she stopped, realizing it had come from just ahead of her. She took a hesitant step back, in time to sense a blur of motion in the periphery of her vision. She felt a terrible pain when her head was struck, dropped her purse, then nothing, and her unconscious body collapsed to the sidewalk.

The red van was parked on the shoulder of the Don Valley Parkway; the driver slouched back in his seat, a cigarette in his mouth, when the police patrol car pulled up behind him. The cop got out and walked to the driver's side. "Everything all right?" he asked the driver.

"Yes, sir. Tired. Thought I would take a short nap."

"It's a bad place to park," the cop said.

"All right, then. I'll be moving on," the man said.

The cop shone his flashlight on the driver for a moment, then directed the beam around the interior of the van before answering. "Yes, sure. Drive safely," he said.

"I will." The engine roared to life and the van drove off.

The cop made a note of the license plate and the time. It was twelve thirty-one.

White steam hissed from under the car hood. The vehicle sputtered to a stop and the driver climbed out. He stood on the grass and cursed his predicament. He was going to be late for his appointment in Markham. He flipped open the hood and watched the steam billow into the sky, then edged to the front door of his car to use his telephone. Traffic on the Don Valley Parkway was at its peak and the long continuous lines of vehicles passed him without interruption. Just as he was about to climb into his car, a fox came out from the underbrush, dragging something with its mouth. The driver stared at the fox in horror, then bent down quickly, picked up several stones and hurled them one after the other at the fox, striking him a couple of times. The fox released the object and raced away. The driver ran to the object and stared down at it – it was the head of a young woman. He ran back to his car and called the police on his cell phone.

I WAS AT my desk at headquarters reading a newspaper when Iris approached. The last few days, our relationship had suffered a downturn. I had a personal problem, and it wasn't my knees, and I guess she did, too. I've seen this situation before between partners and always wondered why they don't talk to each other. Now I was confronted with something that was important and couldn't find the words to share, and it would appear so did Iris.

"We've got another case, Gabe," she said.

"What's up?"

"A woman's body found just off the DVP."

"How'd she die?" I asked as I heaved myself out of the chair.

"Decapitated."

"Geez! That's ugly."

Iris headed for the door. "Who's driving?" she asked.

"You."

"I don't know why I bothered to ask," she mumbled.

I laughed as I tried to keep up with her. "Hey, slow down, will you? You're twenty-eight years younger than I am."

"Lose some weight," she hollered back.

I wish it were that simple. The engine was running by the time I reached the car, and before I had the door shut, we were speeding away. "What's the hurry?" I said. "The woman's already dead."

Iris gave me a hard look. "You got a problem that I should know about?"

"I've had things on my mind."

"What things?"

"Things."

"So *don't* tell me." The car picked up speed.

"Slow down, will you?" I complained. "I want to get there in one piece." We kept the silence for a few more blocks, before I asked, "You got a problem I should know about?"

"I'm working on it," she answered.

"So am I."

Iris ignored me as she wound her way through traffic making for the Danforth ramp of the Don Valley Parkway, then proceeded north until we saw the flashing lights at the crime scene. We got out of the car and approached the yellow police tape. "What do you have?" I asked a constable.

"Forensics is flushing out the area, picking up garbage in case there's a connection, and the coroner's working the body. The woman was beheaded. No signs of rape, no struggle, no torn clothes. Flat on her stomach, hands tied behind her back."

"Any identification on the body?" I asked.

"No. No handbag or wallet. Appears to have been about five-feet two, late twenties, early thirties, straight black hair, about shoulder-length. Nice-looking. The labels on her clothes were from Australia. Good chance the woman was a tourist."

The words hit me like a low blow and I staggered back. A bad coincidence, I thought. It has to be a bad coincidence.

"Gabe, you all right?" Iris asked. "You got no colour in your face."

I didn't answer her, just asked, "Has Forensics taken any Poloroid shots of the head?" My voice sounded like it was being rubbed with sandpaper. My throat was dry. I could feel pressure attacking my head as if a vice was being applied. "Yes, no, what?"

The constable stared at me curiously. "You look kind of pasty. You sick?"

"Have they?" I demanded. I could feel my heart pounding.

"I'll check. Be right back."

I watched him approach Detective Stella Morgan and say something. She looked over at me and smiled. She carried a knapsack over one shoulder and held a camcorder. My focus was on the knapsack.

"Hi, Gabe, Iris," she said, when she came over.

"Do you have any Poloroid shots?" I asked.

"Yes, sure." She glanced at Iris, who shrugged. "You don't look good, Gabe. You sick?"

"Let me see the Polaroids."

She removed a large brown envelope from her bag and handed it to me.

My hands shook as I removed the photographs and stared at them. I couldn't believe my eyes. I slowly replaced the shots in the envelope and handed them back to Stella, then turned and headed back to the car.

"Gabe, what's the matter?" Iris asked as she ran after me.

I shook my head and walked faster.

"Gabe!" she demanded again when we reached our car, "what's wrong?"

My tears flowed unashamedly down my cheeks. "That's my kid," I said. "That's my daughter, Miriam."

"YOU'RE TAKING ME off the case? Why?" I glared angrily at Superintendent Holloway. "You can't do that, Greg."

"I can, Gabe. It's the rules. You're too close to the victim to be objective."

"Objective! That's crap, Greg, and you know it."

"Think a moment. She left Toronto after your wife's death five years ago and has never kept in touch. You know she held you responsible."

"It *was* my fault," I said in a more subdued voice. "I should have known Edith was hurting, but I was too busy playing cop to pay attention."

"See, you're ridden with guilt, Gabe, so how can you be objective? We'll keep you advised. I'm taking you off the case and putting you on leave. You've got time coming to you and I'm ordering you to get lost for a couple of weeks. Go home, Gabe. I'm teaming Iris with Simon Munz. They'll handle the case."

"Simon Munz! He's a Neanderthal. On his best day he's comatose. Come on – let me keep the case."

"No, I'm sorry. You're out and he's in."

"Munz is a bully. You know that? He pushes his weight, not his brains, if he had any."

There was a knock on the door and Munz entered. He had a smirk on his face. "Sorry about your daughter," he said, but his eyes said otherwise.

"Fuck you!" I stormed out of the office.

I DON'T KNOW anyone who's not carrying baggage around in their mind. If the baggage gets too heavy, they drink or withdraw or something like that. Smart ones get help. They see a shrink, wanting to come to grips with whatever they can't live with or accept. It becomes very complicated. Those who don't get help either live with it as I did, block it out, or if the pain gets too bad, remove themselves from it. Permanently. With a gun if they have one, or maybe they jump off a high bridge.

My load was guilt and I bore it for five years because I was unconsciously punishing myself for what had happened. I didn't pour the pills into my wife's mouth, but I purchased the bottle. Now my kid was dead and somehow I knew I was responsible. Sometimes the problem becomes a chain reaction. One begets something else. The baggage gets heavier. Miriam's death cut into me like a dull razor. The pain was everywhere. There was no one I could cry to and there'd never be anyone. Inside, though, I cried. Outside I wanted the killer. I wanted him badly. And God help him when I found him.

I waited outside Iris Forester's apartment the next day for her to come out. I was leaning against my car. She saw me and came over.

"How are you doing, Gabe?"

"You know."

She nodded.

"I want to know everything that's going down, Iris – everything! I won't keep away."

"I didn't figure you would. What are you going to do in the meantime?"

"Investigate. What's Munz planning on doing?"

"He's got a call out for any patrol cop that might have seen or heard something suspicious last night while patrolling the DVP."

"Good. What about evidence? Anything at the scene that's worth following up?"

"Forensics beat the grounds looking for something out of place, but couldn't find anything." She paused and looked away.

"What else, Iris? I want to know everything."

"The splatter of blood indicates her neck was severed while she was still alive – the heart was still beating. The coroner figures it was an axe with a large handle. The severance was clean, all in one motion; they figure it was a man's weight."

"Footprints?"

"Whoever did it brushed the ground and took the branches with him."

"That it?"

"So far."

I tried to digest the news without letting my emotions get in the way, but it was hard. My face tightened, my fists clenched and my lips almost disappeared into my mouth. The scene flashed through my mind and I could picture the events as they took place. Why? Why her? Why me?

"Want to tell me about your daughter, Gabe?"

"What's to tell? I was a lousy husband, a bad father and a good cop. My priorities were out of whack."

"What happened to your wife?"

I focused my gaze across the street. "Depression. Loneliness. Then suicide. A husband too busy being everything but what he should have been." I sighed. "I screwed up, kid. Take a lesson from an expert."

"I'm sorry. Anything I can do for you, Gabe. You know."

"I know. Help me get the son of a bitch." I could feel myself choking up. I turned away so she couldn't see my face. "I'm going to the hotel to see if anyone might have seen her before she disappeared. If something goes down, call me on my cell, okay?"

"Okay, Gabe. Remember, this is Munz's case and he hates you. If you cross him, he'll crucify you."

"Then Munz better watch himself."

"Holloway will be forced to support him, friend or no friend. He can only bend so far for you."

"Then I'm about to find out how far the bow will bend without breaking."

I DROVE DOWNTOWN and parked my car under City Hall, walked across the street to the Sheraton and waited at the main entrance for the patrol cop to meet me. Howard Claremont got me the name of the cop who patrols by the Sheraton and I contacted him at his precinct. Now I sat on a bench waiting for him. Yesterday seemed a million years ago. I had had a sleepless night thinking about meeting my daughter. What to say, what to do...? Should I kiss her? All academic now. To tell her I was sorry would not be accepted, I knew, no matter how sincere I felt. If Miriam still felt the same as when she'd left, there wasn't anything I could say that would appease her anger – or maybe by now it was hate. I had taken too much for granted. There was love in my heart for my wife and daughter, but I doubted she would understand my remorse. Why is it not until you lose something that you begin to appreciate what you had?

Her words on the telephone had been choppy. She was flying to Toronto. She had to see me. She didn't give me a chance to talk, so I just listened. She needed to face me and talk, she said. Would I talk to her? Yes, anytime, I answered. Anytime. And now there was no time. I'd killed them both. She should have stayed away and lived.

I heard the horn honk and looked up. The patrol car had pulled over to the curb. I heaved a big sigh and approached. "Thanks for coming so quickly," I said. "What can you tell me about the woman you saw in front of the hotel last night after midnight?"

"Sorry about your daughter," the cop said.

"About what you saw? Uh, you sure she was alone?"

"Was when I passed the hotel main entrance. Just standing outside the door."

"What was your patrol?"

"I had come along Richmond to York. On York, there were a couple of cars parked on the street and a red van. It's a No Parking zone, but I usually let them alone for one pass. It could be overflow valet parking. When I came by later, they were all gone. Then I passed the hotel entrance and on to Yonge Street. A lot of pedestrian traffic."

"You don't recall anything out of the ordinary?"

"Sorry, no. Nothing. She was wearing a thick sweater and carried a purse under her arm."

"They found no purse."

"One of those long thin ones. No strap. It was black or some dark colour."

"I'll look into that. Thanks. If you do remember something else, ask for Detective Iris Forester or get a hold of Howard Claremont."

The cop nodded and drove away.

It didn't make sense, I thought. After my initial shock had passed, I figured her death might be linked to someone trying to get even with me, but that didn't fit the puzzle. She had only just hit Toronto. No one knew she was coming except me. Was it a random hit? Being in the wrong place at the wrong time? With her purse gone, it could have been robbery. Did one of the homeless on the street decide to jump her? No! Absolutely, no. How would they get the body over to the Parkway? They would have left her where she fell. The killer and the missing purse could be two different incidents. Someone could have picked up the purse after the body was taken away. And what did the severed head mean? Was it a message? Were we dealing with a psycho? Some sick bastard living a fantasy by chopping a head off. If it was a psychopath, there would be other murders.

I entered the hotel and could hear the noise from the main bar. Anyone else in my position would be dead drunk by now, but I don't drink. Even if I did, what could it do for me? A few hours of oblivion? When I came to, everything would still be there. I needed to be sober to figure out what had happened. Drunk, I'm useless. Later, after I tracked the bastard down, I might go for that oblivion. But track him down I would. The thought of killing him didn't seem unappealing either. Right now I needed a lead. My cellular went off and I flipped it open. "Garshowitz here."

"It's Iris. They found another female body without a head."

"Where?"

"In the valley near York Mills Road and the DVP. A jogger found her."

"What do you know so far?"

"She was young, pretty and Chinese. This one had a tattoo on her rump. One of the cops knew her. She's a prostitute. The body was laid out the same way. Flat on her stomach, hands tied behind her back. There's a lot of blood again."

"What's the girl's name?"

"Sandy Tan. She lived in the Mount Pleasant-Eglinton area."

"Any idea about the time of death?"

"Nothing precise, but Forensics thinks this one was killed after your daughter, early in the morning – before six. For sure both murders occurred last night. Your daughter's death was before one, and this one before six. Also got word from Forensics on your daughter. She was not raped. They think the same here."

"Where are you now?" I asked.

"At the scene."

"Good. That gives me a head start."

"What you going to do?"

"I'm going to headquarters to check Sandy Tan out before you get there. The patrol cop said my daughter was carrying a purse. I'll put everything I know down on paper and leave it on your desk. Check out the purse. Have someone check the Dumpsters, or maybe lost and found, talk to the derelicts and homeless, too."

"Anything else?"

"What's Simon doing?"

"Aside from bad-mouthing you and me, nothing much."

"He's an ass."

Iris laughed.

"What's so funny?"

"Sorry. Yesterday you called him a *putz*. Make up your mind."

"I changed my mind, he's no *putz*. A putz has a purpose, an ass is a container."

WHEN I WENT to my desk, I could see those in the room pull their eyes away from me. I've known many of them for years and I knew how they were feeling. I've done the same when someone else was hurting. It's awkward. What do you say? Sometimes I think staying away might be the best medicine. Their looks told me they cared. That was enough. I typed in the information I was looking for and printed out the answer. Another piece of the puzzle was being fitted in. A phone call to Iris and I left.

I saw Iris's car as it made its way down the street. She was scrutinizing the shops as she passed. I waved to her from the curb and she pulled into a vacant spot and got out. It was after seven in the evening, and I had asked her to meet me before going home.

"So where are we headed?" she asked.

"The pool hall on the second floor." I pointed at one of the storefronts. "Rap sheet indicates Sandy Tan's been charged several times and did some jail time; also she had a pimp. He posted her bail. He spends his day shooting pool, and his girls pay him nightly. This is where he'll be from six on. I'll need you as backup."

"Okay. You go up first. I'll follow in a few minutes. What's the pimp's name?"

"Zipper."

"Pardon?"

"He has a scar across one cheek that looks like a zipper. Got it when he was a kid. He likes knives."

"Marvellous. How many are up there?"

"Don't worry, you'll hardly break out in a sweat. I'll protect your back." I grinned.

"I thought I was protecting yours."

"I'm a thinker, not a fighter. That's your bag. Don't hurt him."

"Don't hurt him? He's the one with the knife, remember?"

My grin broadened.

"You seem in a better mood, Gabe."

"No, not better, but now we have a lead. My daughter's death was not an isolated incident. The more involved the crime becomes, the better the chance of finding a clue. My daughter now has company. What I couldn't find in one, I might find in two." I climbed the steps as Iris checked her watch.

There was a haze of smoke in the air and another odour I recognized immediately – marijuana. Iris stayed back, I moved forward. There were four pool players at two tables, the click of the stick striking the ball being the only sound until I coughed to draw attention to my presence. The four Chinese players looked up and one smiled broadly, while the others glared at me stone-faced. They fanned out as I approached.

"Are you lost?" Smiley asked.

"If I was I wouldn't climb stairs to ask for directions. I assume you're Zipper."

The smile quickly disappeared and the man self-consciously ran his hand over the scar. "And who are you?"

"A friend of the law."

"A cop?"

"Homicide. Gabe Garshowitz, Detective."

"Something I can't do for you?"

"I understand you're Sandy Tan's pimp."

"Don't know anyone named Sandy Tan."

"That's funny. The last time she was picked up, you bailed her out. You can relax. I'm not interested in the pimping. I'll let someone else take care of that. What I need to know is where was she working last night?"

"How would I know?"

"We seemed to be going in circles. Maybe we should talk about this at the station."

"Maybe you should get lost. You found your way in, so find your way out."

One of the pool players tapped Zipper on the shoulder and pointed to the door. We all looked at where he pointed.

Iris was leaning against a vending machine.

"That broad with you? You her pimp?" The four laughed and one made obscene gestures at Iris.

Iris sauntered towards them. "We're not looking for trouble, just information. Why not help us and we'll leave as quietly as we came."

"Get lost," Zipper said again, and pushed me against the pool table.

Iris moved between them quickly. "That was stupid," she said. "We're just here to talk."

"Do you need an interpreter? Leave! If the two of you don't leave, you'll be carried out."

We stared hard at each other for a few seconds, then Zipper nodded to his three companions and they closed in on Iris and me. One swung his fist at me – I ducked and dug my elbow hard into his ribs. Iris jump-kicked another in the groin and he doubled over in pain; she followed up with a kick to his head as he was meeting the floor. He lay still. She turned her attention to the one who'd swung at me. He leaped with his foot and swung his arms to catch her as she ducked. She didn't duck, but blocked his leg and pushed it aside, grabbed his arm and twisted it behind his back, while bashing his head into the pool table, then letting him fall to the floor. The third stepped back, grabbed a pool cue and swung it like a bat. Iris ducked and shook her head. "You've been watching too much American television," she said as she picked up a billiard ball and threw it at his head. It struck him in the temple, and he tumbled to the floor without a peep. Man, she was smooth.

We faced Zipper, who hadn't moved. "About Sandy Tan," I said. "Do you know where she was working last night?"

"Why?"

"She's dead."

"Fuck! Whatever was in her handbag is mine."

"You're a real sweet guy," Iris said. "Don't you care?"

Zipper's look was her answer.

"We didn't find a handbag," I said.

"She always had one. She carried her supplies in there."

"What supplies?" Iris asked.

"Are you for real? Mouthwash, toothpaste, water, condoms."

I intervened. "Are you going to answer my question? I'd like to leave. Your buddies are moving again."

"She worked the downtown core. Yonge Street."

"Where did she take her johns?"

"She had a place."

"Hotel?"

"Nah, didn't need one. Her specialty was blow jobs."

Iris's face screwed up in disgust.

Zipper grinned. "Lady, the guys tell me she's so good she makes them feel like a president."

His pals had recovered and were moving in behind him.

"Relax, gentlemen," Iris said, "Too much exercise may be detrimental to your health. Time to go, Gabe. I'm meeting Howard tonight."

I nodded. "You've been a fount of information, Zipper." I slowly backed away. Iris waited until I was close to the door, then followed, hurrying down the stairs to join me.

"Gabe, hold up a minute."

I continued walking to my car, then stopped. "What?" I asked.

"That was my question. What are you going to do now?"

"Cruise downtown and talk to some of the working girls."

"The coroner said that Sandy Tan was struck across the forehead with a blunt instrument. Probably knocked out. Again the head was severed while she was alive."

"What does Munz think?"

"That we're dealing with a psycho. Don't you?"

"I don't know. My daughter was from out of the country. She had to be a random hit. It wasn't planned. The hooker was in a controlled environment. We're looking for someone who knows this city and hookers, and knows where to find one.

Definitely our killer knows the city, considering where the two bodies were found. Whoever we're looking for is home grown. This is no outsider come to Toronto. He's local. And he's partial, maybe to the Don Valley Parkway." I looked at Iris, "Right?"

"Sounds good."

"My understanding of a psychopath is he looks for something in particular. He's reconstructing something in his mind. There is a common pattern." I paused to think. "What's the pattern?"

"Munz could be right."

"Could be. My daughter's body was in an area frequented every day by thousands of motorists, and it's near a kids' day camp. Hidden as it was, the body was meant to be found and the same with the hooker's. If the killer's a psycho, there will be another killing soon, and somewhere in the evidence, he's sending us a message. Like, why the severed heads?"

"Munz is checking with other cities to see if there have been similar homicides."

"Munz hasn't the brains to figure that out. Greg must have told him what to do. Go home, Iris. You have a date. I'll see you tomorrow."

"Just don't do anything stupid, Gabe. You can't change the past."

"It's not the past I want to change."

I GOT A bite to eat in a restaurant nearby and spent the night talking to working girls downtown; actually until three in the morning. It'd been a long time since the mind and the body were in agreement. They wanted to sleep. I seconded the motion and with bleary eyes and a drugged mind went home.

The telephone rang. I rolled over and groped for it. "Yeah?" I mumbled into the mouthpiece.

"Are you awake, Gabe?" It was Iris.

"I am now. What time is it?"

"Why?"

"I didn't get home until after four in the morning. Why are you calling?"

"You were right. We have another one."

I got out of bed quickly. "Where did they find her?"

"How do you know it's a her?"

"Guess. Where?"

"Earl Bales Park."

"What! That's a block from where I live."

"Gabe, that's pretty far from the Don Valley Parkway."

"Yes, but close to Highway 401 and that connects with the DVP. Where in the park?"

"Near the monument. And, Gabe, she's black. The news media's making connections. It will be all over the television at six. They're talking serial killer."

"She's black? That's interesting. Three killings and three different skin colours. I wonder if that's significant? How was the body laid out?"

"The same."

"I'm getting dressed and coming down. I'll walk."

"Munz won't like that."

"Hold his hand. I have to see what the scene looks like."

"*Oy vey,*" Iris said.

"What?"

"Not bad for a *shiksa,* eh?"

I snorted. "No, not bad."

Mystic entered the bedroom, his leash in his mouth. I buckled my belt and hitched up my pant legs, then slipped into my shoes without socks. "Got to run, Mystic. Won't be long." I hurried passed the dog and quickly left the apartment with Mystic staring at the door, the leash still in his mouth.

WAS THIS THE pattern I was waiting for? Was this some nut trying to kill women with different skin colour because of some grievance? I showed my badge to the cop at the Bathurst Street entrance and made my way to the monument. Iris saw me approaching and met me halfway.

"Be nice, Gabe. Munz isn't in good humour."

"Neither am I."

We moved to the area enclosed by the yellow police tape. Simon Munz was talking to Stella Morgan when he saw me. He made his way over. "What are you doing here? This case is off limits to you, remember?"

"I came to look at the body, then I'll leave. Let's not make a big deal out of this."

"Remember chasing me off the Solinus crime scene? Why don't you fuck off and I'll say nothing."

"Have you forgotten it was my daughter who was the first victim?"

"Hey, it should have been her old man instead," he said, his eyes hostile.

"You're a bastard," I snarled.

"Is that envy I detect? Now get out of the park or I'll have you escorted off."

Scowling, I turned and headed for the main road. I saw Stella coming my way.

"How are you, Gabe?" she said awkwardly.

"I'm all right."

"If you come to my office later, I'll let you read the reports on all three deaths."

I smiled. "You're a doll, Stella. Thanks."

"Gabe, do you know Constable Arthur Harris? He patrols the Don Valley Parkway."

"No, why?"

"He's a friend. He reported seeing a red van parked on the shoulder of the Parkway at about the time the coroner figures your daughter died. It was pointed north and the driver was inside, about a hundred metres from where the body was found. Here's his number. Simon will get the report when he returns to headquarters."

A worried Iris approached. She nodded to Stella. "Munz

says to keep moving."

I scowled and muttered a curse. "Thanks again, Stella," I said, and headed for the street. Iris followed.

When we reached Bathurst Street, Iris said, "Gabe...I heard the coroner is releasing your daughter's body."

I gazed solemnly at Iris. "They know what to do. I've made arrangements for a private graveside ceremony."

"Would you like...?"

I offered a weak smile. "Thanks for the thought, but no. I'd like to be alone when she's buried."

"Do you want to tell me the rest of the story?"

"Long story."

"Shorten it. Remember, I'm on your side."

I nodded gravely. "I know." There was a bench a few feet away and I indicated we sit. "Uh, it's hard to put into words. Some people should never get married and definitely should never have kids. That's me. My wife was a Holocaust survivor. What I didn't know was that when she was a kid, the people who hid her from the Germans had repeatedly sexually molested her. When my daughter was eleven, my wife started to have nightmares. I was too busy doing my thing to realize that they were a symptom of a bigger problem. At the time I was trying to be a homicide cop. I passed my exams. I worked long hours. You know what I mean, so I never got to know my kid. She was devoted to her mother.

"My wife died suddenly. It was listed as an accidental death due to an overdose of medication, but I knew it was suicide. Miriam never forgave me. I never forgave myself. Then one day Miriam was gone. Address unknown. That was five years ago. Last week I got a telephone call from her from Australia. She wanted to see me. The rest you know. I ruined her life. Too busy avoiding my personal responsibilities."

"I'm sorry," Iris said softly.

"So am I, but that won't change what happened. I'm going to get the creep who killed her. Go back and check out the scene for me. See if the body is positioned differently, if the hands are tied differently, anything that is different. If this is a serial killer, he's following a pattern induced by his fantasy or rage or whatever makes him do what he does; every killing will look exactly the same. If it's a false lead, there'll be variations. Look for variations."

"What are you going to do?"

"Follow up a lead Stella gave me. I only have a few hours to keep ahead of Munz. Before my daughter was killed, a cop on Queen Street saw a red van parked nearby. Now I've found out that before my kid's body was found, a cop patrolling the Don Valley Parkway talked to someone in a red van. It could be a coincidence, but I don't think so. Last night I talked to several working girls on Yonge Street and they said they saw a red van cruising. So – I got me a common denominator."

"Are you all right, Gabe?"

I mustered a tired smile. "You're a good kid, Iris. I wish I had done as well with my daughter as your parents did with you. I'll be okay." I started to leave, then I asked, "You had a problem when all this started. Can I help?"

Iris smiled. "It's not important now."

"Everything's important. You sure I can't help?"

They say a cop should always expect the unexpected. I got caught then with the unexpected. Iris came up to me and kissed me on the cheek, then briskly walked away.

Men don't cry. Mystic would be waiting. I'll have to remember to carry a handkerchief.

I WAS AT my desk, peering at the screen on my computer when Holloway entered the room about mid-afternoon. I knew I was to stay away, but what I needed was in my computer. I was too impatient to wait for Iris to get it for me. Besides, I knew Greg was aware I was nosing around. He knew me too well. He walked over and read what was on the screen. "Who's Henry Murdock?"

"I don't know."

"This to do with your daughter?"

"Maybe."

"Munz has been bitching about you interfering in his work."

"That was a joke, right?" I swung around and faced him. "I'm off the case, remember? On leave, right? I can go and do what I want as long as I don't muddy the waters. Then I'm safe. That *putz* is in a different stream from me."

"Don't bark at me, Gabe. We've been friends too long. If you think you can help him, that's fine, but it's his case and he makes the decisions."

"So let him. That ape is beating the bushes while I'm tracking the killer. I can't talk to him 'cause he won't listen. I'm keeping a written record of my activities, and if something does happen to me, it'll be in my apartment. There was a red van parked near the Sheraton when my kid was killed, there was a red van cruising the downtown core where the hookers hang out and this new item. Murdock owns a red Dodge van, and the patrol cop listed his licence and time on the DVP the night my kid was murdered. I don't believe in coincidences. There's a connection."

"Okay, I didn't talk to you. But, dammit, be careful!"

Grim-faced, I answered, "I always am." Holloway went into his office. My cell buzzed and I dug it out of my shirt pocket. "Garshowitz."

"It's me."

"Yes, me."

"Gabe, your daughter wasn't the first."

"What?"

"They just found a body in the bushes in that conservation strip park north of Steeles by Dufferin. High grass. Been there maybe a week. Same M.O. Decapitated. But this one was dead before her head was taken off – there isn't the same spray of blood. Also, there are bruises where the axe severed the head. I think you're right about the killer. I don't believe we're dealing with a real psycho. Whoever is doing this is creating a false pattern."

"Shit!"

"I'm at the place now. Body face down and hands tied behind her back. And she wasn't raped. Another thing, Gabe, she's Indian."

"As in First Nations?"

"No. India Indian. That's four different races, four different shades of skin. This killer's killing women of different colours. Do you think this might be a religious thing?"

"No, I think this is a premeditated murder thing. Everything has been a camouflage until now. The marks on the neck of this latest find is a real clue. Looks like she was strangled, then beheaded. Now we have something to work with. What's the woman's name? What does she do? Where's she live? Do you have anything?"

"No. I have some info on the black girl, though. She was a secretary for a law firm on Steeles near the 400. Her boss said they worked late. She left about three in the morning. He called her home to see if she arrived all right, but got no answer. She was single. In the morning he called again when she didn't come to work. He got worried. Then he contacted the police. Her name was Alicea Noble. Does it connect with what you're doing?"

"No. I'm following up another lead. When you're asking questions, ask about a red van. Right now I'm going to see someone who has one." I closed the cellular and stuck it in my pocket, then stared at the screen on my monitor. "Well, at least I have you, Henry. Let's see what you look like." I pressed the keys to clear the screen and left the station.

At Henry Murdock's house, a middle-aged black woman answered. "I'm looking for Henry Murdock. I'm Detective Gabe Garshowitz. Is he home?"

The woman's eyes opened wide with surprise.

"I'm following up on a lead and Mr. Murdock may be able to help me. Is he home?"

"No, sir. He works from four until midnight at a machine shop down on Jones Avenue."

"You his wife?"

She smiled. "No, sir. I'm his sitter, Hanna Johnson. Mr. Murdock and his wife have been separated for more than a year. I look after his daughter until he comes home. She's ten."

"You stay here until he comes home?"

"Yes, sir, until one in the morning. His daughter comes home from school about four and I'm here. I make her supper and do light housework. And he's never late. He knows I want to get home."

"Is Mr. Murdock black?"

"No, sir, he's one of you."

I smiled. "Ever seen his wife?"

"No, sir, not in person. Seen her picture, though. She's from Fiji. Mr. Murdock met her there while on vacation. Pretty woman."

"Is Mrs. Murdock white?"

"No, sir. I think her family was originally from India."

"Really? Do you know her name?"

"He called her Didi. I don't know if that's her real name or just a pet name."

"Do you know why they were separated?"

"No, sir. Not my business."

I had enough answers, so I stopped asking questions. Any other questions Mr. Murdock would have to answer himself. What I asked myself was, was the last corpse, which was the first, his wife? Did the chain of events begin with her and the rest were false leads? "Well, thank you for your help. Tell Mr. Murdock I was here. Here's my card. Ask him to call me tomorrow before he goes to work."

"Yes, sir, I will."

I returned to my car and telephoned Iris. "Have you got a name yet?"

"No. There was no identification on the body."

"Try Didi Murdock."

"I presume you'll tell me why later."

"Just let me know what you find. I'm going home to lie down for a few hours. I've run out of gas. You got me up early and I went to bed late. Call me at home after nine."

"Will do."

I was staring out the window before starting the car when a thought hit me. I hadn't thought about my knees since Miriam's death. I couldn't even remember if I had experienced any pain lately. Was it all in my head?

MY APARTMENT BUZZER woke me from a deep sleep. I was tired. My mouth tasted like last week's pizza. The digital clock beside my bed read nine-twenty. I rolled off the couch and buzzed the front door open, then went into the bathroom and looked at myself in the mirror. I grimaced. One fast look was enough to tell me I needed a shower and a shave. The grumbling in my stomach reminded me I hadn't eaten all day. I did a fast rinse of my mouth just as I heard my visitor knock at my door. I straightened my shirt and opened the door. "I said call me at nine, not come here at nine."

"Thought you might be hungry. Brought you something hot from a Jewish dairy restaurant down the street."

I smiled my appreciation. "No more complaints," I said. "What do you have?"

"Matzah ball soup, tuna salad and a bagel. I asked for chicken salad, but they said not at this restaurant. How come they don't carry chicken?"

"You converting?"

"To get an answer?"

"Traditional Jews don't mix dairy with meat. Kosher restaurants follow traditional rules. I'm more liberal."

"I never thought of chicken as meat."

"*Oy vey*," I said.

Iris laughed. "You've had more practice than me."

Mystic entered the room, his tail swinging like a pendulum when he saw Iris and went over to her. She gave him a hug and he stayed in her arms as we continued our conversation.

"What happened with the name Didi Murdock?" I asked as I spooned the soup.

"Listed with Missing Persons for about a week. Lives with a guy who reported her missing when she didn't come home one night. Doesn't know where she went or if she saw anyone. The file hasn't been followed up because of caseload. They're checking her dental records against the decapitated head and we'll get an answer in the morning. You figure it's her?"

"I do now," I answered as I drank the rest of the soup. "I do now." I opened the lid of the tuna salad container and forked the contents into my mouth.

"If I'd known you were that hungry, I'd have brought you a couple of hamburgers. Without the ham, of course."

"What else?" I said.

"Simon says we'll have more bodies before this is over. He's convinced we're dealing with a psycho. I didn't tell him what you think."

I swallowed the food in my mouth. "A guy with a red van, working the night shift while his ex-wife is living with another man, that's what I think."

"That's a good start. You think he's our killer?"

"Right now it looks good. We need a motive. You check with Family Court tomorrow, while I introduce myself to Mr. Henry Murdock and his red van."

Iris stood. "You're burying your daughter tomorrow – sure you don't want company?"

I shook my head. "No. Thanks for the concern, though."

"You going to be okay?"

"No. But I'll survive. Thanks again and thanks for the food – I was hungry. Now I need a shower and a shave and more sleep, so get lost."

Mystic followed us to the door. "Are you sure you're okay?

Don't you want someone to talk to?"

"I'm fine. It's important I catch the bastard."

"You will."

"I got Mystic to talk to. He has a very sympathetic ear."

Mystic's tail thumped on the hardwood floor at the mention of his name. Iris ran a hand over his head. "Well, if you need someone to answer back, I hope you'll call me."

"Promise."

25

I CALLED HENRY Murdock and told him I was coming over. I led him to believe I was in charge of a team looking into a murder case. I didn't figure he would check me out. We sat in his living room. "As I told you over the telephone, Mr. Murdock, I've been investigating the deaths of four women over the past two weeks, and we believe your wife might be one of the victims."

"Didi!"

"We think so. I understand you are not living together, but did you know she was missing?" I studied Murdock's face, feature by feature, looking for a sign, a twitch that would tell me he was about to lie. I saw nothing but the face of someone in shock.

"No, not at all. We don't keep in touch. We had a difference of opinion, and she left me and my daughter more than a year ago." He got up from his chair and went to a dresser drawer and removed an album. He flipped through it until he found what he was looking for, then returned to his chair. He handed me the open album. "That's her," he said, and pointed to an attractive woman standing in a field, waving at the camera.

I returned the album to him. "It must have been a major difference of opinion to cause you to separate. May I ask what it was?"

I got the impression that Murdock was biting his lips. The answer, whatever it was, was slow in coming out. "She wanted a trial separation. She was having a problem."

"What kind?"

"She needed some time for herself."

"I'm trying to put together a profile of the four women to see if there is a common denominator that might give me a clue about why the killer targeted them. Did you give your wife any kind of an allowance while she was resolving her problem?"

"No, Detective Garshowitz. She left me. She got nothing."

I was beginning to feel like a dentist, extracting the information in bits and pieces. He wasn't being very responsive. "She had her own job?"

"No."

One thing I've learned from Iris was to attack the subject, so I did. "Was she living with a man?"

"Yes."

"Seems to me that would indicate an irreconcilable situation. Were you not going to get a divorce?"

"We hadn't discussed it."

"Did this arrangement satisfy you?"

"I was hoping she would come to her senses and return."

"You would have taken her back?"

"Yes. But I can't give her the time she needs. Only her mother can."

"Did your wife ask for your daughter?"

"No. She's asked me for nothing."

I watched Murdock's face. I knew he couldn't be related to Sarah Silver, but his face had the same cast as hers had when I talked to her. He was lying. "Could you tell me where you were last Tuesday night between midnight and one in the morning?"

"Am I a suspect?"

"No. I'm just trying to eliminate you as a suspect."

"On my way home. It takes me forty-five minutes to get home. Hannah leaves at one."

"I understand you spoke to a police officer that night."

"That's right. I was having difficulty staying awake, so I pulled onto the shoulder of the DVP for a few minutes. I hadn't slept well the night before."

"Before getting on the DVP, did you park your van on York Street? Wouldn't take you long to get there from work after midnight."

"Not possible. I always punch out at about 12:01. That leaves me fifty-five minutes to make a forty-five-minute trip. Could never be home on time if I went to York Street."

"To punch out one minute after, you must get ready before quitting time?"

"I do. The boss gives me permission to get ready ten minutes earlier than the other guys. I also start before the others to make up for it. Hey! The cop on the Parkway should know the time he talked to me. They note those things, don't they? Listen, Detective Garshowitz, my wife and I had our differences, but I still loved her. I didn't kill my wife or anyone else."

I stood. "We believe your wife was the first victim. The second victim, Mr. Murdock, was my daughter, and I'll never rest until I find the killer. Never. Which means I'll find your wife's killer as well."

Murdock stood and met my eyes without flinching. "I hope you do. You have a job to do, Detective Garshowitz. Check my time card. You'll see what I said about leaving is true. I'm not the one you want. Try the boyfriend. Who said their relationship was solid? Him? The last time I talked to my wife, I thought there was a chance she would come back. If there's anyone with motive, it's him. I hear he's very possessive. Check him out."

"I'll do that, Mr. Murdock. Thank you for your time."

Outside in my car, I rehashed what had taken place. The man was cool. More like indifferent. For a guy who wanted his wife back, his display of emotion was minimal. When I said she might be dead, he didn't blink. When I asked would he take her back, he said sure. This man didn't want a wife, he wanted a live-in maid for his kid. I doubted his sincerity. The boyfriend angle had to be looked into if for no other reason than to make sure it wasn't a good clue ignored. My gut was telling me I had just talked to my daughter's killer. All I had to do was prove it.

"I won't say I had tunnel vision, but I admit I was focused. Greg was right about being emotionally involved. It's impossible not to be. But my emotions and my focus were on the same course. Henry Murdock was my man. I had seen his type before. He'd married a pretty woman to show off and be his servant. I knocked on doors on his street after I left him and asked his neighbours questions. There were arguments, I was told. Loud ones. He got angry when he saw her talking to a man and he wasn't there. None of the neighbours liked him. None knew his wife too well. He kept her inside. They only moved into the area about two years ago. One of them told him that they had moved because Henry had a bad fight with a next-door neighbour because he thought he was showing his wife too much attention. The wife told him the story. She was afraid of him. Possessive and jealous. His kind didn't break easy, but I was going to break him. The problem was, how long before he broke. Me, I had forever.

I started following him. At this stage I kept myself back so he didn't know I was around. He seemed to live a normal life. I didn't see him do anything funny or out of the ordinary, except he seemed to have a fixation about his van. He must have taken it to a car wash four times in one week. At home he would scrub the inside. That van looked so shiny, the sun reflected off it, and yet he would wash and clean it every couple of days. I wished I could get a search warrant on the vehicle, but I had no probable cause. I had nothing, including authority.

One day he caught me off guard and drove to the Finch hospital near Highway 400. In fact, the location of the hospital wasn't too far from where Alicia Noble had worked. I watched from the doorway as he talked to the woman at the information desk and entered a corridor. I waited a few minutes and approached the woman.

"Good afternoon," I said. I showed her my badge. "That man who was just here, where was he going?"

Her eyes went to the corridor where Murdock had disappeared. "That man?" she asked, pointing to the empty entrance.

"Yes, that man."

"He asked for cardiac. He had a slip for a nuclear vascular test." She shrugged. "Heart condition, I guess."

I thanked her and returned to my car. I called Iris and asked her to check that out for me. The next day I received a call from Greg to come to the office. It was only a matter of time before he found out what I was doing. I knew Iris was keeping him tuned in to my activities and had expected to hear from him.

"It's time you came back to work, Gabe. I have Simon

Munz investigating your suspicions, even though he claims you're wrong."

"I'm not ready, Greg. As long as I'm on my own, I'm free to concentrate on this case. You know once I'm back on assignment, you'll give me half a dozen other cases to investigate. I'm not returning until I arrest the killer. I know it's Murdock. I checked out the boyfriend and he had an alibi. The time of death was early afternoon. He was at work all day. Murdock doesn't start until four. I'm watching him day and night and he knows it. He killed his wife and then tried to throw the investigation off track by creating the illusion that we were dealing with a nut case who gets his kicks by killing women of different races. It was a sick plan that might have worked, except he included my daughter in his victims."

"Iris tells me you're crowding him and that could lead to trouble. You're all alone out there, and I don't want to lose you if something goes wrong."

"Murdock conceived a desperate plan that went astray. Iris learned that the wife made an application for divorce and asked for custody of their daughter. She did it the day she died. I don't think Murdock knew. He's on a collision course with himself. Everything he did was for nothing, and now he has me to deal with – an avenging father. I'm staying out there until I can bring him in, and then and only then will I come back."

"Do you have any hard evidence?"

"No. Let Munz find that. What I have is fear – fear of me. As long as he knows I'm there, that's pressure he has to contend with, and that's pressure that will eventually break him. What bothers me is I found out he has a heart condition. Apparently he's had a couple of silent heart attacks over the years and goes to a clinic when he thinks something's not working right. I got no choice but to squeeze him. I want him alive though, not dead."

"We checked out his time card," Greg said. "He punched

out at 11:58 p.m. Munz drove the route last night that you described, and it took him too long to get from Jones Avenue to the Sheraton and back to the DVP. The cop is his alibi."

"Did they see him punch his time card?"

"No, they never do. No one saw him leave. Sometimes people punch other people's time cards for them, so everyone was asked if they had punched Murdock's card, and the answer was no. The card was dusted for fingerprints, but by the time we got it, it was saturated with too many overlaps to get a good print. Apparently that night the card was taken from the slot and tallied for payroll. At least four different prints were on there, but none clear. Munz thinks you're wrong and you're taking him away from his own investigation. I can't be a referee forever between you two."

I shook my head. "Murdock gets home at one to relieve his babysitter. He kills my daughter before he goes home. His own daughter is asleep. When the sitter leaves, he goes out and kills again, and returns before his daughter wakes up for school."

"But he couldn't have killed your daughter. His time card and the cop prove it wasn't him. Your theory doesn't work for a one-killer conclusion."

"There has to be an explanation for the time card."

"There isn't. All the employees on Murdock's shift say he was at work. His alibi is strong and your hunch won't hold up against that."

"It's not a hunch anymore!" I was almost shouting. "Get me a search warrant for his van," I said. "He's cleaned the damn thing several times already but maybe not clean enough."

"On what grounds? I'll give you one more week, Gabe. If you don't come back to work then, I'll recommend you for pension."

"You won't. We're friends."

"I will because we're friends. One week, no more."

I WAS HAVING my breakfast at Kiva's. It funny how sometimes

being in a crowded room was no different from being alone. I sat at a table for two and people surrounded me, but I saw only what was before me and listened to my voice talking to me – only my voice. Sunday morning breakfast time had to be the noisiest time of the week at the place. There wasn't a table empty. In fact, there was a small line waiting to get in. As far as eating places go, this had to be one of the most bare-bone places in the city – sterile tables and chairs, nothing of a personal nature on the walls. The décor didn't bring people, and I'm not sure it was the food. After all, what could a fast-order cook do in five seconds with cream cheese, lox and bagels, or onion buns or whatever? Yet, come Sunday, they waited in line.

Everyone was so close to each other it wasn't hard to hear what was said at the next table. Come to think of it, that was how we solved the Charlie Talbot Case, by eavesdropping. That, too, was part of the attraction of this place, the closeness of the tables. Fortunately the waitresses were skinny enough to be able to squeeze between tables carrying several plates at a time, all looking alike – the contents on the plate, that is, not the waitresses.

My inner voice was becoming a distraction. It seemed to be hollering at me for not making a decision. I was in a disagreement with myself. I knew Murdock was my man. I knew it. Couldn't prove it, but that didn't matter, I knew it. There are times when all that is left when investigating is gut reaction. I had it. But the gut and my mind weren't on the same wave length. The gut said, kill, and the head said don't. I held the knife in my hand so hard my fingers tingled.

I raised my head from looking at my plate and saw Iris sitting opposite me. "Hi," I said. "When did you get here?"

"A few minutes ago." There was a look of concern on her face.

I smiled, but it was just for effect.

"I guess I was lost in my thoughts. I didn't hear you."

"You okay, Gabe?" she asked.

"I will be."

"I said hello and sat down, and I could see you were in lala land – you didn't so much as blink."

I nodded.

A waitress came over and Iris gave her order.

"Greg caught me last night before I left the building and asked if I knew what you were doing. I told him you were tailing Murdock."

I cut into my scrambled eggs and placed a forkful in my mouth. I chewed, then said, "Close enough so that he knows I'm there."

"You only have two more days."

I looked at her. "You know?"

This time she nodded. "Greg told me. What are you going to do?"

I tore a piece off the bagel and chewed on it slowly, to give me time to think of an answer. My eyes were focused on the knife. "I'm not sure."

I saw Iris look at my knife and then at me. "Nothing stupid, I hope," she said.

I picked the knife up and smothered some cream cheese on a section of my bagel and said nothing.

The waitress returned and placed the cup of hot water and a carrot muffin in front of Iris and left. "Is it worth it, starving yourself so you can have a thin waist?" I asked.

"What's that got to do with anything?" she asked.

"You made a decision. You deprive yourself for the greater good of whatever you feel is important. I'm trying to decide what is important."

"We'll get him."

"Yes…or I'll get him."

There was a burst of laughter from the corner, and Iris turned to see a double table with eight men around it.

"Do you know why I like coming here?" I said.

"The bagels."

I smiled. "Atmosphere. I feel comfortable here. For a brief moment, I'm not here but elsewhere – a place like this, where I used to go many, many years ago. I was still a patrol cop. I would take my wife and daughter there. It was this bagel restaurant on College near Spadina and it was like we were in our kitchen and everyone was our guest. Of course I never paid anyone but my family's bill." I smiled. "It had atmosphere. A narrow, unattractive strip of a place squeezed between two businesses and it was a Mecca for the Jews. It smelled of life." I inhaled deeply. I saw the look in Iris's eyes and laughed. "I'm okay," I said. "This place has a hold on me, not because of what it is but what it reminds me of. Back then, the bagels were soft and braided. The owner, Ben Posner, would holler at you if you asked for your bagel toasted. "We don't toast bagels, here!" I laughed at my words. "Edith thought the place was dirty, but I saw it as normal. The place was affectionately called 'The Dirty Bagel,' and anyone who was anyone ate there." I pointed to the table of eight men. "Those men are here every morning at seven, every day, seven days a week. They start their day here. God help anyone who sits in their seat. At The Bagel, there was a similar group. One day I was in getting a coffee and Al Waxman was with his cronies at the back. You know Al Waxman?"

"Yeah, sure. The King of Kensington."

"I liked him as the lieutenant in Cagney and Lacey. I loved that program. It had cops with personal problems. They were people. Hey! Do you remember the desk sergeant?"

"I don't think I watched that program."

"That's too bad. It was a great show. The desk sergeant gave the show a light touch. I liked his character. Anyway, Al Waxman was walking out and I stopped him, introduced myself. I was in uniform, and asked what he and his friends do back there. Do you know what he said? He said, the food's not the best, but this is the only place in the universe where everyone is a *maven* – that means expert. Every morning we solve the world's problems. Every one of us has an answer, whereas those who should be making the answers, hesitate. From here the world revolves." I smiled hesitantly. "That's why I have breakfast here, hoping to hear the answer to solve my problem. From here I begin my day."

"And what did you hear?"

I smeared the balance of my bagel with the rest of my cream cheese, plunked a slice of tomato on top and crammed it into my mouth. As I wiped the cream cheese off my moustache, I looked at Iris warmly and said, "I heard your sweet voice." I looked at my watch and got to my feet. "I gotta go, kid. Murdock gets up pretty soon. I need to be outside where he can see me." I left the money on the table and hurried out, Iris right behind.

I got into my car and she came to the window. "You gonna be all right?" she asked.

I am now. "Keep me posted," I said, then drove away.

I KEPT SEVERAL cars between me and the red van. I had made a few moves earlier so that Murdock knew I was behind him, just enough to make him turn his head every so often to see if I was still on his tail. Normally this stunt was done with more than one car. The suspect would spot the car that was obvious, think he lost him, but another had taken its place and then maybe another. The suspect thought he was safe. This time I wanted him to know I was there. He saw me when he awoke, he saw me when going to work and he saw me when he went home. I sat in front of his house during the day and I followed him wherever he went. That man's neck had to be hurting from twisting around. I was running out of time, but it didn't matter. I was going back to work, but I wouldn't abandon my surveillance. Murdock would know I was around as long as he stayed in the city.

My cell phone rang and I groped in my shirt pocket and flipped it open.

"I found the purse," Iris said.

"Where?"

"A bag lady. She said she picked it up that night. Found it on the sidewalk."

"How did you find her?"

"I went to several shelters and let it be known that I would pay for the return of the bag, no questions asked. It was needed in a homicide. She showed up."

"What was inside?"

"You mean what was left?"

"Did she own up to what was gone?" Gabe asked.

"Cash. She says only cash. American and Canadian. And the change."

"What was in the bag?"

"Lipstick, I.D., keys, some Australian money, and Canadian money orders for $500. Oh, and an address book. On the inside cover was a notation that in the event of an emergency, to contact Harry. No last name, only a telephone number. It's an Australian exchange."

"Boyfriend?"

"Don't know. I'll give it to you when I see you next. What's been happening on your end?"

"Nothing, not a damn thing. Murdock went to his clinic yesterday and two days earlier went to Toronto General to see a doctor, I presume. Right now we're on the way to his job. Listen, kid. I got a new thought. Did anyone go on holidays that night and wasn't there for questioning?"

"No."

"Did anyone who worked in the office quit that night and never return?"

"Shit! I didn't ask."

"Okay. When I get to where he works, I'll find out. Hey! Something's happening!"

"What?"

"Damned if I know. His car seemed to go out of control

and he struck a parked car. I'm going to check it out."

"Wait, Gabe! Let me get some police there first. It could be a trap."

"I'll leave the cell open so you can listen to what happens. This is stupid. What could he accomplish by having an accident? I'm getting out of the car."

"Gabe, wait for backup!"

I ran towards the van. Traffic had stopped and people were milling around the vehicle. I pulled out my gun and inched to the driver's-side door and yanked on the handle, sliding it back in one quick motion. Henry Murdock was slumped forward in his seat, his head on the steering wheel. I climbed in.

"Gabe, what's happening?" Iris hollered at me. "Gabe, are you there?"

"Stop yelling! I'm in the van. Murdock's unconscious. Wait a minute until I check him out." I slid in beside Murdock and felt for a pulse in his neck. There was none. "Iris, get an ambulance here. I think he's dead. The bastard's had a heart attack or something."

"We're on the way."

I stared at the body. "You son of a bitch. You got off easy." There were tears in my eyes as I stumbled out of the van to wait for Iris and her backup.

THE TIME CARD was the clincher. Another employee had punched Henry Murdock's card on the night Miriam Garshowitz and Sandy Tan were killed. He had returned to Guyana to live. The night of the murder had been his last day. The next day he had left Canada for South America. When contacted in Guyana, he revealed that Murdock claimed he had to be home early because his babysitter couldn't stay as long as usual. He had left maybe twenty minutes before quitting time. He didn't think it was a big deal. Murdock had planned it well. Forensics went over the van and found a couple of spots of blood that matched two of the victims. Hair fibres found in the van matched my daughter's hair. The case was unofficially closed as unsolved. No trial, no verdict, but case closed.

THE POLICE GYM was empty except for Iris. She pounded the bag, first with her fists, then her feet. She danced around, closing in on the swaying object, faking a counter move by an imaginary opponent, then striking the bag hard with her left foot. She dropped onto her right, pivoting and jabbing with her fists. The perspiration dripped from her face as she bounced on her toes, feeling the energy flow from her body to her limbs.

"Your partner was lucky."

Iris turned to see Simon Munz.

"His luck will run out soon. Farts like him are too old and weak to be useful."

Iris ignored Munz and turned back to the bag and jabbed it hard. She felt a big hand on her shoulder pull her backwards.

"My turn, sweetie. Let a man take a whack."

"Anyone ever tell you you're an asshole?" she said.

Munz's lip curled with anger. "That's your smart mouth again, sweetie. If you don't watch it, I'll forget you're a woman and show you what I'd do to any man who said that."

"First off, asshole, I'm not your sweetie. I'm not anyone's sweetie. Second, you're more shit than man. And third, it's you who are lucky – lucky I don't show you what I do to assholes who push me around."

Munz closed the distance between them. He glared down at her. "I don't like smart mouths and I don't like women who don't know their place. You and the old fart got no business being here. Take my advice and fuck off before I mess up that pretty face."

Iris could see he had clenched his fists. She was mad, really mad. She eyeballed him and with deliberate slowness, said, "Fuck you, asshole."

Munz's right fist swung in a powerhouse swing as he growled his anger. Iris ducked the swing and stiff-punched him in the groin. Munz's mouth opened in silent agony as Iris backed up enough to swing her leg behind his crouched body and topple him to the floor. She stepped farther back as Munz rolled to his knees holding his groin and lifted himself to his feet. There was pure hatred in his eyes as he advanced. He took another swing at her, but she neatly stepped aside. As his off-balance body swept by, she threw three short jabs into his kidney. He howled in pain.

"I haven't got time for this, asshole," she said. "I have an appointment. Do something or get lost," she taunted.

Munz charged her. Iris met his charge with her feet, striking his chest. She twisted in the air and somersaulted backwards onto her feet. He grunted from the blow, staggered, toppling onto his back. Iris moved to his head and dropped on one knee, then jabbed his nose with her fist, breaking the cartilage.

Munz screamed in pain.

Iris got to her feet and walked around his prone body to his legs. "I got to run, asshole, otherwise I'd play with you some more. Anytime you want to show me what you do to the boys again, call on me. I need the exercise. And in case you don't think I can play it your way, if you ever get me shot again, better pray it's for keeps 'cause the next time I'll cut them off." And she kicked him in the testicles.

IRIS STOOD ON the grassy hill and looked down at the section of the cemetery where Gabe's daughter was buried. Gabe was standing before a stone covered in cheesecloth. She wondered if what she was seeing was closure for him. An elderly man approached and the two talked for a moment. The elderly man began to pray, bending his body in rhythm with what he was chanting. When he finished, he removed the cheesecloth, shook Gabe's hand and left.

Gabe stood staring at the monument for a while, then

bent down, picked up a pebble and placed it on the ledge of the gravestone. He stared at the monument for a minute more, then turned and walked down the hill to where his car was parked.

Iris waited for him to drive away before she descended the hill. She read his daughter's name, Miriam Ruth Garshowitz, her date of birth and the date she died. It was the inscription that told her what she wanted to know. It read: *Born and died, but didn't have a chance to live. And it wasn't her fault.* He still blamed himself. She picked up a pebble. She didn't know what the significance of that gesture was, but since Gabe had done it, it seemed necessary for her to do the same. She placed the pebble next to his.

She looked at the monument, then noticed the one directly behind for Annie Kapinsky Weisz, which read, *She lived with hope and love.* Iris shifted her gaze back to Miriam's gravestone and rested the palm of her right hand over Gabe's pebble. "He's really a good guy," she said, then sighed and returned to her car.

Epilogue

THE LONG-DISTANCE operator made the connection for me. I had wanted some privacy and had gone out into the hall and used the pay phone. The only thing that remained to be done was to contact this Harry and tell him about Miriam. Whoever Harry was, he'd obviously meant something to her. I waited for Harry to answer.

"Hello. Yes." The voice was old, weak, with a European accent. "Yes, who is this?"

"Hello, sir," I answered. "My name is Gabriel Garshowitz. My daughter was Miriam Garshowitz. Your name and phone number were in her address book to be contacted in case of emergency. I believe you were friends?"

There was a long period of silence before the voice answered. "You said, 'were.' Are we not friends anymore?"

"I'm sorry to tell you she's dead."

There was another long period of silence. I waited patiently. "How?"

"A random murder. A stupid man who thought he could solve his problem by destroying the lives of others. It was a senseless death."

"I can relate to that. I'm so sorry. I liked her. Liked her a lot."

I could hear his breathing and could tell he was having difficulty talking. "Sir. Are you all right?"

"Yes. Did you two meet before she died, Mr. Garshowitz?"

This time it was my turn to remain quiet until I finally forced out the answer. "No. It happened before our meeting. And you, sir, I sense by your voice that you might be older than me. I can tell she meant a great deal to you. Uh, did you take my place in her life?"

"No, Mr. Garshowitz, I replaced no one. I, too, am a Holocaust survivor. I, too, experienced hidden pain, but I was able to make a life for myself. Not the life I would have preferred, but still a life. I am now eighty-three."

There was a few moments of silence, as I listened to his breathing.

"I was in a concentration camp. Auschwitz. I was tortured. I lost my wife. Losing my wife was more painful. When I returned home, there was no more Warsaw. Most had died. Circumstances brought me to Australia. I decided to stay here. No matter how far away a person goes to forget, the memory follows. My pain followed me, as it did your wife. I buried it, too, but it always resurfaced."

He coughed several times.

Again I asked, "Are you all right, sir?"

"Yes."

"Did my daughter tell you everything?" I asked.

"What, Mr. Garshowitz, is everything? Did she tell me something, yes. Was it all? I doubt it."

"Do you know why she returned to Toronto?"

"Yes. Your daughter and I spent many an evening talking. I tried to explain what it was to live with bad memories. I tried to make her understand as best I could that when the pain and the memories become too much, then death becomes an answer. Your wife's pain could no longer be treated. I told her, her death was not your fault, Mr. Garshowitz, but the fault of what she had experienced."

"Did Miriam understand?"

"She was able to understand her mother's need for death. She made peace with her and wanted to make peace with you. I'm sorry that never happened."

"So am I. I'm glad she met you. I'm relieved that Miriam was able to come to grips with what happened. I'm sure you were instrumental in her healing. My wife was a victim of the war and I'm afraid I made my daughter a victim by not being a father to her."

"We are all victims, Mr. Garshowitz. Even you. As unlikely as that might appear, even you. Whether it be because of events or choice, all humanity has to overcome the obstacles of life. Some do this better than others. Guilt is a luxury. To feel sorry destroys the ability to survive. Remembering and learning are the only choices worth pursuing. I remember my life before the war and live. So should you."

"That's good advice, Harry, but circumstances have a way of making good advice difficult to accept. I'll try."

"Ah, circumstance. It is a powerful word, Mr. Garshowitz. Circumstance presented itself, and I met my wife in a library. Circumstance presented itself to me in Auschwitz and I leaped at it to seek justice. It brought me to Australia, where after I completed my task, decided to stay. There are good and bad circumstances and they take hold of your life and direct you to acts that bring pleasure or resolve." He coughed again. His breathing was more laboured.

"I'm sorry, Harry. I don't know your last name. All Miriam wrote on her note was your first name and telephone number."

"My name is Hershl Weisz, Mr. Garshowitz. Everything has to come to an end – even life. I am afflicted with cancer. Soon I will be with my wife. It is time. Miriam was my last responsibility. I found that in trying to help your daughter, she was also helping me. My words to her were words that I had to hear. By speaking them I had a better understanding of why I survived. By living, Mr. Garshowitz, I believe I performed a mitzvah. I kept alive the memories of those I loved. I perpetuated their life and in doing that, it gave my living a purpose.

"I'm sorry we could not have met under better circumstances, but life has a way of unfolding that cannot always be controlled. Feel no remorse, Mr. Garshowitz. We are all in God's hands. I see life as a ship and we are its passengers. There will be storms and calm seas. Many of us will drift apart, but in the end, we will meet again. I only hope that my Annie is waiting for me. We have been apart a long time."

I recognized the name immediately. How complicated life can be. Annie had been right, her Hershl had survived. Love can be pleasure and pain, ecstasy and depression, an invisible cord that stretches into eternity, and Annie and Harry were tied to it. They lived because of their memories. I decided to let things remain the way they were and say nothing. "I'm sure she is, sir," I said. "Thank you for your words and for your friendship to my daughter. Goodbye."

"Goodbye."

I replaced the receiver and looked down at the piece of paper with Harry's name and telephone number. Annie Kapinsky Weisz and Edith Garshowitz, two lost souls whose lives would be forever locked together without ever knowing the link. And then there was Hershl Weisz and me. Hershl had moved away from his past thinking it dead, and I had lived for the present, not thinking about the future, victims of our own folly. I folded the sheet into a small square and tucked it into my wallet, a reminder that we all have a purpose in life – to remember. I intended to live a long life. I had a responsibility to keep alive their memories. I owed them at least that.

"Gabe, I've been looking for you," Iris said as she came around the hall. "We got us another case."

I smiled. "I'm right behind you, sweetie."

If you enjoyed
THE UNLIKELY VICTIMS
be on the lookout for the next
Gabe and Iris Adventure!